TORRES STOOD AND LOOKED AT THE CREATURE FOR A LONG TIME.

Doubtless, had a full-blooded Klingon killed it, he or she would be whooping and dancing in triumph. She felt no sense of giddy pleasure. She actually felt sick to her stomach at what she had just done, even though she had been fighting for her life. Still and harmless in death, the *grikshak* looked beautiful to her. It was only doing what instinct told it to do—find food and stay alive, just as she was.

Slowly, she walked up to the creature and, on impulse, dropped down beside it and placed a hand on its bloody head.

"I thank the spirit of the *grikshak,*" she said aloud, feeling that what she was doing was both foolish and appropriate. "I will use its flesh for sustenance, and its hide as protection from the elements."

She would need a sharp stone to cut it open. . . .

STAR TREK VOYAGER®

THE FARTHER SHORE

CHRISTIE GOLDEN

Based upon STAR TREK®
created by Gene Roddenberry
and STAR TREK: VOYAGER
created by Rick Berman &
Michael Piller & Jeri Taylor

POCKET BOOKS
New York London Toronto Sydney Singapore

An *Original* Publication of POCKET BOOKS

POCKET BOOKS, a division of Simon & Schuster, Inc.
1230 Avenue of the Americas, New York, NY 10020

This book is published by Pocket Books, a division of Simon & Schuster, Inc., under exclusive license from Paramount Pictures.

ISBN: 0-7434-6755-8

First Pocket Books paperback edition July 2003

10 9 8 7 6 5 4 3 2

Manufactured in the United States of America

This book is humbly dedicated
to the Columbia *Seven:*

Rick Husband
William McCool
Ilan Ramon
David Brown
Laurel Clark
Michael Anderson
Kalpana Chawla

We mourn you and salute you.
May your spirits dance with the stars.

Now the laborer's day is o'er;
Now the battle day is past;
Now upon the farther shore
Lands the voyager at last.

—"HYMN," JOHN ELLERTON

THE FARTHER SHORE

PROLOGUE

Age Twenty-one

She graduates at the top of her class, and she has learned more from the Academy than anyone could have suspected.

She has learned how to feign, to imitate the behavior of others, to blend in. She has been elected head of her class, and students and teachers alike often express their admiration for her intelligence, her leadership. She has learned when to laugh and when to express sympathy, who to cultivate and who to avoid, and what exactly to do to get ahead with every person who crosses her path. She is a master at finding and exploiting weakness, at uncovering secrets, at telling people what they want to hear and getting them to do what she wants them to do.

Her father is killed a few years later, by a Borg at-

tack at Wolf 359. She and her mother appear stoic at the funeral, but she knows that inside, her mother burns with the same fierce, hot joy that the girl does. At one point, she turns to her mother, and recognizes the glee, swiftly hidden, in her mother's blue eyes.

She understands that the massacre is a tragedy, that many are suffering from the loss of people they loved. But she cannot feel anything but relief and savage pleasure. That, and rage and hatred, are her limited palette of emotions, and the pictures she can paint with them are dark and clear.

At this moment, celebrating her father's death while wearing a mask of sorrow, she experiences another emotion: gratitude toward the cybernetic monsters who have finally done what she has longed to do all her life.

Chapter 1

THE WATER WAS hardly inviting. Its surface was coated with some kind of algae and it smelled faintly of decay. Nonetheless, B'Elanna Torres scooped up the water with her hands and drank deeply.

It had been almost a week since she had first stepped out on trembling legs into the wilderness of Boreth. Her first instinct had been to wash off the sticky, foul-smelling combination of ash and blood that coated her body. However, it had taken her some time to find water, and by then, she had changed her mind.

The coating that the priestesses had smeared all over her naked body as part of her ordeal had distinct and important advantages as well as disadvantages. The vile stuff prevented insects from bothering her, and in this tropical climate, they were thick as, well, flies. It also helped protect her skin from the merciless rays of the sun, and even provided a sort of insulation during the chillier night. And when she walked right past a grazing *maasklak,* an unexpected encounter that had startled them both, she realized that it helped mask her scent as well.

She imagined rolling in feces would produce a similar effect, and frankly, she wasn't sure that she wouldn't prefer the latter. It had taken nearly two days before her nose had become inured to her own reek. But here in this place, she realized she needed every edge she could find.

B'Elanna hadn't been overly worried at first. Starfleet was quite thorough in training its cadets to handle emergency situations, and she had certainly had enough experience thinking on her feet in the seven years she'd spent on *Voyager.* But Starfleet had also tended to assume that when one crash-landed on an inhospitable planet, one would usually have one's emergency medical kit, phasers, and so on. At the very least, they'd assumed one would have clothes.

B'Elanna had nothing but her own two hands and her wit.

One of the first things she had done was to find water. She dimly remembered something about a few of Boreth's plants that weren't deadly, and began to forage berries, fruits, and edible tubers and roots. After about day two, she'd overcome her repugnance sufficiently to add insects to her diet. Making fire was easy—she'd always had a knack for it and teased Chakotay about it mercilessly.

She had two goals that were occasionally in conflict with one another. The first was to simply stay alive and as healthy as was possible given the circumstances. The second was to keep moving in the direction her mother had indicated on the map. Both were challenging, but the latter more so. With no compass and a complete unfamiliarity with the terrain and even the stars that speckled the sky that arched over this world, Torres had very little frame of reference.

The map had indicated that Miral would be waiting for her somewhere to the northeast of the temple. Torres had wasted two precious days traveling in the wrong direction before she remembered that Boreth's sun rose in the south and traveled north during the day. Upon realizing her mistake, B'Elanna Torres raged with a fury that would have impressed Logt, had she been witness to it.

Her redundant organs were serving her well during this time of extreme physical duress. She recalled the conversation she had with the Doctor, when he had argued as persuasively as he was capable of doing in favor of the extra lung and other organs little Miral would have. Humans would have had a very difficult time of this, and even she, half-human as she was, fell into exhausted slumber at the end of every day.

Her feet started to blister at the end of the second day. She rubbed them with mud to soothe them and started to think about what she could use to create makeshift shoes. Her first try, wrapping large leaves around them, was a complete failure. A half-hour's worth of walking on not-very-rough terrain shredded them. She realized that she was going to need something sturdier than plants.

She was also going to need something more substantial to eat than roots and grubs. Torres began walking at first light and didn't stop until dusk, when she would search for shelter and make a fire. She was burning calories like mad and was starting to feel weak and shaky.

Reluctantly, she came to the conclusion that she would need to make a weapon. Boreth was rich with all kinds of wildlife. A single *maasklak* would provide both food and clothing. It was a logical deduction, but the thought made her feel even sicker. Torres took no pleasure in killing. She fought when she had to, and had killed in self-defense more than once, but that was a long way from deliberately setting out to take a life, even an animal's life. She imagined that for most Klingons who undertook the Challenge of Spirit, coming to grips with killing an animal was probably the least of their worries. But it disturbed her greatly.

She'd talked to Chakotay once about hunting, back in the early days when she was first getting to know him. He was, as she ought to have expected, quite philosophical about the whole thing. He seemed to have no qualms about it in theory or in practice, if there was a need.

"But you're a vegetarian," she had pointed out.

"I have access to a replicator," he had countered. "I don't need to go out and hunt my meals."

"But you would if you had to?"

"Absolutely."

"Without batting an eye."

He'd smiled then, indulgently. "Hardly. My people have elaborate rituals to prepare for hunting. We make ourselves worthy of success in the hunt by purifying our minds and body through meditation and bathing.

We call on the spirits of the animals we are about to kill, asking permission to take what we need. And when we do make a kill, we thank the creature's spirit. Nothing is wasted, not bone or sinew or flesh or horn or hide. It is all viewed as a gift from the animal, and it is part of the cycle. But in today's world, there's no need to take a life when we can program the replicator for everything from stuffed mushrooms to chocolate cake."

She supposed he had a point, and had thought no more about it, even as she often asked the replicator for a thick T-bone steak, extra rare. Tom liked his steaks medium, with a baked potato and—

Just that quickly, Torres was crying. She had deliberately pushed thoughts of her husband and child to the back of her mind when they arose, because she instinctively knew she couldn't spare the energy of missing Tom and Miral. There had only been a handful of days over the last seven years when she had not seen Tom. He was a fixture in her life even before they had gotten married, and she had carried Miral within her, brought her forth into this universe, and now keenly missed feeling the child nursing in her arms. By her count, Miral was nine weeks old today. Nine weeks. Torres suddenly realized she had been away for two-thirds of her daughter's entire life.

She had really had no choice but to leave them behind and embark on the Challenge. Intellectually she knew that, and even in her heart, she knew that. But a part of her, the part that was wife and mother, deeply mourned the abrupt severance. The tears were hot as they trickled down her face, and B'Elanna knew they were making pale furrows in the gray ash that was her mask.

At least they were safe. Tom was probably with Harry Kim right now, relaxing and joking, while Miral slept peacefully in her nursery. The Doctor, no doubt, would be making a sarcastic comment or two, but she knew better than most the depth of tenderness of which the hologram was capable. He adored Miral, and no child could have a better godfather.

She cursed. She was wasting precious water on these stupid tears. Torres gulped and wiped at her eyes, then cursed again as the motion got dirt in them and they stung.

It was only then that she heard the *grikshak*.

Its growl was low, soft, and as menacing as anything she had ever heard. Her thoughts focused to laser-sharp clarity. All distracting images of husband and child fled before the more urgent need to be alert and stay alive.

She froze, remembering just in time that movement antagonized the creature. Only her eyes darted rapidly about, trying to locate it. There—in the tall blue grasses. Its azure coat was the perfect camouflage, but its constant low growl revealed where it had hidden itself.

She had only been permitted a few hours to read up on the flora and fauna of Boreth, but one thing had stuck in her mind. The *grikshak* was the most dangerous predator on the planet. It had little fear of humanoids, it had more teeth than any self-respecting creature ought to, and it was really, really big.

They faced each other, the animal and the half-

Klingon. Torres mentally kicked herself. She knew there were *grikshaks* on this continent. She ought to have fabricated weapons on day one. Instead, she'd almost been killed because she'd succumbed to maudlin recollection. At once, she amended that thought. She might yet be killed.

She had caught a break in that this *grikshak* was a juvenile. Its coat was still bright blue, not the silver-blue of a mature female, and it was barely the size of Earth's grizzly. Its teeth, bared in challenge, were only as large as her hand. A black, wet nose moved as it snuffled the air. It seemed confused that it couldn't scent her. Torres figured that her lack of smell was the only reason she was still alive; the thing was still trying to determine what she was.

Her gaze flickered to the earth. By her foot were stones a little bigger than her hand. They would make pathetic weapons, but they were the only ones she had. She'd have to time it just right. Torres fixed in her mind the exact position of each stone, even as she returned her gaze to meet that of the creature.

It crooned and cocked its head, still trying to figure out what this scentless, still thing in its path was.

At that moment, Torres squatted, grabbed three stones, and dove for a nearby tree. She scrambled up the rough trunk as fast as her feet and hands would take her. Her movement broke the spell that had kept the *grikshak* immobile and it charged, its roar nearly shattering her eardrums. Long blue-black claws tore the earth where she had been standing a fraction of a second earlier, and it whirled with shocking speed to charge the tree.

Hanging on determinedly to the shaking branches, Torres took aim and threw the first stone. It was a perfect blow, catching the creature between its large eyes. She heard a crunch. The animal staggered, but did not fall. Torres saw a welt begin to rise and knew she'd managed to fracture the skull. Again she threw with all her strength, willing the stone to strike home. This one struck the *grikshak*'s right eye. It shrieked in agony, bringing a forepaw up to its face in a very human gesture.

She had only one stone left. She had to make it count. The animal was bellowing, its sharp-toothed mouth wide open. Torres summoned all her courage, dropped from the branches to the earth, and ran toward the creature. She shoved the stone deep into its open gullet and snatched her hand back before those dreadful teeth could clamp down and sever her arm.

She wasn't quick enough to avoid a glancing blow from the *grikshak*'s huge forepaw, though, and cried out as she felt the white-hot pain of claws scraping her back. She began to run as fast as her legs would carry her through the tall grass, feeling blood trickle down her back and legs, knowing that the scent was enraging the beast.

It gave chase, but in silence. The only sound was the crashing of the vegetation it trampled in its path. Torres wasn't stupid enough to slow down and look over her shoulder. She ran for all she was worth, pumping her legs faster than she had ever done before, willing her feet to find sure footholds and not slip. Three lungs gulping air filled her blood with oxygen, and adrenaline lent extra speed.

After a couple of minutes she realized she no longer

heard any sound at all behind her. She kept running for another moment or two, then decided to risk a backward glance.

There was no sign of the *grikshak*.

Torres slowed and gasped for breath, glancing around for any trace of it circling to approach from another direction. She saw nothing.

Her breathing slowed. Carefully, grabbing up more stones as she saw them, she retraced her steps. She tensed as she heard a thrashing sound up ahead, but kept moving.

The *grikshak* flailed frantically on the earth, churning up huge clumps of bushes and grass in its death throes. Its mouth was open and its forepaws clawed its own face to ribbons as it tried futilely to extricate the stone Torres had shoved deep into its trachea. The struggle reached a crescendo and then the massive animal lay on the earth, shuddering only slightly, until with one final twitch, it lay still. Blood and saliva slowly trickled from its sharp-toothed mouth.

Torres stood and looked at it for a long time. Doubtless had a full-blooded Klingon killed the creature, he or she would be whooping and dancing in triumph. She felt no sense of giddy pleasure. She actually felt sick to her stomach at what she had just done, even though she had been fighting for her life. Still and harmless in death, the *grikshak* looked beautiful to her. It was only doing what instinct told it to do—find food and stay alive, just as she was.

Slowly, she walked up to the creature, and on impulse, dropped down beside it and placed a hand on its bloody head.

"I thank the spirit of the *grikshak,*" she said aloud, feeling that what she was doing was both foolish and appropriate. "I will use its flesh for sustenance, and its hide as protection from the elements."

She would need a sharp stone to cut it open.

Chapter 2

LIBBY WEBBER was beginning to think her plan wouldn't work.

It had seemed so easy, so foolproof. Each step would lead naturally to the next, and the final step would get her what she wanted. Except it just wasn't working out that way.

She'd done her research on Trevor Blake. The first thing she noticed while perusing his file was how ordinary he looked. There was almost nothing at all distinctive about him. He was Caucasian, age thirty-seven, of average height and weight. His features weren't homely, but neither were they handsome. His profile stated that his eyes were hazel, but she couldn't really name the color even though she'd intently scrutinized the image. His hair was . . . brown. Not dark brown, or light brown, or walnut or mahogany or even mousy brown. Just plain brown. He wore nondescript civilian clothing. He was completely, utterly overlookable. Which, she mused, would ironically make him the perfect spy, had his temperament been suitable.

But it was clear from the moment she began reading his bio that he was destined for science. He suddenly seemed much less ordinary to her as she read his list of accomplishments. He'd been breaking through scientific barriers since he was a young man, and the list of his achievements just kept going. Until, abruptly, it stopped four years ago. Libby assumed this was when Covington had commandeered him for Starfleet Intelligence. This bio had been cleared for a very high level; obviously, what Covington had him working on now was top secret.

She determined where he lived and began to shadow him. He was, not surprisingly, as predictable as clockwork. Every morning at 7:45 precisely, he left his small apartment carrying a briefcase and walked the three blocks to the official, public headquarters of SI. He worked until exactly noon, at which time he left and walked two blocks to a small outdoor café called The Stop Spot. It was a serve-yourself establishment with several replicators and small places to sit in the sun. A couple of human waiters kept the place tidy. He ordered the same thing every day—an egg salad sandwich on white bread with an apple and a large cup of coffee, heavy on the cream and sugar, and a single chocolate chip cookie for dessert.

At 6:30, he left SI with the same briefcase and walked home. She didn't know what he fixed himself for dinner, but she was willing to bet it was the same thing every night. At precisely ten o'clock, the lights went out.

Very ordinary. Very predictable. Very boring, but also very convenient for Libby's purposes. Which was why she was so exasperated that it wasn't working.

She'd prepared her props and her dialogue carefully, then put her plan into action. She had watched him walk to The Stop Spot, and five minutes later walked there herself. He was already sitting at a table, eating his sandwich. She instructed the replicator to produce an egg salad sandwich on rye bread, with an orange and a large coffee, heavy on the cream and sugar, making sure she spoke loudly enough so that Blake would overhear. She watched him out of the corner of her eye. He was intently reading a padd and didn't appear to have noticed.

She sat at a table a little distance away from him, facing him. Libby tried to catch his eye several times, and utterly failed. She finished her sandwich in silence, reflecting on how much she disliked egg salad, then rose. She took exactly four steps in his direction before she "dropped" a small padd. It hit the cement and she kept walking.

She had almost turned the corner when she heard a voice behind her calling, "Excuse me! You dropped this!"

Libby turned, putting on her sweetest smile, only to see the young waiter chasing after her. Inwardly she sighed; a whole day wasted.

She put on a convincing show, though, as she took the padd from the young man, who smiled shyly at her. "Thank you so much!" she said graciously, then went home.

She tried it again the next day. This time, the waiter

didn't see the dropped padd, but neither did Trevor Blake. She had to go back and pick it up off the ground herself an hour later. Libby waited a day, so it wouldn't be too obvious. She was beginning to suspect, however, that she could beat Trevor Blake over the head with the padd and he wouldn't notice.

Today, she choked down yet another despised egg salad sandwich, finished her orange and coffee, and rose to leave. Again, the padd slipped out of her bag and fell to the ground. This time, however, it was close enough to Blake that he heard the sound. She saw his brown head move in the direction of the padd and quickened her pace. There was an automated transporter around the corner. She got to it just in time, for as she dematerialized, she saw him start toward her.

Perfect.

She rematerialized in her cabin and wondered how long the next step would take. The longer, the better; it would give him a chance to read the fake journal she'd compiled. And the more he read of that, the more he'd want to see her.

It was late that afternoon when he finally contacted her. She had carefully applied makeup and tousled her hair just so before she sat down at the computer.

"Hello?" she said, with just the right amount of warmth and caution.

"Um . . . Miss Webber?"

"Yes," she said, looking confused. "May I ask who you are, sir?"

He cleared his throat. "You don't know me, but I found a padd that I think belongs to you. I think you dropped it at The Stop Spot earlier today."

"I'm certain you're mistaken. . . . Wait a moment, will you?" She rose and pretended to fumble in her bag. "Oh my God . . . you found my journal? Please tell me you didn't read it!"

He flushed bright pink and lied, "No, of course not. I just wanted to see if there was any contact information."

Again, perfect. She collapsed into the chair and sighed deeply. "Thank you so much. You're such a gentleman, Mr . . . ?"

"Uh . . . Blake. Trevor Blake."

She unleashed the full force of her smile upon him, and she could swear he quivered. "Trevor," she said sweetly. "Thank you so much. You don't know how devastated I would be if that had gotten lost. Clearly I'll have to guard it more closely."

"Do you have lunch regularly at The Stop Spot? I can meet you there tomorrow and give it to you then."

"I really don't think I want to wait that long," she said. "But I'm certain you've got plans for tonight."

Again, he cleared his throat. "Ah, no . . . tonight I'm free, actually."

Of course you are. I knew that. "I'm surprised, but that's my good luck. Please—let me take you out to dinner. It's not enough to repay you for what you've done."

He hesitated, and for a bad moment she thought she'd lost him. Then, "Okay. If you're sure."

"Oh, I'm quite sure." She gave him another smile. "Shall we meet at The Stop Spot at seven?"

She chose her outfit with care. She wanted to be enticing, but not overly so; tasteful, yet with just the barest hint of eroticism. By the way his eyes widened and he swallowed, she thought she'd succeeded.

Libby strode toward him, hand extended. "Thank you again for safeguarding it."

"You're very welcome." Again, he revealed himself by blushing. Libby wondered how far he'd gotten in the juicy, utterly fabricated "entries." Far enough, she supposed.

"What's your pleasure?" she asked.

His no-color eyes widened. "What?"

"For dinner. What's your pleasure? I know all kinds of great restaurants. Do you like Ethiopian, or maybe Thai?"

"Um . . . I kind of like plain food."

Of course you do, she thought. His food preferences hadn't been in his bio, but she couldn't imagine this fellow being adventurous in any fashion.

"I know just the place," she said. In a few moments they were sitting at a restaurant called The Garden of Eatin'. It was a bit on the rundown side, its one redeeming feature that it was consistent in its mediocrity. She knew that the chef, for oddly enough there was actually a live human in the kitchen, varied his menu not a whit, and that it offered such uninspired choices as Cobb Salad, grilled cheese sandwiches, and hamburgers.

She was not surprised when Trevor ordered a medium hamburger, no onions, extra pickles, and french fries. Libby had eaten meat before when she felt it was vital to her assignments, but she disliked to do so. She ordered a grilled cheese sandwich with a house salad and oil and vinegar dressing.

By sheer will she kept the conversation alive, asking as many questions as she could, which he replied to with monosyllabic answers. At one point, though, when the conversation lagged severely, he took the initiative and asked her about what she did. Knowing that the truth was best whenever it could be applied, she told him she was a musician. He didn't seem particularly interested.

Even when the talk turned to his work, he didn't have much to say. Libby found this quite odd. Usually people loved to talk about themselves and their work. She was beginning to despair of the evening working out as she had hoped when, after they had finished dessert, Trevor cleared his throat and asked, "Would you like to come over to my place for a nightcap?"

She tried not to look as startled as she felt. Judging by his expression, he'd spent all evening working up his courage to ask her. For a brief moment, she felt sorry for him. He wasn't unattractive, and the work he did was fascinating. He just needed to polish himself a little. She suspected this was his first date in a long time, and that was a shame.

Libby immediately set his expectations by saying, "I've got to be up early for a rehearsal tomorrow, so I can't stay too long, but yes—I'd love to have a nightcap with you."

His smile was sweet, sincere, and boyish, and again, she was sorry that he wasn't out with someone who could really appreciate that smile.

Trevor's apartment was exactly as she had imagined it. It was tidy and organized and devoid of anything resembling imaginative furnishings. She'd stayed in hotel rooms with more character. But then, she wasn't here to analyze his decor. Her experienced gaze swept the room with icy detachment, searching out what she had come for. There it was, on a table in the far end of the room. Trevor Blake's computer.

"What would you like?"

She smiled at him. "Whatever you're having," she said.

Trevor looked slightly distressed. "I'm not sure what I'm having," he said. It was rather endearing.

"Well," she said, "do you have any wine?"

"Red, white, or rosé?"

At least he understood the differences. "Red," she said.

"Cabernet, merlot, shiraz—" Trevor was actually counting them off on his fingers.

"A merlot sounds wonderful!"

"Okay," he said, and rewarded her with that sweet smile again. Clearly, he felt more comfortable in his own surroundings. He left and went into another room.

She listened for a moment, then jumped to her task. Quickly she removed a small mechanical device, no bigger than her thumbnail, from her purse. She attached it to the back of Trevor's computer and counted the seconds it would take to perform its task, then snatched it back. From the kitchen, she heard the sound of the cork popping and wine being poured. Libby had just dropped the device back into her purse and sat back on the sofa when Trevor reappeared with two glasses.

He handed one to her and she noticed how well-shaped his hands were. A faint stab of guilt knifed through her. This was the part about her job that she hated—using the innocents. Trevor struck her as a decent, if boring, fellow. But she had to do this.

He raised his glass. "A toast," he said. "To fortunate coincidences."

She clinked her glass against his. "I'll drink to that." She looked into his eyes and saw that they weren't a muddy, unnamable color after all. They were a lovely shade of olive green flecked with gold.

The wine was excellent. They chatted for a while and then Libby exclaimed loudly at the time.

"I'm so sorry to have kept you this late," she said, rising. "I've got to be up very early tomorrow." She extended her hand, and this time when he shook it, his grasp was strong and warm.

"Libby," he said, "I've—I had a wonderful time." He seemed to be about to say something more, then apparently lost his nerve. Libby was profoundly grateful.

She playfully waggled the padd he had returned to her. "I didn't know that losing this would lead to such a pleasant evening." It wasn't entirely a lie. The last half hour had been quite pleasant. Before he could gather up his courage to say anything more, she had taken a few steps toward the door. She could almost see Trevor shrink back into his protective shell of ordinariness.

He walked her to the transporter site. She kept expecting him to make an overture, but he seemed distracted, lost in thought, and when she said goodnight again he barely seemed to notice. Libby was vastly relieved.

Trevor watched the beautiful young woman dematerialize and began cursing himself the minute she was gone. Damn it! Why did he always . . . why did he never . . .

Against his better instincts he had read a few entries in the journal she had dropped. He had blushed at the frankness displayed therein and when she had suggested going out with him, he had been stunned. Libby had seemed so nice and sweet. So beautiful. And he had done nothing, said nothing. By her attitude he could tell she, like everyone else, looked at him and dismissed him. He couldn't blame her. There was nothing to set him apart, to make him someone anyone would want to really *see.*

But they would see him soon enough. Everyone would see him and be unable to avert their eyes from what he had done.

Everyone.

Libby lifted the hypospray to her throat and pressed. Instantly, she felt more alert. The pleasant haze of the wine and food departed, leaving a sharpness and focus in its stead. The drug wasn't supposed to be used often, but she'd wrangled permission. Time was fleeing and if she was going to stop Montgomery, she needed something on him. Fast.

She sat down at her computer and attached the small device. Instantly it began downloading its contents to her own computer. Libby didn't utilize a lot of gadgets, but when she did, she always found them amusing and useful. The computer would be able to decrypt everything up to the second top-secret level clearance.

"Complete," said the computer.

"Read names of files," instructed Libby.

"Experiment H247. Analysis of Parker's Second Theorem." On and on it went. Libby's shoulders sagged. There was a lot of long, detailed, boring reading ahead of her tonight.

"Memo from Admiral Kenneth Montgomery, stardate—"

"Stop." Excitement rushed through Libby. Her hunch had been right. This guy did have something on Montgomery, or else why would he keep the memos?

"Compile all documents that have any reference to Admiral Montgomery."

"Compiled."

"Display." There were hundreds of them. "Jackpot," she said softly. She read the first one:

TO: All members of Section 9
FROM: Admiral Kenneth Montgomery
RE: Lieutenant Hegwood's Party

Friday is Lieutenant Hegwood's 40th birthday. He thinks we don't know, but we admirals have our sources. We're planning a little surprise for him, so

"What the . . ."

She went on to the next one. This one concerned Commander Grafton's maternity leave. The next one was a reprimand concerning filched office supplies. The one after that urged all members of Section 9 to keep to the requested limit of fourteen teraquads of data for personal use on the computer.

Slack-jawed, Libby plowed through a few more startlingly banal memos and then leaned back in her chair, thinking. These just couldn't be what they seemed to be. Sudden inspiration struck—maybe these were fakes. Maybe they had hidden messages encrypted in them. She ran them through, but no luck. Hard as it was for her to comprehend, it appeared as though Trevor

Blake had simply never gotten around to deleting commonplace office memos from four years ago.

"No wonder you haven't had a date in a while, Mr. Blake," she murmured.

There remained the possibility, however unlikely, that there was something of substance in the memos, so she continued reading. She read all 420 of them. She read a data comparison between Setoya's Theory and Parker's Fourth Theorem. She read about experiment F638-H. She read Trevor's grocery lists from the last eight months and noticed without surprise that he almost always got the same thing.

She had endured stoically, and then she got to Royal Protocol.

"Oh, please God, no," she moaned.

The lengthy and ponderous Royal Protocol essay was the bane of everyone—*everyone*—in Starfleet Intelligence. It was a long-winded document that dealt with the various diplomatic nuances involved in dealing with royal families throughout the Federation.

With little pleasure Libby recalled a few. In the Royal Family of Tarkulis, one first dropped to one's knees in front of the youngest member of the family, then to each in succession. When greeting the Malshu of Verjuu, one covered one's eyes until one was graciously given permission to look upon the Blessed One. There were about a million things to memorize and well over a million things one could to do give offense and quite possibly start a war. The Royal Protocol document was, among Starfleet Intelligence members, a symbol of everything that was exquisitely boring and yet required one's full attention.

She wondered why he had it. It was more likely to be found in her computer than in Trevor Blake's. And she wouldn't have had the nasty thing in her house if she could have avoided it. Why would Trevor?

He was not the most socially adroit person she'd ever met. Maybe he simply wanted to get a few "pointers." Or maybe he was hoping to shift fields. Neither explanation seemed very likely. Probably what had happened was that Trevor had been issued a copy when he first started out in Section 9 and had just never bothered to delete it.

Feeling slightly sick, Libby realized she was going to have to plow through the damn thing. No stone unturned and all that. Even though she knew full well that anything that might reveal a connection to Montgomery was not likely to be found in the single most boring document to grace Federation Intelligence records.

Libby closed her eyes, gathering strength, and dove in.

It was an enormous file, in alphabetical order. And it had been added to considerably since Libby had first joined SI. By the time Libby had waded through the Acamarians to the Gorn, she felt she'd rather face an old-fashioned firing squad, a cigarette clenched between her teeth and a blindfold over her eyes, than keep reading.

The sentence she was reading turned to utter gibberish. For a moment, she thought that she was simply so exhausted that the words just weren't making sense anymore. She rubbed her eyes, willing herself to stay awake.

Then she realized that the rest of the document was encrypted. Suddenly wide-awake, Libby used her limited skills and after a grueling few hours was able to decipher a few words.

"Oh my God," Libby breathed. She glanced at the chronometer to see that she had worked clear through the night. Six thirteen was early, but not too early for something of this magnitude. She was just about to contact Covington when her computer chirped. Her nerves frayed, she jumped and squeaked. Recovering, she touched the button.

Brenna Covington's face appeared on the screen. *Perfect timing,* Libby thought.

"Good morning, Agent Webber. I know it's a bit early, but as I recall you tend to be an early riser."

Libby made a wry face. "Usually," she said.

"I'll get right to the point. Why did you meet with Trevor Blake last night?"

Libby blinked, surprised. She had no idea Covington watched her people that closely. "I heard Admiral Montgomery mention Trevor's name in your conversation and I thought I'd see if he knew anything that could help us ID Montgomery as the mole." She took a breath and was about to tell Covington what she'd found buried inside the Royal Protocol document, but Covington spoke first.

"He's a dead end. Anything he knows about Montgomery is at least four years old. Don't contact him again, it's a waste of your time. I'm sending over some more documentation on Montgomery that will be much more helpful in your search, I trust."

Libby's stomach clenched. Of course. She'd been so tired, her brain had been too sluggish to put the pieces together. Trevor Blake didn't have the drive to have done his . . . research . . . on his own. He was a man who acted on orders.

And he was on orders from Brenna Covington.

"Agent Webber?"

Libby licked lips suddenly gone dry and reached for the skills that had saved her life before. She laughed easily.

"You don't have to tell me twice, ma'am. Trevor Blake is a nice enough fellow, but let me put it this way—it was a *long* evening!"

Almost imperceptibly, Covington's face relaxed, further confirming Libby's fears. "I thought as much," she said, and chuckled. They smiled at one another as if they were two girlfriends sharing boy talk. It almost made Libby sick.

"You look a little tired, Agent Webber."

"I am," she said. "I've been up all night reading reports."

"Take a break before you start on the next batch," said Covington. "Better to be sharp."

"Understood. Is there anything else?"

"Just keep up the good work. Covington out." Her image disappeared and Libby sagged in her chair.

Never in her life had she felt more alone or lost, not even when *Voyager* was reported missing. She had just uncovered some terrifying information and discovered that her boss was up to her neck in it. Someone had to know about this, try to stop it. But who could she trust?

Chapter 3

CAPTAIN JEAN-LUC PICARD looked as startled as Admiral Kathryn Janeway had ever seen him.

"This is highly irregular, Admiral."

"I realize that," said Janeway, "and because it's so irregular, I insist you call me Kathryn."

A flicker of mirth briefly curved Picard's lips. "Usually requests of this sort come through the proper channels of Starfleet Command. May I ask why you chose not to pursue that venue?"

"Because Starfleet Command would want to know why, and if I told them, they'd say no." She shrugged. "Simple as that."

Picard chuckled. "Despite your protestations, I'd say your time in the Delta Quadrant has given you a touch of the renegade. Can you tell *me* why?"

She hesitated. "You have to promise me that if you

deny my request—hell, even if you agree to it—you won't tell Starfleet Command my reasons."

He frowned. "I don't like where this conversation is going." He thought it over, then nodded. "Very well. You have my word."

"Commander Data is an android. It was acknowledged in a court of law on stardate 42523.7 that he be granted the full rights of any human being in the eyes of the Federation, even though he's not even made of flesh and blood." She leaned forward into the screen. "I want those same rights granted to my friend the Doctor."

"I can certainly sympathize with your feelings," said Picard, "but it's my understanding that the hologram is suspected of crimes that have led to the deaths of eight people."

"He hasn't even been read his rights!" Janeway snapped. "He was arrested on no charge, is being held on no charge, and is probably going to be deprogrammed or worse simply because Starfleet can do it. You didn't stand by and watch Data be dismantled because he was viewed as Starfleet property. Do you expect me to do anything less for one of my people?"

Picard sighed. "No, I don't," he said. "It's not for us to decide if he was or wasn't involved. He should have the same right to trial that every Federation citizen has."

The sense of relief that washed over every person in the room was almost palpable. Janeway smiled. "Thank you, Jean-Luc. I won't forget this."

"Don't thank me, thank Commander Data, providing he agrees. I'll recommend that he assist you, but of course, you realize that in the end, it's his decision, not mine."

"As a person, as an individual, he has the right to make his own decisions. Of course I understand. When can I expect to hear from him?"

"Not as soon as you would probably prefer," he said, and the smiles around the room faded somewhat. "There are certain duties he needs to perform before I can permit him to take a leave of absence. We'll be in touch." He hesitated, then added, "I wish you the best of luck. And if there's anything more I can do, please ask."

"Again, thank you."

He smiled, briefly. "Picard out."

Janeway sighed and sat back in the chair. "Well, we've done what we can," she said.

"That's it? Data will contact us when he gets around to it?" asked Lieutenant Commander Tom Paris. He looked strange to Janeway without his daughter in his arms. Ever since he had been brought in for questioning, as they all had been a few days ago, Miral had been in her grandparent's care. Not having her to worry about seemed to have given Tom a headstrong, dangerous edge. Janeway hadn't realized to what extent marriage and fatherhood had tempered Paris.

"For now, yes, Mr. Paris," she said. She had deliberately used his last name and there was a warning note in her voice.

"I can't believe this is even happening in the first place," blurted Kim. He'd been sitting quietly and this outburst surprised Janeway. "We shouldn't have to be begging favors like this. They're imprisoning innocent people and holding them like—like they're animals. They're grilling us to death and not letting us help, which we could do if they'd just realize it."

Gently, Janeway said, "The Borg are so familiar to us, they're like old friends." She wrinkled her nose and amended. "Perhaps more like old enemies. We know them in a way Starfleet, indeed no one who wasn't on *Voyager,* can understand. We've lost a lot of our fear of them out of necessity. I think we've forgotten just how terrifying they are. Seven and Icheb are like family to all of us. I look at them and I don't even see their implants anymore. But that's all that Starfleet could see when this new virus started cropping up, and I suppose we can't blame them."

"I had hoped for better from an institution that preaches compassion and tolerance for differences," said Chakotay. "Icheb was beaten by his own classmates."

Tuvok looked up sharply, and if Janeway didn't know better, she could have sworn she saw righteous anger in his dark eyes. "Rest assured, Commander, that will be addressed. All of those who participated have been suspended. It is likely they will be expelled."

"If they weren't kids, I'd like to bloody a nose myself," said Tom.

"That's enough of that line of talk!" Janeway snapped. "There's a holographic uprising that was clearly inspired by the Doctor. Starfleet is right to assume he had at least a modicum of involvement. There's a Borg virus spreading across the Earth coinciding with our arrival home. Starfleet is right to investigate to see if there's any connection. It's how they're going about it that I don't like. We'll do what we can, but we are all sworn Starfleet officers. Now. We'll just have to see if Data is willing to help us, and wait until he arrives. If we have him on our side in time, that's a huge step forward."

"And if we don't?" asked Chakotay.

For just a fraction of an instant, she hesitated. What would they do? She didn't know. There had been many moments like this in her life, where she had absolutely no idea what to do next. But one thing she did know was that eventually, solutions would present themselves if she trusted that they'd come.

"We think of something else," she said simply.

It was late—or early, depending how you looked at it—when Harry Kim returned to his apartment. He wanted badly to talk to Libby, but she had been asleep for hours at this point. He was angry and frustrated. He felt helpless to do anything useful, and it chafed.

He and Tom had returned to Tom's apartment for a while, talking, after Janeway had dismissed them. They'd said a few dark things he supposed they didn't really mean about "Data's duties" and drunk a beer or two, then Harry had said goodnight. Tom looked as though he didn't want Harry to leave, and Harry supposed he knew why. Without Miral or the Doctor in the apartment, the place felt dreadfully empty.

He was surprised to see a light blinking on his computer at this hour. Probably Tom, he thought. "Computer, play message," he said, shrugging out of his shirt.

He was surprised when no image appeared on the screen, and he heard no voice. For a moment, he thought that his computer must be damaged, but then he saw the old-fashioned text scrolling across the page. The hairs on the back of his neck prickled as he read.

You will not be able to trace this message so please do not try. I am a friend. I am sending you this missive to warn you about a threat to humanity itself. There is a Borg virus spreading across the globe. Starfleet is attempting to keep this quiet so as not to cause widespread panic, but certain people in the Federation itself are responsible for the virus. There is a conspiracy. You must take steps, but as secretly as you can. Be safe.

Kim didn't try to trace it. Any message sent in this fashion would be so heavily encrypted that it would be virtually impossible to trace. He also that knew that only a handful of people had been briefed about the Borg virus, so whoever his mysterious contact was, he was for real. He couldn't believe that the Federation itself was involved, though. Why? How? Who?

He downloaded the data onto a padd and contacted Janeway. When he read her the message, he could see the color literally drain from her face. In a detached part of his brain, he marveled at the image; he'd always thought that a cliché.

"Thank you for that information, Mr. Kim. Do you have any idea who this person or persons might be, and why they decided to contact you?"

"Not at all, Admiral. The statement 'I am a friend' can't be literal. I don't know anyone who'd have connections like that."

Janeway leaned back in her chair and rubbed at her tired eyes. "I wonder what steps your friend expects us to take. In case you haven't noticed, we're somewhat persona non grata these days." The last words were harsher than Harry might have expected from her, but he thought he understood.

Janeway had worked so hard to bring them all home, and she had mostly succeeded. A few friends had fallen in the Delta Quadrant, but Janeway had gotten her ship and most of its crew back where they belonged. Except it felt as though they didn't belong. The Quadrant had moved on without them, thank you very much, and Kim felt left behind, left out, more than anything. The only real notice they'd attracted had been as suspects.

"Admiral," he said, "You've got to get Data on our side. Starfleet can't keep excluding us. And by us I mean the Doctor and Seven and Icheb. Especially if what this person is saying is true, that there's a conspiracy involving the appearance of Borg on Earth."

"This whole thing could be some kind of elaborate setup, Harry," said Janeway. "You do realize that?"

"I do. But what if it's true? Can we afford to just ignore it?"

Janeway shook her head. "No, we can't. If there's anyone who'd be angrier that someone in Starfleet was actually helping the Borg assimilate Earth more than myself or my crew, it's Picard. Don't mention this to anyone, Harry, not even anyone else from *Voyager* until I tell you. That's an order."

Oddly, Harry smiled. It was good to hear Janeway giving him an order again.

"Aye, ma'am," he said.

The nights were the hardest, Seven thought.

The people who guarded them dimmed the lights, as if any of the three prisoners would be able to sleep. Things quieted down, and Seven's body screamed louder for regeneration than at any other time. During the day, she could force her exhaustion away. She had visits to Dr. Kaz to keep her mind occupied; they were daily now, sometimes two or three times a day, depending on well or how badly her body was handling the situation. There was the occasional visit, too, from Janeway, Chakotay, and Tuvok to divert her. The Doctor did his best to keep them entertained, but the constant strain was affecting even the hologram.

But at night, all efforts at pretense were revealed as the hopeless straws they were. Conversation wound down and they all sat silently in their cells, the hologram and the two former Borg. Seven and Icheb would close their eyes and lie down upon their beds. Even if they could not sleep as normal humans did, even if they could not regenerate as the Borg needed to, they had been told by both the Doctor and Kaz that simply resting the body and trying to quiet the mind would help. At least a little, Kaz had told her, looking miserable. And "little" was the operative word.

She wondered how long it would take before her body shut down completely. She had gone for several days before without regeneration, but that had been aboard *Voyager*, usually when there was some pressing emergency that, in her mind at least, required her to stay functional. But now there was nothing to divert her mind from gnawing at the same worry: How long would it last? Would they let Icheb regenerate when he collapsed into unconsciousness? Would they let her do so when she started raving like a madwoman?

She knew the signs to look for: increased appetite, a drop in body temperature, shakiness, headaches, increased pain sensitivity. She was experiencing all of these physical effects of total sleep deprivation, and the psychological effects—irritability, poor concentration, apathy, paranoia, among others—were also starting to manifest.

Icheb was suffering, too. Just today he'd told her that he was having perceptual disturbances and he'd had a long conversation with someone who wasn't there. Seven knew that the Vulcan "interrogator" had "examined" Icheb, too, and wondered why they didn't just let him go. He was just a boy. He'd only even been an active Borg for a little while.

She watched him as he lay on his pallet, longing to reach out and stroke his hair but afraid of waking him.

He made a soft, rumbling sound. She started to her feet immediately and was about to reach for him when the Doctor's sharp whisper interrupted her.

"Don't, Seven!"

She turned to look at him. "He may be choking!" she shot back, also in a whisper.

To her surprise, the Doctor smiled. "That's not choking. That's snoring."

She continued to look at him blankly.

"Don't you understand?" he said, still whispering. "He's asleep. Icheb has fallen asleep."

Seven turned back to stare at the boy. His chest was rising and falling rhythmically, and he kept making that soft noise.

"It's not possible," she said, more to herself than to the Doctor. "We cannot sleep as humans do. We must regenerate."

"He's younger than you, and was Borg for a much

shorter time," the Doctor reminded her. "I think he's learned to . . . adapt to his new situation."

Seven felt tears welling in her eyes. She tried to blink them back but they would not be stopped. They were tears of gratitude, of relief, and they poured down her face like a waterfall coursing down a mountainside.

"Thank you," she whispered, to who or what she did not know. "Thank you."

It had been a long night for Lieutenant Vassily Andropov. He'd been doing the graveyard shift for over six weeks now, and he still couldn't get his body to get used to it. He was not a night person and it was with reluctance that he agreed to do the shift at all. He hated materializing in his apartment as the sky was turning gray outside, and the birds were just starting their daily songs. Having to drink too much coffee during his shift simply to stay alert made him jittery, and it was hard for him to unwind when he did get home and have a chance to catch a few hours' sleep. He was grateful that he lived alone. It would be nearly impossible to maintain a relationship with this maddening schedule. And he'd be so grouchy, no one would want to live with him.

Andropov never called for lights when he materialized at home. He wanted it as dark and easy on his eyes as possible. There was only the simplest of routines—appear in the bedroom, undress, and fall into bed. He sank down in his favorite chair and groaned with pleasure at the comfort of it. He was so tired. Well, he told himself, taking off his boots and yawning, it wouldn't be for too much longer. He just had to soldier through a few more weeks and then—

Hands clamped down on his shoulders, holding him down in the chair. He cried out and tried to break free, but they were implacable and strong, like iron bands. A figure stepped in front of him.

"Lights," called the stranger.

Andropov blinked a few times, then stared. "Oliver Baines," he said, hoarsely.

Baines smiled. "Well, not really, but close enough. I'm a holographic version of Baines."

Hologram? Impossible. Andropov's apartment wasn't fitted with holographic emitters. He couldn't possibly—And then Vassily's gaze fell to the small black rectangle at Baines's feet. It was the size and shape of a briefcase, but with the swiftness of one trained to recognize a possible threat when he saw it, Andropov made the jump. It was a portable emitter. Even though such things didn't exist, as far as he knew, that was what it had to be.

Andropov struggled with renewed energy. It was futile. The being behind him—another hologram, he guessed—held him firmly. Damn it, he was one of the top people at the corrections institute, his apartment was well protected, they ought not to have been able to get in here—

"Yes, I know, you're wondering how we managed to surprise you with our welcome home party," said Baines idly, taking out a piece of equipment that looked both familiar and strange to Andropov. "I don't want to reveal my tricks just yet. But let's just say this—your security needs an upgrade."

He smiled broadly, as if he had just said something that was actually funny.

"What do you want?" Andropov demanded.

"Why, you, Lieutenant. Or at least, your appearance." He looked at his apparatus and nodded, as if satisfied. "Excellent. You may step out now."

The pressure on Vassily's shoulders was gone. At once, he tried to bolt upright, thinking to go for the phaser he had so carelessly tossed on the dresser. How easily he had been lulled into a false sense of security. But even as he tensed to rise, Baines pressed something and a force field descended. Trapped in his chair, Andropov swore angrily.

The other hologram moved into Andropov's field of vision. He was about as tall as Baines, and clearly male, but he had no face. Andropov gasped, taken aback. The faceless hologram turned toward him, then back to Baines.

"Here we are, my friend," said Baines, his voice kind. He touched a few things on his apparatus and the figure beside him began to change in front of Andropov's eyes. It grew slightly taller and broader across the chest. Its black jumpsuit changed color, turning to gray, black, and yellow, with exactly the right number of pips in its color. Hair undulated across its naked skull, hair that was black shot through with a streak of gray. Eyes began to take shape, dark brown and large, over a hawk nose and thin lips.

"Oh my God," breathed Andropov, staring into a face he knew from forty-two years of looking into a mirror. His doppelgänger smiled at him.

"Vassily, meet Vassily," said Baines. He chuckled again.

Now Andropov knew what Baines's plan was. "It won't work. He may look like me, but he doesn't know what I know."

"Oh really? I think I might," said Andropov's double in flawless Russian.

"They will find out, eventually," Andropov insisted, though with less certainty than before.

"Perhaps," said Baines. "But not before he's done what he needs to."

Andropov swallowed hard. "Listen, Mr. Baines. We know the eight deaths were accidental. But if you deliberately murder a Starfleet officer—"

"Who said anything about murdering you?" Baines seemed genuinely upset. "I'm not a monster, Lieutenant."

"Then . . . what are you going to do with me? Just leave me here, trapped in a chair by this force field?"

"Of course not. I have a little trip planned for you." Baines smiled. "Call it a cultural exchange, if you will."

And then Baines, the double, and the room began to shimmer as Andropov dematerialized.

Chapter 4

SEVEN OF NINE screamed as the implacable Borg seized her and forced her down on their monstrous parody of a biobed. Janeway stood and watched, frozen, unable to move, unable to even look away. The Borg moved about their business, and merciful tears blurred the image of Seven's arm being severed. The Borg performing the operation looked up, and Janeway stared into the dead eyes of Admiral Kenneth Montgomery.

Resistance is futile.

Janeway bolted upright, covered with sweat, safe in her own bed. Her heart was racing. The sound came again, as if an echo of her nightmare, but it was real and all too familiar—the sound of her computer alerting her that someone was trying to reach her.

Still slightly disoriented from the vivid nature of the

dream, Janeway grabbed a robe, ran a hand over her hair, and sat down at the computer.

"Dr. Kaz," she said, surprised.

"Good morning, Admiral. I'm sorry to have awakened you. I thought you'd already be up."

She glanced at the chronometer and grimaced when she saw it was well past nine in the morning. "By all standards I ought to be, but I haven't been getting a lot of sleep recently."

It was a true remark and she had thought an innocent one, but something flickered over Kaz's features. "I understand," he said, his voice a bit harsher than it was before. "I know a couple of people who haven't been getting enough sleep myself."

The silence lay heavily between them as they looked into one another's eyes.

"I see," said Janeway, waiting for him to make the next move.

"I think proper sleep is vital to healthy functioning," Kaz continued. Janeway knew they weren't talking about her. "In fact, I feel so strongly about it that I'd like to discuss some strategies for treating insomnia with you."

Kaz had assured her that his sickbay was not monitored, but apparently he wasn't as certain about his computer. "I'd appreciate that," she said heartily. "I bet you're going to tell me I need to cut back on my coffee."

He laughed, caught by surprise at her quip. "Well, it would be a start," he said.

"Not a chance. I've got seven years of drinking replicated stuff to make up for."

"Well, why don't we meet for a cup and discuss . . . other options for getting a good night's sleep?"

"Sounds good to me. I know a little café in Santa Barbara." She gave him the coordinates.

"Shall I meet you in an hour?"

"I think I can be presentable by then." She sobered slightly. "Thank you, Doctor."

"Just doing my job." His face blipped out.

Janeway leaned back in her chair, then rose to get a pot of coffee brewing. As the delicious aroma filled her apartment, she returned to her computer. "Computer, call up records for Dr. Kaz, Jarem."

She perused his official file and was impressed by what she saw. He had told her the truth about two of his symbiont's histories. One, Radara Kaz, had indeed been a hugely popular and greatly honored poet. Janeway had even read some of her works. A phrase from one of Radara's works floated to her mind:

The Soul flutters on, in torment from its own belief
That it is alone in the vastness of the universe;
But Soul, extend to what you cannot see or sense,
And brush the tentative fingers
Of the Souls reaching blindly
To you.

His Maquis host, Gradak, had been equally as impressive. He had been one of the very few to survive the massacre at Tevlik's Moonbase, though he hadn't lived very long after that dreadful incident. Grievously wounded himself, he helped fifteen other injured, including four children, escape in a shuttle, heading straight for the nearest Federation base. Gradak had known they would be captured, but at least they would be alive. Refusing treatment for himself, he brought all his charges to safety. He was unconscious by the time a Federation starship took them aboard, and died on the operating table. Fortunately, the symbiont was successfully transplanted in time to the only Trill aboard the ship, who happened to be one of the doctors. Jarem Kaz.

Jarem himself was no slouch, either. He had a mind that liked a challenge and had developed a vaccine for Lhaj Fever in his "spare time," according to the records. Lhaj Fever was rare but 97 percent fatal. The vaccine would save thousands on developing worlds. Even before he had been given the Kaz symbiont, he had been on record as speaking out against the Cardassians, although there had been no sign of any action on his part. His captain had been sorry to see him go, but acknowledged that Starfleet needed Kaz's skill, intelligence, and compassion elsewhere.

It was the last quality that intrigued Janeway most. According to both Seven and Icheb, Kaz was indeed compassionate. She'd seen his caring and intensity for herself.

Looking at the handsome face on the screen, she said aloud, "I do hope I can trust you, Doctor."

They ordered their coffees to go and strolled along Santa Barbara's quaint downtown area. For a while, they simply shared pleasantries and idle chitchat. Their meandering steps took them down to the beach. It was a gorgeous day. The sky was an intense blue, interrupted only by the wheeling of gray-and-white seagulls.

Finally, Janeway broached the subject. "Flattered as I am to think that you sought me out for my sparkling conversation, Dr. Kaz, I suspect that's not really the case."

He sipped his coffee and didn't look at her, his eyes, as blue as the sky, fixed on the ocean. "No, Admiral, it isn't. I wanted to pass on a warning—and an offer."

Janeway tensed, but tried not to show it. She, too, sipped her coffee and didn't look at her companion. "Go on."

"I have tried repeatedly to convince Montgomery to allow Seven of Nine and Icheb to regenerate. He has refused my request every time. I understand his reasoning, but there are steps we could take to reduce the chance of anyone contacting Seven or Icheb in their regeneration state." He grimaced. "As if anyone would actually try to contact them. I have done everything I can with medication to simulate the effects of regeneration, but eventually there will be nothing more I can do. The effect on both of them is similar to total sleep deprivation."

"Which, according to Starfleet regulations, constitutes torture."

Kaz nodded. "Icheb, remarkably, has been able to get some sleep."

She turned to him now, pleasure filling her. "Really? That's wonderful news."

"Not as wonderful as it seems. He still needs regeneration. Let me get straight to the point: If they are not allowed to regenerate soon, they will die. Seven first, most likely, and then Icheb."

"And Starfleet won't allow them to regenerate," said Janeway bitterly. "Seems the outcome is inevitable then."

"Not necessarily," said Kaz. "And your Doctor—I told you I feared for him. I was unfortunately correct. It seems that the EMH Mark Ones don't really need surgical and medical knowledge to mine dilithium and haul rocks, so they're going to be reprogrammed with only the most basic subroutines. Your Doctor is going to be the first so reprogrammed. Montgomery wants to set an example and send a warning to those who would participate in the HoloRevolution."

He turned and looked at her at last, and his blue eyes were filled with sympathy. "If he were human," he said softly, "we'd call this a lobotomy."

Despite herself, Janeway's hand flew to her mouth. It took her a moment to recover from the full blow of Kaz's predictions of the fate of three friends.

"Why are you telling me this?" she said at last, regaining her composure.

"Because I took a vow before I joined Starfleet to harm no one," said Kaz. "I won't sit by and watch them do this to three innocent people. I *can't*."

"You can't get them released," said Janeway, hoping he'd contradict her.

"No," he replied. "But I can get them out. With your help."

She scrutinized his face. "You're taking a great risk, Doctor," she said. "You could be court-martialed for this, barred from practicing medicine."

He shrugged his broad shoulders. "Part of me has died before doing what it felt was right. Sitting in a comfortable Starfleet prison for the rest of my life pales in comparison. Even if I die, the symbiont lives on. So in a sense, I'll go on. Life and freedom are deeply precious to me, as they are to any living creature, but they're not quite what they are to humans. Joined Trills have a bit of a longer view. Besides, you run the same risks as I do, Admiral."

"But they're my crew," she said. "They're my friends. They'd do the same for me."

"From what I've seen, I believe they would."

Janeway hesitated, then said, "I don't suppose you're particularly close with Harry Kim?"

"Lieutenant Kim?" At her nod, he continued. "I examined him, of course, and we chatted a bit, as you and I did. But no, outside of that one encounter we'd never met. Why do you ask?"

"No reason." She'd been hoping to learn that Kaz might be Harry's mysterious contact, but no such luck. She switched the subject quickly. "Radara and Gradak would be proud of you."

His lips twitched. "You've been checking up on me."

"I'm willing to bet you've been doing the same, or else you'd never be walking along the beach with me having coffee and proposing a jailbreak," she replied.

He heaved a mock sigh. "Guilty as charged."

"So, Dr. Kaz, what's your plan?"

When Janeway returned to her apartment, she saw that her computer light was blinking. She mused on the fact that although she was technically not on assignment, she was almost busier than she had been aboard *Voyager.*

When the gold-skinned, yellow-eyed face appeared on her viewscreen, her heart leaped.

"Good morning, Admiral Janeway," said Data. "Captain Picard has granted me shore leave for the next ten days. I am looking forward to meeting you."

Nothing more. No indication of whether or not he was game for the plan—which, of course, had suddenly and quite drastically been changed. Just a willingness to meet.

Fair enough. She really couldn't ask for commitment from someone she'd never met, especially given the present circumstances. She sent him a reply, asking him to come to her apartment at 1800 hours. She then began firing messages off to her former crewmen.

When Commander Data arrived, he seemed surprised to find that Janeway was not alone in her apartment. Nonetheless, his expression was pleasant as he looked around at the expectant faces.

"Greetings!" he said.

Janeway made the rounds, introducing Chakotay, Paris, Kim, and Tuvok. Everyone, of course, had heard of Commander Data, but only Tuvok had actually met him. Data politely shook hands with the humans and gave Tuvok the traditional spread-fingered greeting.

"Live long and prosper, Commander Tuvok."

Tuvok returned the gesture. "Peace and long life, Commander Data."

Data cocked his head. "An interesting wish for an android, who is technically not alive."

Janeway smiled. "An apt comment, Commander, considering the nature of the issue which brought you here." She indicated a seat and he took it. She sat on the sofa next to him.

"I assume Captain Picard filled you in . . . on everything?"

"If by that you mean did he inform me that you desire to utilize my skills as an advocate for the EMH Mark One who served aboard your vessel, that you are certain that this same hologram can be invaluable in helping to halt the Borg virus that is currently spreading across the Earth, and that you suspect that Starfleet itself may be responsible for the implementation of said virus, then yes."

Janeway smiled. "I wish we'd had you with us during our time in the Delta Quadrant, Mr. Data."

"Thank you, Admiral. I doubt, however, that Captain Picard would share that desire."

"I'm certain he wouldn't." Her smile faded. "Tell me, Mr. Data, may I take it that your appearance here implies that you are willing to help us?"

"I am inclined to do so, but I would like to hear more."

She leaned forward, her eyes searching his. "You're about to get an earful. I invited my former senior staff here tonight to tell you about . . . a slight change in plan. You're welcome to rake us over the coals if you like."

He looked puzzled, then his face brightened. "Ah. Rake one over the coals. To take to task, or to interrogate vigorously. Another slang term is, to grill. It is curious that there are so many cooking metaphors involved in—"

"Data," said Janeway, "time really is of the essence."

"Of course. Please proceed."

It was nearly 2200 when Janeway put through a final message to Kenneth Montgomery. He seemed in unusually good spirits when he answered. She wondered what had happened to put him in such a cheerful mood.

She thought about asking, but was worried that it would turn into a sarcastic remark, and that wasn't what she wanted right now.

"Good evening, Admiral," he said. "Who will it be this time, Seven, Icheb, or the Doctor?"

Janeway forced herself to smile pleasantly. "Why, all three. Let me get right to the point. You've held Seven and Icheb for almost two weeks now without allowing them to regenerate. Dr. Kaz tells me that he can minimize the risk of any Borg contact while in their regenerative state."

Montgomery sighed. "The key word in that statement is 'minimize.' We can't be certain. There's a Borg virus running around striking apparently at random. Surely you can see what a security risk they are."

"If they don't regenerate, they'll die," she said quietly. "Are you willing to have the deaths of innocent people on your hands?"

Montgomery made a dismissive gesture. "That's an overstatement," he said.

"Your head doctor doesn't think so."

"Kaz is an alarmist. Probably that poet/Maquis combination in his symbiont. The other doctor on my team assures me that it's nowhere near that dire. And even so, the answer to your question is yes. To prevent every person on the planet from turning into a Borg, I'd sacrifice two innocent people. From what I know of your encounters with the Borg, you'd do the same."

For just a moment, Janeway pondered the statement. Would she? The answer grieved her but did not surprise her. Yes, she would sacrifice Seven and Icheb . . . if she knew, without a doubt, that it would halt such a terrible thing.

"But you *don't* know that their deaths will stop the virus. In fact, utilizing their knowledge would be more helpful than letting them go insane and die in a Starfleet prison."

"I don't agree," said Montgomery. "Let's go to the next battle so we can both get to bed at a decent time, shall we?"

"Fine with me," said Janeway. "Even if I agreed that the Doctor was involved in the HoloRevolution—hell, let's go for it, let's say he was the ringleader. Even so, he knows more about the Borg than anyone else except for the other two people you're keeping locked in prison. Why not let him help you find a cure for the virus? Why reprogram such a vital resource into a mindless automaton shoveling dilithium?"

"Janeway, you're like a damaged data loop, endlessly repeating yourself," snapped Montgomery. "I have reasons and orders for doing what I'm doing, and while your compassion for your crew does you credit, I think you're just a little bit biased in this particular situation. The needs of the many outweigh the needs of the few."

"I'm getting mighty tired of that phrase being thrown up as an excuse," said Janeway. "So you're going to keep two people imprisoned who could very well be innocent, knowing that they face the possibility of insanity and death?" she pressed, wanting him to say it himself.

"Yes, damn it, yes, for the good of the Earth!"

"And you're going to lobotomize a being that could

very well help you stop the virus simply because you *think* he might be involved in an uprising?"

"We need to make an example. You've seen what a simple strike can do. Eight people are now dead. We've got to stop this thing before Baines can get any deeper into our systems."

"Thank you, Admiral. That's what I wanted to hear. Janeway out."

She took a perverse delight in the shocked, insulted look on Montgomery's face as she touched the control panel. Janeway looked over at Data, standing to her left, out of Montgomery's view.

"Well, Mr. Data? Will you join our merry little band of traitors and radicals?"

It was a long moment as she watched the android consider. "It is a difficult decision," he said. "But . . . I have learned the right ones often are."

Like all of Baines's modified holograms, the one wearing the face and body of Lieutenant Vassily Andropov had been designed to be confident, but not reckless. So when he walked into the correctional facility at 2100 hours, he moved with the same ease in his body as the real Andropov moved in his. He had thoroughly studied the man he was to impersonate, and had all his mannerisms, ticks, expressions, and even his slight Russian accent down perfectly. No one would know the difference.

Barbara Robinson, the other lieutenant who manned the first security entrance into the building, was already there, a cup of coffee in her hand. She smiled at him.

"Evening, Vassily," she said.

"Evening, Barbara," he replied. "How's the coffee tonight?"

"Slightly more viscous than usual, but with that same bitterness we've grown to know and love," she quipped, taking a sip.

The hologram chuckled. "Sounds about right," he said. He stepped through the checkpoint as if he had done it a thousand times before, as if it was all routine, as if he was going to put his briefcase down and go for some coffee himself.

When the alarm sounded, he looked as startled as Robinson did.

"That's weird," said Robinson. "Try it again."

Shrugging, the Vassily hologram stepped out, then stepped in again. A second time, alarms shrilled. Robinson shook her head and touched a few buttons, silencing the sound.

"Security here. What is your condition?"

"Code green," she said. "False alarm. Lieutenant Andropov tripped the alarm." Deftly she pressed control pads on her console. "There's got be a misalignment in one of the bioscanners—no, wait, both of them are malfunctioning. Damn it."

The hologram groaned. "So I get to stand here for a few hours, is that it?"

Robinson grimaced sympathetically. "Sir, request permission to check him in manually."

"Granted. Let him in and get him to work fixing the problem. We're trying to sleep up here." The hologram heard laughter in the background, met Robinson's eyes, and grinned.

"Will do, sir. I'll let you know when we've corrected the problem. Robinson out."

Still grinning, she reached for her tricorder. "Silly stuff, but hey, regs are regs."

"I know. I could be an alien in disguise," he said, as he permitted her to scan him. He was completely at ease.

She found what she expected to—that the figure before her was a flesh and blood human, particularly, one Vassily Andropov. "Nice briefcase," she said, taking it from him.

"Thanks. Just got it." Again, the hologram was not worried. When Robinson flipped it open to scan it, she saw only a few scattered padds, a small tool kit, and a private communicator. She did not see the complex array of equipment, blinking on and off as it went about its job of projecting not only the hologram of Andropov, but a smaller hologram of normalcy about itself. Unaware of what she beheld, Robinson snapped the case closed and handed it back to him.

"Come on in," she invited, teasingly.

"Why, thank you," he said, and stepped forward. As long as the "briefcase" was within two meters of his projection, he would not dematerialize. It was he who had suggested putting Vassily's very real tool kit into the briefcase, along with the holographic projection of ordinary items. It gave him the perfect excuse to carry the case with him at all times as he went about his "job." He recalled the pleasure he had felt when Baines's eyes had lit up with approval at his shrewd thinking.

It would have taken the real Vassily a couple of hours to "repair" the problem of misaligned bioscanners. The hologram would have to work for the same length of time to do what he had come here to do—adjust every bioscanner in the building to analyze a holographic signature as if it were a biological one. He was the vanguard of Baines's troops. Once he had rendered it as easy for them to enter as if they were human, the floodgates would open.

As he passed Robinson, sitting at her desk with a padd and her sludgy coffee, he thought to himself: *We'll get you next.*

Chapter 5

LIBBY ALLOWED HERSELF a few hours of sleep. Her mind chafed at the forced inactivity but her body, screaming for rest, fell asleep almost immediately. She awoke still groggy but slightly more refreshed.

She had an odd ache in her chest and it took her a while to figure out what it was. At last, she realized it was a sense of betrayal. She had liked and respected Covington. To think the woman was somehow involved . . .

No, that was jumping to conclusions. Covington was clearly trying to redirect her efforts away from Blake and his Borg expertise and onto Montgomery, that much was certain. The question was—why? Libby had high levels of clearance, but not the highest. Perhaps it was just routine. Covington was, after all, the Director of Covert Ops. There were some things Libby wasn't supposed to know, and that didn't mean they were sinister things.

Libby could understand it if Covington were simply doing her job and protecting classified information. But why put her on the trail of an innocent man? Nothing Covington had given Libby had lent credence to her hints that Montgomery was a dangerous mole.

Libby brushed her teeth, thinking hard. If Montgomery was being set up, someone out there had a reason for doing so. Who would benefit if Montgomery's hands were suddenly shackled, if he were put in jail for being a traitor? It hadn't taken a genius to observe that Covington and Montgomery knew and disliked each other a great deal. Could Covington be that shallow, that she would go to such efforts simply to one-up a personal enemy? Libby couldn't imagine anyone who would waste resources on such frivolous goals getting far in SI, and Covington had gotten far indeed. No, if Covington had her reasons for getting Montgomery out of the way, they were big ones, bigger than any personal vendetta.

Which led, inevitably and chillingly, back to what Libby had been able to learn. She had only been able to decode the barest fraction of the Royal Protocol document, but that was enough to scare her to death. She needed to know more, but frankly, was afraid of what she would find.

Slightly refreshed from her nap, Libby sat back down at the computer and suppressed a groan. She hated this stuff. The hours wore on. Libby decoded a few more key words, and they did nothing to assuage her distress.

Finally, rubbing her grit-filled eyes, she decided to try to take stock of what she'd been able to uncover.

One: It was clear that the Federation had been aware of a potential virus for at least the last five years. Long after *Voyager* had been pulled into the Delta Quadrant, and certainly long before its return just a few weeks ago. The not-so-subtle efforts to somehow shift the blame onto the ship, its crew, or both were obviously in the wrong.

Poor Harry, she thought.

Two: As anyone would logically expect, ever since the disaster at Wolf 359, Starfleet Intelligence had been furiously studying everything they could about the Borg. To know one's enemy was to be able to prepare to fight it. It made sense that they would collect every bit of debris from the destroyed Borg ships—past and present—and study it thoroughly.

"Past" referred to the Borg vessel which had almost caused Zefram Cochrane to miss his date with destiny in 2063. The *Enterprise*'s role in what amounted to saving humanity and probably the universe into the bargain had been well documented. Debris from the Borg sphere destroyed by the *Enterprise* had been scattered into space. Some of it had been caught in Earth's orbit, and, as was virtually inevitable, much had eventually found its way planetside. Where it was found, it was gathered up for investigation.

So far, so good, Libby thought. No indication of anything other than expected procedure to safeguard the Federation from one of its most deadly threats.

Here things began to get spotty and Libby was forced into conjecture. She got a few words here and there that gave her some idea as to what SI was looking for as it analyzed this debris: "syntax," "structure," "computer." Borg were part machine, part person. What made them so was the computer protocol, which somehow produced the nanoprobes, controlled the collective, and linked the queen so expertly to her hive.

What wasn't immediately clear was where the virus had come from. Something in what SI had been studying contained the virus—she'd been able to get the word "dormant." She could make a good guess that the Borg vessels had been booby-trapped in some way, that even in destruction, they could somehow plant this virus and make more Borg. But why hadn't that happened? What flipped the switch, to use an old metaphor, from dormant to active?

Libby realized that she had done all her limited decryption skills would permit her to do. She'd have to bring someone else in, someone who could decrypt the whole damned document. This was the Rosetta stone to the entire present Borg threat, she knew it in her bones. There were answers in here, but for the moment, they were tantalizingly out of reach.

She gnawed her lip. Who to trust? There was one person she could think of, but she cringed from the task. Then she thought of what the world would be like if the virus went unchecked, and began sending a message.

After everyone else had left, Chakotay lingered behind. Janeway set a fresh pot of coffee to brewing—"Decaf," she said, "none of us has been getting enough sleep"—and almost collapsed on the couch beside her former first officer. With the ease of old friends, he draped his arm over her shoulder, and she leaned against his chest.

"You look exhausted," he said.

"Flattery will get you nowhere," she replied. He chuckled and his warm breath stirred her hair. "Do you know," she continued, "for the first time since this whole thing began, I really think we might succeed."

"That depends on what we want to succeed at," Chakotay responded. "I think we'll succeed admirably in getting everyone thrown in the brig for the rest of their lives, which would be something of a record."

"You don't mean that."

"Only a little bit."

She punched him playfully and rose, getting out two mugs. "You may be right at that," she said, "but I'd be willing to trade that for Seven and Icheb's lives, the Doctor's mind, and the continuation of the human race."

"Everyone who was here tonight is," said Chakotay, taking the mug of steaming brown liquid she handed him. "Even Data."

"That's part of why I feel we'll be able to pull this off," Janeway said. She took a sip. Even decaffeinated, the elixir was heavenly.

Her computer chimed softly. She groaned. "Who is it this time?" she asked rhetorically, rising and going over to the computer. Harry Kim's face appeared on the screen.

"Got another one," he said.

She knew at once what he meant. "Put it through."

For the second time in as many days, Janeway found herself looking at old-fashioned white lettering on a dark screen. Odd, how the highest level of computer sophistication manifested itself in such a comparatively unsophisticated fashion.

* * *

Hello again, Lieutenant Kim. I have some more information for you. Starfleet has known about a potential Borg virus for over five years. Voyager *is not in any way responsible for it and I will be able to help you prove it shortly. The key to this puzzle lies in what Starfleet has been researching—the Borg computer protocol. Starfleet has been examining Borg debris, and this debris is what carried the virus. I will have more for you soon. Your friend, Peregrine.*

"My God," breathed Janeway. "I wish there were some way to verify that this person is genuine."

Chakotay, who had come to stand beside her and who had also read the missive, said, "I think he or she is genuine. You can't send that kind of heavily blocked message without having a certain level of clearance. The real question is, are we being fed disinformation?"

"You think someone is trying to set us up? Make us act precipitously?"

"Entirely possible," said Chakotay.

Janeway turned back to the message and read it again. "But it all sounds so credible. It's exactly what we would do—analyze the debris, try to figure out how their computer systems worked. And from what we know of the Borg, I wouldn't put this virus idea past them."

She touched a control pad and Kim's face again appeared on the screen. "Thanks, Harry. Any time you get a message, day or night, I want to hear about it."

"Aye, ma'am."

"Harry, does the name Peregrine mean anything to

you? It's not a typical type of code name for Intelligence agents."

Harry shook his head. "I know it's a type of hawk, but no, it has no special meaning."

"You've done good work tonight, Lieutenant. Get some sleep."

"Thank you, ma'am. Goodnight, Admiral."

Chakotay took her half-empty cup. "Let me get you a warm-up," he said, heading into the small kitchen. Janeway had turned to follow him when her computer chimed yet again.

"Good heavens, Starfleet Command isn't this busy," she grumbled, and touched the pad.

She froze. She recognized the face on the screen. She'd seen it last in Kaz's sickbay, on a small screen, admitting to the deaths of eight innocent people. She'd seen it on a large scale, telling people in a South Carolina restaurant that a strike was in progress.

"Oliver Baines," she said, keeping her voice cool and professional. "What a surprise."

He smiled. "But not a pleasant one, I gather. Ah well. But I think you'll be glad that I contacted you once you hear what I have to say."

Her voice was steely. "Go on." Subtly, so he wouldn't notice, she pressed a keypad and started a trace.

"You and I have something in common." At her skeptical expression, he added, "We both care about the fate of the Doctor. He's . . . he's a hero to me. I've read your logs and I know that you have come to respect him as a person, with the same rights as organic beings. I don't know if you've heard, but the Federation is planning on deprogramming him and all the other EMH Mark Ones they can get their hands on."

"I'm aware of that, yes."

He looked at her closely. "Do you really understand what that means?"

"I do. The Doctor will have only a limited set of basic subroutines. He'll be little more than an automaton."

"His love of opera, his writing skills, his affection for the crew he served so well for seven years—all gone. He'll be a mindless, lumbering—"

"If you've got a point, get to it." Out of the corner of her eye, she saw a light flash on her computer. The trace had failed. Whatever blocking system he had, it was a damn good one.

"I will. Sorry about the trace." He smiled. "You know that I can't stand by and let them do that to the Doctor, or the other EMH Mark Ones. Nor, I think, will you."

"I'm pursuing every avenue I can think of."

"Including getting Mr. Data to perform as an attorney, I assume. Oh—surprised you again. I'm not superhuman, Admiral. But I have been watching you. It doesn't take a genius to assume that an android who's been declared sentient would want to do what he could to save a sentient hologram."

With respect, Janeway said, "Your talents were wasted on Lynaris Prime."

The smugness faded. He seemed genuinely pleased when he said, "Thank you, Admiral. I think we could be allies."

"I don't ally with terrorists and murderers."

"The deaths of those people were a tragic accident. All of the bombs were set to detonate when the buildings were supposed to be empty. They are casualties of war, Admiral, and I'm sorry. But steps need to be taken, or there will be more casualties—holographic causalities. I know that you would mourn the deletion of your Doctor as much as you would the death of any flesh person, and because of that, I'm giving you this warning."

He leaned forward into the viewscreen, his eyes intense. "We are planning to liberate the Doctor."

"How?"

"There are many at the prison site who are not flesh beings anymore. I've replaced key personnel with holographic doppelgängers."

"But how can—"

"Your Doctor is no longer the only hologram with a portable emitter. Mine aren't quite as sophisticated, but they will do."

So the Doctor had been right. Baines had been able to create a portable emitter for his holograms.

"Don't think about warning anyone," Baines continued. "I'm going to put my plan into action the minute we terminate this conversation. I didn't know your timetable, if any, for any rescue you might be planning. It's my understanding that you have three friends in that prison. I didn't want you to get hurt if by chance you were . . . involved."

"You don't seem to care much about human life," Janeway said.

"That's not true! I only—"

"Why are you warning me?"

"As I said, we could be allies. At the very least, the old adage applies—the enemy of my enemy is my friend. We're more alike than different. You are one of the few organics in any position of power who understands what I'm fighting for."

Chakotay had remained utterly silent and immobile. Neither he nor Janeway wanted Baines to know that anyone else was overhearing this conversation. She felt his eyes on her but didn't give him away by even glancing quickly in his direction.

This was no short warning. Baines was sincere, at least in part—he did want her as an ally. He wanted to talk. A thought flickered in her mind. Perhaps she could take this opportunity and dissuade him. After all, he was right—they shared a common goal, although they were worlds apart on how to achieve that goal.

"You're right, Mr. Baines," she said smoothly. "I want the Doctor whole and unharmed. I have no desire to see the other EMHs' potential so degraded. I do think there should be rights granted to holograms."

His body posture softened slightly. "Yes," he said, "Yes, I knew you would understand."

"You and the Doctor had a brief conversation, is that correct?"

"Yes, and for that he was sent to prison. Which is why I must ensure that he is freed before they do this terrible thing to him!"

"The Doctor told me that he tried to dissuade you from violence."

"He did. And I listened to him. A strike isn't violent. I did nothing to interfere with any EMHs or any holograms that were in a position to save lives."

He desperately wanted credit for what he'd done right, Janeway thought. Almost like a child.

"You did. But—"

"And I told you, the bombs weren't supposed—"

"But they did, Mr. Baines. They *did* kill people. You made that decision to destroy property and took some innocent lives right along with it. You've got to live with that choice, but you also have the chance to not make things any worse. You say this attack on the complex where the Doctor is being held is going to be violent. That's escalating things from accidental deaths to deliberate deaths. No one is going to listen to you if you do that. No one is going to believe you're on the side of the angels if you start piling up corpses in your wake."

He stared at her, stunned at the frankness of her speech. Out of the corner of her eye she saw Chakotay start smiling. He knew where she was going with this.

"I think the Doctor is very wise, Mr. Baines, and the advice he gave you was excellent. Slaves in the 1800s would never have been freed if the people in power at the time had not realized the injustice of their ways and pushed to end a dreadful institution. A hundred years later, the Civil Rights movement would have been a failure if it had only been African Americans protesting discrimination. And violence against women would not have ended had not men worked alongside women to make it stop. It's fine for the holograms to stand up for their rights, and they should. But if you keep pushing this, those of us who are actually on your side are going to be forced to turn against you and decry what you are doing."

"But how can I make them see?" he cried, his voice breaking. If nothing else, Baines was no cynic. It was obvious he cared passionately about his holographic friends.

"You lived with the Doctor for seven years. You had a chance to see him rise above what he was designed for, to learn to like him as a person. Everyone else thinks of holograms as slaves or servants, not people. How can I make them understand without something being at stake if they don't?"

"It seems to me that the Doctor did a fine job of conveying what it was like to be a hologram, destined to be at the beck and call of his creators," said Janeway. "His holonovel really made the reader feel the humiliation, the fear. He got that information across clearly and profoundly, with not so much as a scratch. Don't underestimate the power of words, Mr. Baines. You don't always need to hurt people to get their attention."

He had seemed to be listening, but now he was shaking his head. "Your way will take too long," he said flatly. "Too many will be taken off-line, or reprogrammed. I can't afford to wait."

"Maybe you won't have to."

He looked at her suspiciously, but said, "I'm listening."

Janeway made her decision. It was all or nothing now.

"I'll admit it. We were planning a jailbreak of our own to free Seven, Icheb, and the Doctor, all of whom are in what I believe to be immediate danger. I can't afford to wait, either. You can help us, if you will. Help us to buy some time and minimize loss of life."

Baines snorted. "It's a trap. I'm not an idiot, Admiral."

She shook her head, aware that Chakotay was staring at her. Apparently, he *hadn't* known where she was going with this.

"No trap, Mr. Baines. I give you my word. If you assist us, I promise you will have a chance to talk to the Doctor within a few hours of his liberation."

He shook his head so violently his hair flew. "No. I don't trust you. You'll betray me. The Doctor will never be free if I—"

"How dare you!" The words cracked like an old-fashioned pistol shot. Even Chakotay started, and Baines shut his mouth so quickly that his teeth snapped together. Janeway rarely gave in to her emotions so freely, but she couldn't help it and frankly didn't want to.

"How *dare* you!" she repeated. "You say you understand the depth of feeling I have for the Doctor. If that's true, how can you accuse me of sitting here worrying about setting a trap for you when they're about to destroy him? He's an icon to you, a symbol of your revolution, a tool. But he's a hell of a lot more than that to me. He's my friend. I'll die before I let them harm him, Mr. Baines, and if you believe nothing else I say, then you'd damn well better believe that."

They stared at one another for a long moment. Finally, Baines spoke.

"I do believe that, Admiral. And I will help you in any way I can."

Chapter 6

THE RAIN WAS surprisingly cold.

B'Elanna huddled miserably under what little shelter she had been able to find, a cluster of enormous leaves close to the ground. She was grateful for her new "clothes," although the skin she'd been able to get from the *grikshak* still smelled of carrion and her flesh cringed from the moist underside where it touched her. But, beggars couldn't be choosers.

"You know, Mother," she said aloud, just to hear her own voice, "we could have had a nice, traditional reunion in some pleasant café over a cup of coffee."

The soft, seemingly endless patter of rain was her only answer.

Even had her mother not decided to play this potentially deadly game of hide-and-seek with her only offspring, Torres knew that Miral wouldn't be caught dead in a pleasant café. No, if they weren't here in this miserable wet wilderness, they'd be knocking back mugs of bloodwine and singing loud, grating Klingon songs. Maybe this was better.

She didn't want to admit it, but a part of her—a very small part—was enjoying this. B'Elanna had always thrived on pushing her own limits. She dove on every engineering challenge with gusto that would have pleased Kahless himself. She couldn't count the hours she had lain awake in bed, in recent years with Tom snoring softly beside her, staring at the ceiling while her mind chewed on one problem or another. Her desire to excel, to make a difference, had driven her all her life. But Torres had never really thought about it too much.

Except now, she had a lot of time on her hands with often nothing to do but think. And she wasn't necessarily happy with what she saw floating to the top of her consciousness.

Why had she been so driven? It was easy to lay the blame on her parents, but that was not really the whole story. Her mother had pushed B'Elanna into Klingon culture with too much enthusiasm and too little preparation for it. Everything she had done had been done full tilt, with lots of yelling and broad gestures. Her quiet father had not been able to compete. B'Elanna still hadn't had a chance to talk to him, to ask him, as one adult to another, what had really transpired between him and Miral. That had been one of the things she had wanted to do, but she hadn't expected this, hadn't expected her mother to throw still one more impossible challenge at her half-human daughter, hadn't expected to be sitting naked but for a dead animal skin alone in the wilderness while cold rain sluiced down—

Torres wiped at a face that was wet with more than raindrops.

This was no game. This was no stint in a monastery, or lecture, or four-hour excursion to sit, bored to death, at a performance of Klingon opera. This was very real, was very deadly, and Miral had done this for a reason.

Torres reviewed her time on the Barge of the Dead. Even now, her heart sped up at the recollection. What a terrifying experience that had been. All her repressed memories of Klingon myth and legend had shot to the surface, with sharp teeth, sharp weapons, and sharp, painful memories of failure and disappointments.

She'd done what she'd needed to, in the misty realm of whatever it had been—spirit, shared dreaming, subconscious. And beyond all the logic with which the very pragmatic B'Elanna Torres understood, somehow Miral had known about it.

"But that wasn't enough for you, Mother, was it?" she said, again speaking aloud. "I couldn't just save you in the spirit world, I had to come here and do it all over again in the material world. How many times do I have to prove myself worthy to you?"

And the answer came almost like a physical blow inside her skull: *Until you believe it yourself.*

She laughed, shakily, more unsettled than amused by the forceful revelation. "Well," she said, "that could take forever."

But even as she said it, she knew it had better not. It had been fine to be the sullen rebel, the wild child, when it was only herself who stood to lose. But things had changed. Now, there were others. Her mother, stubbornly ensconced in the wilderness until Torres came to find her. Her father, who so clearly wanted to make things right again, if he could. And her own, immediate family: Tom, whom she loved more than she hated herself, and her beautiful, perfect daughter, named for her grandmother. Their fates all hinged on what B'Elanna did this moment, this hour, this day, this month. It was a weight she never thought she'd have to carry, but she found the burden a sweet one.

She was so lost in reverie that she didn't noticed the rain slowing down until it had almost completely stopped. She blinked as the dark green light of the jungle shifted slowly to brighter hues, and the steady, soothing rhythm of the rain gave way to first silence, then the tentative calling of birds and animals.

She crawled out from under her shelter of leaves and her hand immediately sank wrist-deep in mud. Only a few days ago that would have produced a snort of disgust. Now, she stepped forward, dropped the cloak for the time being, and slathered the protective mud all over her body.

She was adapting. She was growing.

She was meeting the Challenge of Spirit, and as she smoothed the smelly, goopy stuff over her arms and torso, she understood why the priests and priestesses had chosen that name for this ordeal.

Libby waited nervously for him to appear. She had made a halfhearted attempt to put on some makeup, but then at the last moment had washed it off. There was no need to dress up. This wasn't a date, it was business. Deadly, dangerous business.

Tourists didn't frequent the site she had chosen for their rendezvous. It was a rocky shoreline about a mile or two from her little cabin, without the long stretches of white sand that sunbathers flocked to. She had walked here; the brisk wind had brought some color back into her pale cheeks and the exercise had helped her to feel slightly more alert.

He materialized about five minutes after she had arrived. She hadn't seen him since Covington had requested the temporary transfer. He looked good.

Tall, slender, his golden hair turning silver, he was dressed informally, as she had requested, in slightly baggy pants and a sweater. She recognized the sweater. She remembered pulling it off him the first time they had made love.

He saw her and waved, walking toward her carefully amid the rocks. She tucked her hands under her arms and smiled back, somewhat tightly. The wind was having far too much fun with her thick, curly hair, and she knew it'd be a rat's nest by the time she had a chance to comb it out. If she'd been thinking she'd have pulled it back in a ponytail, at least.

He stood beside her now, much taller than she. It was the first time they had met in private since he had gently taken her hands, looked into her eyes, and said that they needed to end it.

"Hello, sir," she said, and extended her hand.

He shook it, his hand warm and strong as it closed about hers. She knew he hadn't wanted to end it, had in fact wanted to take it further, but Assistant Director

Aidan Fletcher realized before Libby had that their romance was destroying their working relationship. They'd remained good friends and in the end, the supervisor-employee relationship hadn't been damaged. He'd been right to break things off, though she had cried for days at the time.

"It's good to see you, Agent Webber. Though considering the distinctly informal aspect of our environment, I'd prefer it if you called me Aidan."

"All right." She pressed a small button in the pocket of her jacket. Almost immediately she heard a small chirp from Aidan's jacket. She blushed.

He laughed. "You tried to put up a dampening field without telling me," he said. "I see Covington's taught you how to sneak."

His easy manner was calming her. She gave him a quick grin. "Impossible to sneak past you," she said.

His smile faded a little. "Listen, um . . . It's no secret that you've gotten back together with Harry Kim, so I assume you wanted to see me on business."

Harry. If she hadn't been disentangled from Aidan, she never would have been free to rediscover him. She had told Harry, at the banquet, that she'd slept with a few men and fallen in love with one. She felt a surge of gratitude toward that one man, who now stood before her, for being wise enough to let her go.

"You're right," she said. "This is business. Deadly business, I think."

"How very cloak and dagger of you, Miss Webber."

"Don't joke!" At her expression, he sobered at once. "I'm onto something big."

"Go on." He listened intently, his gray eyes fastened

on hers, as she told him what had happened. She left nothing out—not Covington's order to start dating Harry again, not the story of a fictitious mole who would eventually "turn out to be" Kenneth Montgomery, not her stalking of and eventual meeting with Trevor Blake.

That did get a reaction from him. "Blake?" Aidan said, startled. "I had no idea he was borrowed expertise. He showed up one day with not much fanfare and just stayed. We all kind of forgot about him. He's—well, I suppose you know."

She nodded. "He's not particularly memorable," she said. "He kept every memo from Montgomery in his computer. I mean every single one—birthday parties, baby shower announcements, you name it." She hesitated, then asked, "Aidan—does the term Royal Protocol mean anything to you?"

"It's a horrible document that Starfleet ought to have banned as torture," Aidan said. "Is there any other reference?"

"It was one of the files on Blake's computer. I was slogging through it like a good little agent when all of a sudden it turned to gibberish," said Libby.

"Gibberish?"

"As in deeply encrypted information. I've got the basic decryption skills they teach every agent at my level, but there's much more there I simply can't crack. Here's what I have learned, though. This Borg virus didn't come to Earth with *Voyager*. It's been around for a long time—say, for a few hundred years. I think the Borg booby-trapped their vessels, trying to find a way to spread the virus eventually even if they were destroyed."

Aidan nodded. "It makes sense, but why hide this? It's exactly what we should be doing. Investigating."

"That's what I thought. I guess Starfleet doesn't want everyone to know they knew about this virus and did nothing to stop it, or even warn anyone about the debris." Bitterly, she added, "I just broke a few more words that lead me to believe that the virus is spread by physical contact."

Aidan stared. "You mean, if anyone touched the debris, they'd become infected?"

"It sounds that way."

"But then why hasn't it happened long before now? We've had some of that debris around for years."

She shrugged helplessly. "Who knows? It could be a set program—the thing doesn't become active until after a certain number of years."

"Or the virus could be mechanical, not organic," mused Aidan. "We know the Borg use nanoprobes for many things. Maybe it needed a command."

"Then what's the command? Who gave it? Why? But again, Aidan—my skills are so basic it's entirely possible that I'm deciphering it all incorrectly. There's so much I still don't know and I don't want to jump to conclusions."

He smiled. "As a famous Baker Street detective said, 'It is a mistake to theorize without all the data.' "

She looked at him steadily. He made the leap quickly and said, "Oh. Now I understand why you contacted me."

"I need your help. I need one of your cryptographers to do a blind decoding."

"Impossible," he said. "I can't authorize that."

"You have to," she said. "If this goes as deep as I think it might, you would be put in danger."

"And you won't be?"

"I'm already in danger. If Covington is going to suspect me, she suspects me by now. This could be nothing. As I said, I may be seeing conspiracies where none exist."

"If the public policy is to shift blame to *Voyager* when it's Starfleet poking and prodding that's let the genie out of the bottle, that's a conspiracy right there."

She waved her hand impatiently. "A minor misdirection, easily rectified by a public apology when the virus is cured. If that's really all it is. But things aren't adding up, Aidan. It's just too strange. My gut is telling me that there's something more, a lot more, and I need to know what it is."

"So do I. I'm your boss, remember?"

"Please just do this for me. As a favor. I've never asked anything from you before. You're the only one I can trust." She was aware that she was pleading, and she didn't like it, but she saw no other course. She also didn't tell him that she wasn't even completely sure she could trust *him.* She had no idea how deep things went at Starfleet Intelligence. It was possible that Aidan was involved.

If he was, she was literally living on borrowed time.

His eyes searched hers for a long moment. "All right. On one condition—that if there is something here bigger than finger-pointing, you call me in the minute you know anything. Do you promise?"

She nodded, vastly relieved. She would, of course, make that call when she had all the information.

"Okay." He shifted uncomfortably on the jagged rocks. "I don't suppose I can take you out for lunch?"

"I don't know that our being seen together is a wise idea right now. If something big is going down, and I go with it, you'll need to be free from Covington's suspicion to act."

"If you were anyone else, I'd accuse you of melodrama," he said. "But I know you too well. All right. Send me that information and I'll have someone get on it immediately."

Impulsively, she reached for his hand. "Thank you, Aidan," she said, her heart full. "Thank you."

Chapter 7

AFTER AIDAN had dematerialized, Libby walked on the beach for a while, absently picking up rocks made smooth by the ceaseless rhythm of the sea, caressing them, and then returning them to the ocean. The action calmed her thoughts. Yes, she was doing the right thing.

She returned to her little cabin in a better mood than when she had left it, but her tension returned when she saw there was a message.

"I hope it's Harry," she muttered under her breath. She tapped the screen and Covington's face appeared.

"Hello, Agent Webber. Just wanted to check in and see how you were progressing with the material I sent you. I'll want an update by this afternoon. And if I may offer some advice, woman to woman—it's always a bad idea to date the boss."

She smiled and winked in a sisterly fashion, and then the screen went dark.

Libby almost couldn't breathe. She had debated the necessity for putting up the dampening field at all, considering how isolated she and Aidan were. Now her legs went weak and she fell into the chair, her stomach churning. Thank God she *had* used the dampening field. Covington was still watching her.

She and Aidan hadn't shouted their relationship from the rooftops, but they hadn't made an effort to hide it, either. No doubt Covington knew they had once been involved. Thank God for that, too. All Covington suspected was that Libby was thinking of cheating on Harry, and she could handle that.

At least, Libby desperately hoped that was all that Covington suspected. Suddenly shaky and feeling extremely paranoid, she removed a small, round object from a drawer and began to check her room carefully for bugs.

Brenna Covington finished her message to Libby Webber, then leaned back in her chair and stretched. The man in her bed said, "God, I love it when you do that. You look just like a cat."

Slowly, she turned and gave him a wide, sultry smile.

"You still here?" she teased. "Don't you have things to do, misinformation to spread, quarrels to start, suspicions to plant?"

Commander Brian Grady stretched in the sheets, imitating her.

"Oh, yes. But you make it damned hard for a man to leave." He beckoned lazily. "Come back to bed. We've both got time. Rank hath its privileges."

Resentment stirred faintly inside her. Brenna Covington knew how to give a lover pleasure, how to feign delight and lust and passion. She had learned those lessons well, from observation in her safe place deep inside. But no man's caresses ever truly moved her.

The Hand had seen to that.

It took her utmost skill to not cringe from Grady's caresses and kisses, to smile up into his face as if she was as enamored as he.

But it was not that he was a cruel or even an unskilled lover. Every man's hand was the Hand. Her deliberate, calculated response of feigned desire was her revenge. She had used her body, tall, taut, and well-shaped, as a tool, as she had used her powers of observation, her brain, her detachment as tools, and all had served her well. Brian Grady was useful to her now. He was in a position where he was trusted and well liked. Those were his tools. She told him what to say and do, and who to say and do it with, and he obeyed. It was easy to manipulate him. He had been hers for three years now. She had something he wanted, wanted desperately, and she exploited that mercilessly to get him to dance to her tune.

So she returned to the bed, and put her tools to work. At one point, he seized her roughly and said, "You know what I want."

"No," she said. "Later. Tonight. It takes too much time."

Disappointment and anger flickered across his face. Denying him anything always frustrated him, so she tried to do so only when necessary. That was part of her power over him—she knew how often he had been disappointed, been overlooked, been denied. She didn't care, but she knew, and utilized that knowledge.

By all rights, Project Full Circle should have been his. She, too, was disappointed that he had not been selected to lead the project; it would have made her job so much easier had her lackey been given such power.

Instead, Starfleet had appointed the hero of the hour, Admiral Kenneth Montgomery. He had courage, intelligence, and tenacity, and, unfortunately for Covington's ultimate plans, scruples. The man was incorruptible. Covington knew; she'd tried, several years ago. She had done nothing to truly compromise herself or her plans, of course. She was far too sharp for that. But she had done enough for Montgomery to regard her with suspicion and distrust.

She had to get him out of the way, or at least hamper him as much as possible. He wasn't a fool, and sooner or later, he'd be onto her. So Covington had searched for the perfect innocent agent to take him down. Libby Webber's name had reached her desk. Libby's former connection with *Voyager* made her someone that Covington needed to redirect as soon as possible. The pretty thing was an information gatherer, nothing more, and Covington found her sweet, malleable, and eager to please.

So Covington had spent some time putting together some false evidence and put Little Miss Music on Montgomery's trail. Although Covington had to admit, Libby was better and had more initiative than she had suspected. Libby's decision to track down Blake came perilously close to jeopardizing the entire plan. Fortunately, Blake, though brilliant, was utterly devoid of social graces and probably wouldn't know what had happened if Libby had actually seduced him.

One thing Covington knew for certain, though, was that, seduced or not, Blake would never utter one word of the plans he, Grady, and Covington had been working on over the last several years. He had too much at stake.

And seeing Aidan Fletcher . . . Covington dismissed it. She knew he and Libby had an affair a while ago. She made it her business to know these things. Apparently, boring good-boy Harry Kim wasn't enough to keep Libby's attention for long.

Voyager's return played right into Covington's hands. It couldn't have been timelier. There it was, complete with two Borg and a host of futuristic refits. All attention was focused on it. It was unknown, unfamiliar, and she understood well that it was never a big leap from "unfamiliar" to "suspected."

Grady, acting on Covington's instructions, was the first to voice suspicions about the Doctor when the strike erupted, and the Borg when the virus began to manifest. She didn't have the pleasure of seeing him do it, but she knew how he would look: reluctant to cast blame on returning heroes, embarrassed to think bad thoughts about them, but . . . just worried enough so that Montgomery would be worried, too. And Montgomery was one who didn't sit on his hunches, but acted.

She had watched with amusement, standing just out of viewing range, one time when the meddlesome Janeway had contacted Grady. How easily he lied to

Voyager's former captain, that boyish freckled face screwed up into an expression of concern. It had been all Covington could do not to give herself away by an injudicious snicker.

Janeway had been a problem, that much was certain. Covington had not fully appreciated the depth of Janeway's devotion to her crew, even the Borg, even the artificial doctor. They needed to be safely away under suspicion, of course. The last thing Covington needed was two Borg and a doctor putting their heads together with Starfleet trying to figure out the virus. They would, she was certain of it. And both Covington and her carefully laid plans of the last several years would come to ruin.

Janeway was like the dogs Covington learned the admiral loved: dedicated, loyal, and not likely to surrender something once she had gotten her teeth into it. Her continuous yapping, fortunately, had alienated the one man she ought to be courting—Montgomery. The more Janeway demanded, the more he dug in his heels. It was all working out better than Covington had feared.

Not soon enough for Covington, Grady was spent. He whistled as he put on his uniform. He would be in top form today, she knew.

Harry didn't say much during their lunch together. He toyed with his noodle salad and let his coffee get cold. When Libby tried to make conversation, her only reward was a monosyllabic response.

The average girlfriend would start getting suspicious at this point. She'd feel hurt and rejected, wonder if there was someone else, or if her sweetheart was growing tired of her. Libby knew better than to jump to such outrageous conclusions. For one thing, she knew Harry. For another, she knew what Harry was involved in.

She didn't know for certain, of course, what his specific plans were. It was a pity they couldn't trust one another, but that was something she had accepted going in to Starfleet Intelligence on the level she desired. No one outside of a very few people in SI was to know what she was doing, or else she'd be of very little use. That included friends, concert managers, family . . . and Harry.

She even wondered if she'd made a foolish slip by giving him the "code name" of Peregrine. No one in Intelligence used code names like that. But she needed a moniker of some sort and what had first flashed into her mind was the sight of the great, glorious falcon wheeling above them during their trip to the desert. She'd seen it shortly before sunset, when she was partway through the delicious meal with her beloved in the middle of nowhere, only a few hours before they had made love for the first time in over seven years.

The bird symbolized hope for her, and before she knew it, she'd picked it as her contact name. Fortunately, she had kept the peregrine close to her heart. Harry had noticed her looking at it but they had discussed it only briefly. With luck, he wouldn't make the connection.

Her hunch that something big was going down with Harry and probably several other *Voyager* crew members was confirmed when, at the end of the meal, Harry pushed aside his half-eaten entrée and announced, "I just wanted to let you know that I might be out of touch for a while."

She sipped her tea. Her own lunch hadn't stood a chance against her appetite and she'd almost licked the lasagna plate clean.

"Really?" she asked, hoping she had the proper mix of concern and trust in her voice. "What's going on?"

"I can't tell you."

Mentally, Libby shook her head and chuckled. Good heavens, but he would make a lousy spy. Aloud, she said, "Why not?" as she reached for his hand.

"I have orders."

That confirmed what Libby suspected. Whatever Harry was planning, higher ranks than the junior officers were involved. She wondered if Harry realized how much information he was conveying while explaining that he couldn't tell her anything.

He turned his hand over so he could entwine his fingers with hers.

"A mission?" Libby pressed.

He squeezed her hand, and then released it. "I told you, honey, I can't discuss it."

"How long will you be gone?"

To her surprise, he laughed, then sobered at once. "I've no idea." Again, he had told her something. He wouldn't just be out of touch, he'd be physically away from San Francisco.

"I know it's hard for you to understand," he continued. "You're a musician. You've got your concert schedule to honor, but you're the one who makes that schedule. When you're in Starfleet, you don't get to make the decisions."

"I do understand," she said. He would never know just how much. "It's all right." She smiled. "You've been too much of a distraction anyway. I need to get a lot of practice in if I'm going to be ready for that Vulcan tour next month."

Even as she said it, she saw him visibly tense, and she knew why. There was a very real chance there wouldn't be any more humans on the planet by next month.

The entire population of the Earth could be Borg. *Would* be Borg, if something weren't done to stop it. One thing she had said to Harry had been the honest-to-God truth—he was a distraction. She had work to do.

When he kissed her good-bye, he was at once more intense than usual and more distant. She stroked his cheek and looked into his eyes lovingly, trying to convey nothing more than girlish sorrow at parting and hoping to hide her worry. Something big was definitely going down, and she wished she knew what it was.

When she materialized in her cabin, she saw a blinking red light. Adrenaline flooded her. She desperately hoped the message was from Fletcher, not Covington.

Instead, the face that appeared on the screen was Harry's. His brown eyes were large and his handsome face somber.

"Libby, once before I left on a mission on *Voyager.* I was gone for seven years. I don't know what's going to happen, so I—hell, I'm breaking every rule in the book by talking to you, but I just couldn't walk off and leave you, knowing I might not come back. I wanted to say a proper good-bye, in case . . . in case things didn't work out. I love you, Libby. And when I get back," he paused and smiled, "you and I are going to have a nice long talk about a few things."

His image disappeared. Libby blinked back tears. "I love you, too, Harry," she said into the silence.

Covington went through her day as usual, showing up at her office and conducting the day-to-day business of Covert Ops as if it actually still mattered. And as usual, she stayed late, saying a cheerful goodnight to her staff as they went home. They thought her a hard worker. They thought her pathetic and lonely and married to her job.

She was content to let them think that. She knew why she was staying late.

Around two A.M., after taking a last scan of the entire building to make sure she was alone, Covington took a deep breath. Excitement and anticipation shivered through her. What she was about to do aroused and excited her more than any clumsy male touch.

Here was intimacy. Here was connection and power and fulfillment and passion.

Here was love.

It was late when Libby finally heard from Fletcher. His face was unreadable and his manner uncharacteristically brusque.

"I did as you asked, Libby. The decrypted file is now in your computer. Contact me once you've read it." And without another word, his image disappeared.

Her initial surprise at his rudeness gave way to apprehension. Suddenly Libby didn't want to read the document she'd breached all kinds of protocol to read. Suddenly she wanted nothing to do with this whole spy business. She wanted to just be what the world thought she was, a concert performer, utterly ignorant of espionage and lies and Borg threats like the rest of the world.

But she was who she was, and knew what she knew, and it was with trembling hands that she pressed the key and the file sprang to her screen.

There was a lot of technical jargon that she vaguely grasped. She could reread all that later, after she'd gotten the gist of the file. As her eyes flickered over the words, her breathing became shallower.

This was horrible. This was beyond imagining.

The question as to why the Borg virus had remained dormant for so long was an easily answerable one, and she wondered why neither she nor Fletcher had figured it out before now. Or maybe it wasn't that great of a mystery. Maybe they just hadn't wanted to acknowledge the dreadful truth. In order for the Borg virus to be activated, someone had to issue a specific command. That someone could be none other than the Borg queen.

The virus was active and had been for several days now. Which led inevitably to the conclusion that somewhere not too far from Earth, the queen lurked.

But how could this be? Starfleet knew how to find a Borg ship. There was none anywhere in the quadrant that they knew of.

Libby swallowed and read on. Her stomach churned and suddenly she wished she hadn't eaten quite so much of her lasagna at lunch.

Trevor Blake went on at great and monotonous length about theory and execution thereof. She had to rub her eyes and reread a sentence here and there to make sure she understood it. Exciting and fast-paced, Blake's writing wasn't. At one point, she saw something and did her usual rub and reread, certain that she'd misinterpreted it. After the third reading, she desperately wished she had misinterpreted it, but was sickly afraid she grasped the meaning all too well.

Trevor Blake had demonstrated a bit of a sense of humor in selecting the Royal Protocol document as the cover for his treatise on creating a Borg queen. Not only did it serve as a powerful deterrent in case anyone downloaded it—no one in his right mind would voluntarily slog through that mind-numbing document—but there was a second, terrifyingly ironic twist as well.

It sank in slowly, sickeningly, like the news of the death of a loved one.

Oh God. Oh God. Oh no.

Bile rose in her throat. She stumbled toward the kitchen and barely made it to the sink before she threw up, sobbing as she did so. Tears poured down her face in a flood as she sank to the floor, holding herself and shaking. Indigo and Rowena hastened to her, rubbing their furry faces against her bare shins.

Royal Protocol—this Royal Protocol—had nothing to do with etiquette. It had nothing to do with anything sane.

"Royal Protocol" was the name of the computer protocol used by the Borg to create a queen.

And it was already happening.

Brenna Covington rose and went to the small sonic shower she'd requested two years ago. She worked so late, she had explained; sometimes a shower revived her. Of course they installed one for her.

First, she removed her clothes. She took out her special contact lenses, carefully placing them in solution. She didn't need them to see. Then the blond wig went, draped on its stand. She stepped into the shower and closed her eyes as the sweat, dirt, and makeup almost magically dissolved from her body, leaving her feeling reborn.

She stepped out of the shower and regarded her perfect body in the mirror. Long, strong legs. A flat abdomen. She touched it briefly, acknowledging what lay within, unseen.

The scars were all inside. The scars were always, ever, all inside.

Her gaze traveled up past small but firm breasts, to her eyes. She smiled at her reflection.

Get a hold of yourself, Elizabeth, Libby thought fiercely. *You're no good to anyone shivering here on the floor.* Her limbs felt as if they were made of rubber, but she managed to clamber to her feet. She rinsed her mouth out and splashed her face with cold water, then stumbled like a drunken woman back to the computer.

Starfleet Intelligence, with Trevor Blake as head researcher, had spent the last several years deciphering this protocol. They had enough information to create a Borg queen, but had, at least at the time this document was written, not yet deciphered the entire protocol. Pieces were missing. There was a queen somewhere with enough power to activate the virus, but she couldn't yet turn it into the sweeping epidemic that would nearly instantaneously destroy the Earth.

Not yet. But soon. Trevor Blake felt it would be soon.

The Borg had many advantages, but one thing they could not escape and that was almost a disadvantage was the nearly flawless logic by which they operated. Organic beings could bluff, go off on tangents, have inspired insights. But the Borg were as ruthless in their functioning and structure as they were in their decimation of worlds. It made a sort of frightening sense, and Libby wondered why no one had figured this out before Blake had.

Organic beings had created machines. But it was the machines that made organic beings into Borg. Without their technology, the Borg were like an old-fashioned lamp that had been unplugged. Everything the drones did was in response to orders from their queen, her instructions to the hive mind. Damage the queen, and the whole thing fell apart. The queen made drones. How, then, was a queen made?

She was an organic being who would have to become not just Borg, but almost a super-Borg. She was the complete operating system for the entire mammoth structure. She was more than a single being—she was the program made flesh and machine.

In one of those odd connections one sometimes makes when under duress, Libby's mind flashed back to a theater term: deus ex machina. In ancient Greek dramas, occasionally the day was saved by a god from mythology descending onto the stage by means of a mechanical device. It had become a slightly derogatory term in theater and literature, used when an author grafted on a miraculous happy ending when logically there was none to be had.

She didn't give a damn right now about poor plotting and cheesy endings in books and holonovels. Her mind seized on the literal translation of the term "deus ex machina" and worried it like a terrier with a rat:

God from machine.

Clothing largely disguised the sickly gray pallor of Covington's skin, except for hands and face. Special makeup designed by the doctor who had operated on her so well these past several years made her skin seem merely porcelain, not bloodless. Eyes that saw better than any human's met those in the mirror.

But it was the back of her bald head she loved most. This was what Brian Grady so loved to fondle when they coupled; what drew him and held him fast, like a fly in her mammoth spider's web.

No . . . a spider wasn't quite right.

The Borg had figured out how to create a god from a machine. Take an organic being, make her Borg, and give her access to the Royal Protocol . . . and you had a queen. So this was how, when the *Enterprise* destroyed the Borg cube that had been host to Picard and also presumably the queen, she had come back. This was how the Admiral Janeway of the future had been able to slay the queen, and yet there was one somewhere on Earth right now.

You couldn't ever really kill the queen, because the queen wasn't a person. It—she—was a program.

It was so simple. So logical. So terrifying.

For a long moment, Libby's mind refused to function. It was trying to wrap itself around the almost inconceivable reality that Starfleet Intelligence was well on its way to creating a complete Borg queen who would utterly destroy humanity. Why? It was good to know how the bastards did it, of course, but who the hell would—

And then she knew.

Covington went into her office and settled herself at the computer. With the touch of a button, a hidden panel revealed itself. She licked her lips, drawing out the moment of pleasure, and then stepped into the secret alcove. Green light bathed her gray body.

At once, voices flooded her mind, but she was not overwhelmed. She reached out in joy, touching each mind one with her own, feeling the surge of their responses. Their need and desire for her. Tears filled her eyes and spilled down her cheeks, as they did every time she connected with them thusly. Their unconditional, unwavering, undying devotion and love flooded her, and she heard and responded with every cell of her body.

They were hers, better now for being hers than they had been before she had sought them out. And there would be so many more to come, soon, soon. Each one a part of the nearly perfect whole. She loved them, would protect and defend them, even as she gave them their orders, even as she instructed some to die in order to preserve the whole. They fed her spirit in a way that no single human ever had. They nourished her as she took care of them. Humans thought it all went one way, but they were wrong. Terribly wrong.

They were her beloved subjects, her precious drones, and she was their adoring queen.

Chapter 8

MONTGOMERY WAS just returning from another meeting with his staff when Kaz stopped him in the hall. Sighing, Montgomery said, "Don't tell me, let me guess. You want a regeneration chamber for the Borg."

Kaz glared at him. "They're not Borg, and it's too late for that."

Montgomery started so violently he spilled his coffee. "What? Are they—"

"No, not yet, thank God. I've had both of them in my sickbay this morning and their vital signs are showing severe distress. We've got to do what we discussed."

Montgomery frowned. "I don't much like that," he said.

"I like even less the thought of these two dying on our watch," said Kaz.

"You're absolutely certain?"

"Stasis has its own risk, especially when the subjects are this weak. I would indeed have to feel this was the only alternative, and I regret to inform you that I've reached that point," Kaz answered.

"Damn it. I don't like the idea of them being difficult to question if an emergency arises," said Montgomery. Kaz said nothing, almost literally biting his tongue to avoid exploding at his commanding officer. Finally Montgomery said, "We can wake them if I need them, right?"

"As I told you earlier, sir, it's risky, but if need be, we can revive them, yes."

"Very well. You may proceed."

Janeway, Data, Chakotay, and Tuvok entered the correctional facility. Janeway felt she was becoming far too familiar with this place. She was getting to know all the security personnel by name. Of course, now every time she met someone, she wondered who was human and who was one of Baines's decoys.

"Good morning, Lieutenants," she said to Andropov and Robinson. She was almost on a first-name basis with Robinson, but Andropov was new. "I think you know who we're here to see."

"Indeed we do," said Robinson, motioning them to step through. "Good morning, Commander Data. It's an honor to meet you, sir."

"Good morning," Data replied. "I only regret that our meeting is taking place under such circumstances." Everyone but he passed through the security systems. Data set off the alarm. Of course, Janeway thought, calming herself. Data was a machine. The bioscanners wouldn't recognize him as human. Lieutenant Andropov scanned him with the tricorder, after apologizing profusely, then waved him through.

He touched a pad on his console. "This is Lieutenant Andropov," he said. "Admiral Janeway and Commanders Data, Chakotay, and Tuvok have arrived to see Seven of Nine, Icheb, and the Doctor."

There was a pause. "I'm afraid they're too late," came the voice from the other end.

"What?" cried Janeway. "What do you mean?"

"Seven of Nine and Icheb are going into stasis. It's a precautionary measure suggested by Dr. Kaz," the voice continued.

"Put me through to Dr. Kaz immediately," Janeway demanded.

"Admiral," said Andropov, "if the doctor is readying stasis fields, then it's not advisable to—"

"That is an order, Lieutenant," snapped Janeway. She felt the blood rise in her cheeks and knew her eyes were probably bright. She only hoped that the lieutenant would take it for anger, not the apprehension she was really feeling.

"Yes, Admiral, of course," said Andropov, visibly subdued. "Dr. Kaz, this is Lieutenant Andropov from Admissions. May—"

"Not now, Lieutenant," came Kaz's voice.

"Dr. Kaz," said Janeway, "It's Admiral Janeway. Is there any way we could talk to Seven and Icheb, or are you too far along in the process?"

There was a pause, then Kaz replied, "If you come up right away you might have a moment or two, but no more. I'd advise haste, Admiral. They won't be coherent for very long."

"You heard the doctor," Janeway told the two security guards. "Let us through. Now."

The four strode briskly along the corridors. To Janeway, the turbolifts seemed unusually slow, but she was certain it was just her anxiety. Human or hologram, Andropov and Robinson had alerted the other guards at each of the three security stations en route to sickbay. They were all prepared to rush them through as quickly as possible, providing of course that all proper security measures were observed. Janeway felt sure they could see the sweat gathering at her hairline each time they stopped, but they made it through without incident. While she was grateful for Baines's thoroughness in this particular situation, it was alarming how easily the security systems at such a pivotal institution could be breached. Once her promise to Baines had been satisfied, she'd notify Starfleet immediately.

She always hated deals with the devil.

The guard posted outside sickbay stepped aside so they could enter. The door hissed open. Kaz turned around to see who his guests were. He looked preoccupied. Seven and Icheb lay on the beds. Icheb had his eyes closed and Seven turned her head with apparent effort to gaze at them with half-lidded eyes.

"You're just in time," Kaz said. He nodded at the guard. "Dismissed, Lieutenant. Thank you."

The guard nodded and returned to his post. The minute the doors closed, Kaz let out a huge breath.

"We did it," he said.

Seven swung her legs over the bed and stepped lightly to the floor. Icheb did likewise. There was no hint of grogginess about either of them.

"You are premature, Doctor," she said. "We still have to effect our escape."

"We got this far, that's a good sign," said Kaz. He glanced at his four visitors, then his mouth curved in a wry smile. "So, which of you are the holograms?"

"We are," said Chakotay and Tuvok. "Were you able to adjust the system?"

"Indeed I was," said Kaz, "though I'm no engineer and I regret to say that it took me a while to figure out how to bypass the alert system. Seven and Icheb were able to double-check it for me when she arrived about a half-hour ago."

Of course, Janeway thought. In order for the ruse to work, the holographic emitters placed in every Starfleet medical facility would have to be operating. Otherwise, there'd be no point in having an EMH. However, if they were activated, someone would notice. Kaz had had to figure out how to activate the emitters without attracting attention.

"They're on. You may, uh, transfer your briefcases," he told "Chakotay" and "Tuvok."

They looked at each other, then nodded. With the touch of a button in their briefcase-size portable emitters, they shimmered and reformed as Seven of Nine and Icheb. There was a brief, uncomfortable moment as the real former Borg stared at their doubles.

"I realize it is unusual to see oneself so realistically portrayed," said Data, "but we do not have much time."

"Data's right," said Janeway. "Let's do this and get the hell out."

The holograms of Icheb and Seven walked to their flesh counterparts.

"Here," the false Icheb said to the real one, "this button will activate the holographic field. You will look and sound like Commander Chakotay, and if you're stopped and searched, the briefcase will look as if it just contains ordinary items. They won't be able to see the controls."

"When you are safely away, this button will shut down the field," said "Seven." "It will also reveal the controls in the portable emitter, just so you know."

"I understand," said Seven, and then, hesitantly, "Thank you."

The hologram smiled at her, then he-she-it lay on one of the beds. The one who looked like Icheb followed suit. The doctor pressed a few buttons, and a stasis field sprang into place around the two of them.

Data examined the display. "Well done, Doctor. Everything appears to confirm the illusion that Seven of Nine and Icheb are present and in stasis."

"Thank you, Commander Data." Kaz turned to face Janeway. "I've done everything I can to play up how ill Seven and Icheb are, which, unfortunately, is not much of an exaggeration. They'll need several hours of uninterrupted regeneration as soon as possible."

Janeway nodded. "I'll see that they get it, though I'm certain Seven will argue that she'd be more valuable plowing ahead."

Seven raised a blond eyebrow in indignation. "I had hoped to begin work on analyzing the Borg virus immediately," she said.

Janeway grinned. "See?"

Kaz grinned back. "Tie her down if you have to, but make sure she regenerates. Icheb, too. His newfound ability to sleep a little bit has helped stave off much of the damage, but he needs several hours as well." He hesitated. "I'm not certain I approve of your choice of allies, but as the saying goes, desperate times call for desperate measures."

"I'd say these are desperate indeed," said Janeway. "We'll be in touch." She glanced at the holograms. "You're sure they won't be disturbed?"

"I'll do what I can, of course, but Montgomery does have the right to sever the stasis if he sees fit."

"Let's hope he doesn't." Her gaze shifted to Seven and Icheb and she smiled slightly. "Suit up, you two. It's time for our next abduction."

Janeway, Data, "Chakotay," and "Tuvok" were admitted into the Doctor's cell. A guard, as usual, stood outside. It was Lieutenant Debby Garris, who smiled when she caught sight of Janeway. The admiral was a frequent visitor, and she always made a point of being pleasant to the guards she encountered. Although she disagreed with them this time, she knew they were good people just doing their jobs.

She returned the smile. "Good morning, Lieutenant Garris."

"Good morning, Admiral. Commanders." She looked slightly troubled and glanced into the now-empty cell across from the Doctor. "They were put into stasis this morning, for their own safety," Garris said quickly. "They're all right."

"Your compassion for my concern does you credit, Lieutenant," Janeway said warmly. "We were just in time to talk to them before Kaz completed the process."

She relaxed, relieved. Janeway briefly glanced up to see the small red light glowing steadily. Not unexpectedly, she saw they were still under surveillance.

The Doctor had risen to greet them. "Commander Data," said the Doctor, clearly surprised. "May I ask why you're here?"

"A few years ago, I was put on trial for my own rights as an individual, Doctor," said Data. "When Admiral Janeway informed my captain of your situation, I realized that it was necessary for me to assist you in your own quest for the same recognition. A Federation citizen should not be held against his will with no charges."

"They think I've got something to do with Baines, but they've yet to present any sort of case," the Doctor said.

Data nodded. "I see." He turned to Garris. "Lieutenant Garris, I am here to act as the Doctor's legal counsel."

Garris looked confused. "But he's just a hologram," she began.

"And I am just an android," said Data. "And yet I am recognized as a person."

Janeway felt a bit sorry for poor Garris as she opened and closed her mouth, uncertain as to how to reply. She stepped in and saved the younger woman the trouble.

"Whether or not the Doctor is a person has yet to be proved, but until it is, it might be a good idea to err on the side of caution and assume individuality until that's proven not to be the case. Therefore, he's entitled to a private conversation with his legal counsel."

"I really should get permission from Admiral Montgomery," said Garris.

"Go ahead," Janeway said. She said it lightly, as if the outcome was certain, but in reality, such was not the case. Montgomery might deny her just to be unpleasant.

"He's unavailable right now. Perhaps if you return tomorrow—"

Data shook his head. "That would not be advisable," he said.

"Commander Data's an extremely busy man," said Janeway. "Captain Picard would be disappointed that he gave his crewman leave and Data didn't even get to meet with his client."

She wasn't above exerting a little pressure if need be. They'd gotten used to her and her crew by now, which was well and good; but the names of Data and Captain Jean-Luc Picard still dazzled the younger members of Starfleet. The name-dropping had the desired effect. Pushing her advantage, she said, "I'll take full responsibility if Montgomery has any sort of problem with this."

That did it. Relief spread over Garris's young, attractive face. "Very well, Admiral." She lowered the force field and Data stepped inside. The field snapped back into place, but Data and the Doctor remained standing.

Janeway indicated the red light. "*Private* conversation, Lieutenant," she reminded her gently.

"Oh, yes, of course." Garris touched another button beside the door and the light went off.

"Would you care to sit?" said the Doctor, indicating the small bed.

"I do not tire, nor do you," said Data logically.

Gently, Janeway took the lieutenant by the arm and steered her down the hall, out of earshot. "Tuvok" and "Chakotay" followed.

"I understand you've just returned from your honeymoon. How's married life treating you?" she asked in an amiable fashion.

She listened with half an ear, nodding in the right places as Garris told her about her honeymoon in the tropics. But her mind was not on sunny beaches and waving palm trees. She was trying to figure out how long they would need. She suspected that the plan would be carried out in a matter of seconds, but that Data and the Doctor would linger over their conversation so as to make the fabrication of legal consultant and client more believable.

It was a full half-hour before she heard Data's voice calling, "I have completed my consultation, Lieutenant Garris."

Garris hurried down the hall. The Doctor sat on the bed, his hands clasped loosely. A small padd sat beside him. Data stood, hands folded behind his back, awaiting them. The force field was deactivated.

Data turned back to the Doctor. "I will be visiting you again soon. In the meantime, please review the documentation I have provided."

"Thank you, Commander Data. I will," said the Doctor earnestly. He turned to Janeway. "Thank you, Admiral, for believing in me."

She smiled. "We'll drop by again soon, Doctor. Good-bye, Lieutenant. I enjoyed our chat."

"As did I, Admiral. Good day."

They strode down the hall. Janeway muttered under her breath, "How did your consultation go?"

"Successfully," said Data, but nothing more. Elation filled Janeway.

They might just be able to pull this off, after all.

It seemed to take forever before the four of them safely materialized in Paris's apartment. The real Chakotay and Tuvok were anxiously awaiting their arrival, along with Tom and Harry. When Janeway met her former first officer's gaze and said, "We did it," sighs of relief and not a few whoops filled the room.

Grinning fiercely herself, Janeway nonetheless held up a calming hand. "Let's make sure it went as well as I hoped first." She turned to the doubles. "We'll start with you two. Disengage holographic camouflage," she said.

The false Tuvok and Chakotay opened their briefcase-size portable emitters and touched a few buttons. There was a humming sound, and then Seven and Icheb stood before them.

Even as their friends rushed toward them to offer hugs and pats on the back, the former Borg both stumbled. Tuvok caught Seven as she fell.

"I apologize for my weakness, Admiral," Seven mumbled. "Perhaps Dr. Kaz was correct in his assessment of my need to regenerate."

Tuvok gently led her to a couch and sat her down. Icheb wasn't far behind her. Pale and shaking, he propped his head up on his elbows and held his head in his hands.

"We'll get you both to a chamber as soon as we can," Janeway promised. "But we have one more person to check on."

Data reached up to his head and deftly removed a chunk of his skullcap. There was a sharp intake of breath all around the room. It wasn't every day one watched a friend remove a piece of his anatomy so casually.

Red and green dots chased each other on Data's head. He walked over to one of the holographic emitters and his face went slack. His head twitched.

"Processing . . ." he said in a dull voice.

There was a crackle, and then the Doctor stood before them. His dark eyes were wide with delight. He clutched his chest as if ascertaining the reality of his form.

"I'm here. You really did it! Thank you so much, Mr. Data."

"Do not thank me yet, Doctor," warned Data. "You may still have your program altered or perhaps deleted entirely. We have not yet proven your viability as a unique individual, which would be the only means by which—"

"It's good enough for now, Commander," said Janeway, walking over to the android and putting an affectionate hand on his shoulder. Her eyes took in the scene fondly. It was good to see her friends on the right side of a prison force field.

Her next task was to see to it that they stayed there.

"I'm afraid I have to ask you to download the Doctor once more, Data. And you two," she said to Seven and Icheb, "will have to hang on for a little bit longer."

"Where to now?" asked the Doctor.

Janeway smiled, softly. "We're going to go visit an old friend," she said.

Chapter 9

THERE WAS a chirping sound, and Libby started. Dimly she realized someone was trying to contact her. Automatically she touched the button, trying to compose herself. If anyone asked, she'd just say she'd been sick. Which was the truth.

It was Aidan Fletcher. She opened her mouth to speak, but he spoke first.

"I can tell by your expression that you've read the document," he said.

Her mind worked sluggishly, then she said, "How do you—you read it!"

He nodded. "Guilty as charged."

She seized on the anger. It was much nicer than nauseating, numb horror. "You son of a bitch!" she exploded. "You promised!"

"I know, but come on, Libby—you know I had to."

He was pleading with her, and her brief fire of outrage flickered and went out. She sagged in her chair.

"I suppose you did." Now that she looked at him, she could see that he was much paler than usual as well. "You look about as bad as I feel," she said.

"I feel pretty bad," he admitted. "I wanted to let you know that we'll take it from here. This can't be Starfleet-authorized. Someone is acting on his own."

"Her own," Libby corrected, "and you are not going to take it from here."

He frowned. "Agent Webber," he began calmly.

"Don't Agent Webber me! This is my case and has been from the beginning."

"But you know what's at stake!" he cried. "The virus is spreading every minute. The doctors estimate that soon healthy adults will become infected."

"They're not there yet," Libby replied. "If Covington were able to issue an instruction for them to activate, she'd have done it by now. She can't command them as completely as she'd like. We've got a little time."

He shook his silver-gold head. "Supposition. No. I'm sorry."

"Aidan, you wouldn't even be aware that this was going on if it hadn't been for me!" Libby protested. "Besides, everyone who works at that building is in danger. Don't you think she hasn't anticipated possible discovery? Don't you think you're already infected?"

He paled. "I haven't been exposed to any debris."

Exasperated, Libby cried, "Do you think that matters? Your desk is probably covered with nanoprobes."

His gaze fell to his desk and he scooted his chair back. If it hadn't been so dreadfully serious it would have been funny.

"If she thinks she's in danger from anyone in SI, she'll activate the nanoprobes. You are probably among the first who'll be stricken, Aidan. She picked me because—" Oh, how she hated to say it "—because she didn't deem me any kind of threat. Because she thought I was too stupid to figure out her game. I've got a lot more room to maneuver than you do. Please. Give me some time. I have some . . . some contacts. Some names to clear."

"Harry," he said. "Of course. I'm afraid I—"

"Twenty-four hours."

"What?"

"Twenty-four hours. Give me twenty-four hours. Please, Aidan."

He looked at her helplessly. "Libby, this isn't a game."

"Believe me, I know. Twenty-four hours. Please."

His eyes searched hers. Finally, he said, "Twelve hours. And while you're doing . . . whatever it is you'll be doing, you should be aware that I'm assembling a team of my own. At precisely twelve hours and one second from now, I'll be executing my plan."

"The minute you move against her, Covington will activate the virus," Libby warned.

"We all run risks doing what we do, Agent Webber."

"Twelve hours, then."

Aidan sighed. "Damn it, Libby . . . you watch your back, okay?"

"Okay. Thanks, Aidan."

"I'm not sure you should be thanking me at all," he said, and terminated the conversation.

The talk with Aidan had calmed Libby somewhat and had helped lift the veil of fear and confusion. She was alert and focused now, and knew what she had to do.

The trouble was, how to get in touch with Harry? He was going off on some mission. She guessed it was something to do with Admiral Janeway and the rest of the former *Voyager* command crew, but that did her no good. Where would they go? What would they try to do?

And suddenly, she knew. Harry, bless him, had told her, though not in so many words.

"Sweetie," she said aloud, chuckling despite the direness of the situation, "you're just too easy to read."

And she began to compose her message.

"Vassily," came a voice, low and urgent. "Vassily, wake up."

Slowly Vassily Andropov opened his eyes. Robinson was bending over him. Her eyes were encircled with black liner, and there was a beauty mark on her cheek. Her hair, which he had always seen neatly pinned in a regulation bun at the back of her head, was loose and flowed down around her shoulders.

Her *bare* shoulders.

He bolted upright and scrambled away, vastly relieved to see that she wasn't entirely naked. She had a swath of shimmering blue satin that covered just enough of her body to keep Vassily from mortification. Next to her was a girl who couldn't have been more than twenty. She was petite and frightened-looking, with large green eyes and short, light brown hair.

"Thank God you're awake," Robinson said, her voice a harsh whisper.

He looked down at himself and found that he, too, wore only the barest scrap of clothing. His muscular chest and strong legs were bare for the world to see.

"What the hell . . ." Then he remembered. Remembered Oliver Baines breaking into his house, remembered the hologram that resembled one Vassily Andropov in every single aspect.

"Baines?" he asked Robinson. She nodded.

"Broke into my own house," she said bitterly. "So much for security systems."

Andropov looked around. They were not alone. At least four dozen people, all clad in the same shimmering blue silk, were also here. But where was "here"? Why had Baines . . . ?

He blinked at the sun, a dazzling light in an azure sky. Beneath him was sand, creeping uncomfortably into his not-very-concealing loincloth.

"What have you learned so far, Lieutenant?" he asked, hoping the usage of her formal rank would help things feel a bit more professional. It was hard to feel professional in a loincloth.

She reached to touch her own clothes, trying to secure them and stretch them to cover more of her pale flesh. The girl at her elbow followed suit.

"Not much, I'm afraid. Allyson here tells me everyone was kidnapped by Baines and replaced with holograms."

"There doesn't seem to be a pattern in who he picked," said Allyson, speaking for the first time. Her voice was soft, shy. "You're both with Starfleet. I'm just an artist. Others here are mechanics, scientists—people from all walks of life."

"This doesn't make sense," said Andropov, getting to his feet and brushing sand from his backside. "Holding us is dangerous. We're a liability. Why didn't he just vaporize us?"

"Hostages?" offered Robinson.

"No, he doesn't want anyone knowing we're gone, remember?" Andropov said.

Suddenly dozens of creamy white horses galloped over the hill. Their riders were resplendent in shimmering white and gold. Both males and females were beautiful and proud, tall and strong-looking.

All the prisoners, for prisoners they were, rose and clustered together. The riders halted their mounts, and one of the bright white horses stepped forward. Andropov recognized its rider.

"Baines," Robinson whispered. "Bastard."

Oliver Baines was clad in a tunic. Sandals laced up his legs and a large gold crown glinted in the sunlight. He looked like a desert king, but the garb was preposterous—surely no real desert chieftain had ever worn such flimsy material. His eyes raked the prisoners with contempt.

"Welcome to my world, ladies and gentlemen," he said. His voice shouldn't have been able to carry that far, but it did. Vassily frowned. Something was not right here.

"A while ago, you were leading your ordinary lives. Many of you served in Starfleet. Others are civilians. All of you are here, now. Back in your world, no one even knows you are gone. My holograms have seen to that. You think you are so unique, that you are irreplaceable. But you're not.

"In your world, you were the organics—the masters. Here, you will experience what it is like to be the slave class. This is a pleasant little fantasy world that I have created, much the same way you," he said, pointing to one man, "or you," he added, stabbing his finger in the direction of another, "have created such simulations to while away the time. In these little fantasy worlds, the creator has everything he desires. He uses holograms to achieve his pleasures."

Baines looked around, smiling slightly. "Now the shoe is on the other foot. I hope you enjoy your time in this particular holosuite."

The prisoners exchanged uncertain glances. Vassily felt Allyson's hand steal into his own. He twined his fingers around hers. There was no desire, no passion—just the desperate contact of flesh on flesh, an intense need to connect with another human being.

The moment was shattered as the holographic riders spurred their holographic horses into action. Neighing fiercely, the beasts charged the crowd. Andropov felt Allyson's hand being torn from his grip. He stumbled and fell, and other bodies landed on top of him.

They all struggled to their feet. Andropov coughed, his mouth full of sand, and that was when he felt the sting of the whip. In a fraction of a second, his back was laid open from shoulder to buttock. Despite himself, he cried aloud, with pain and surprise.

"Up, slave," snarled the rider. He was a large man, brown-skinned and dark-eyed. His muscles gleamed with sweat. "We have monuments to build." He turned his head and his eyes fell upon Allyson, who stood with a cluster of other prisoners. Andropov could already see a bruise welling on her face.

White teeth showed in the rider's brown face as he leered, his gaze caressing her from head to toe.

"Behold a rose blooming amid the dung pile," he said, his voice sultry. Allyson, green eyes wide, cringed and tried to cover herself.

"Leave her alone," said two voices at the same time. One voice was Vassily's. The other who spoke was a tall, attractive woman. Her skin was as brown as the rider's, and her long, straight hair as black. Her body was strong and athletic, and her almond-shaped eyes snapped defiance.

Briefly the rider glanced in Vassily's direction. Almost absently, he cracked his long, thin whip. This time it caught Andropov across the cheek, narrowly missing his eye. He clapped his hand to the wound and blood flowed between his fingers. The rider turned back to the other woman, clearly much more interested in her than in Andropov.

"Another flower," he said. "My chieftain Baines has an eye for beauty, I see. And such fire, to rush to the defense of her friend!"

"She's not my friend," Allyson said quickly. Andropov saw that she was shaking. He knew what she was doing—trying to protect the other woman.

"It does not matter," said the dark-skinned woman. Her voice was deep and musical. "You will leave her alone. You will leave all the women alone, and you will cease injuring the men. Your 'chieftain' will return us to the places he has stolen us from, or he will face the wrath of the Federation."

The rider threw his head back and laughed heartily. He turned to his comrades. "Listen to her!" he crowed. "As if she actually has some say in what becomes of her!" His friends laughed along with him. He turned back to the woman, and although desire still gleamed in his eyes, his voice was harsh.

"You are nothing, do you understand? You've got no name, no rights, no reason for existence except to please us. You'll do what we tell you to do and you'll do it with a smile on that pretty face. Or else," he said, and casually drew a sharp, curved dagger, "I can make that face not so pretty."

"I do have a name," said the woman, practically spitting the words. "I am Lieutenant Akolo Tare. I am a pilot aboard the *U.S.S.*—"

Andropov never learned the name of her ship. The rider spurred his horse and bore down on Tare. The crowd hastened to get out of the hologram's way. All except Tare. She stood her ground, and as he galloped straight toward her she leaped at him. He was clearly surprised at the attack and seemed even more shocked when she grabbed him around the waist and pulled him off his horse.

It was a short struggle, however. Strong and fit as she was, it was obvious that Baines had foreseen something like this and programmed his holograms to be much stronger than a human. It wasn't more than a second or two before the rider had pinned Tare beneath him.

But Tare's actions had inspired the prisoners, and

they descended on the rider, pulling him off the gasping woman. Tare scrambled to her feet. Her hand went to her throat; bruises were already starting to appear.

The small revolt was brief. The other riders galloped toward their friend's defense, and this time when the whip struck Andropov he fell to his knees. It wasn't just a whip sting this time. Whoever was manning the controls in this hellish simulation had just programmed the whips to deliver a powerful shock. His body was still thrumming and his bones ached as he climbed unsteadily to his feet.

The riders had trussed up Tare as if she were an animal, and the first rider flung her over his saddle. Her eyes were wide and filled with fear now, and although she struggled, everyone present knew it would avail her nothing.

"You are slaves!" bellowed the rider. "You exist to serve at our pleasure. How is it to be on the other side of the simulation?"

And Andropov suddenly got it. He wondered why it had taken him so long to figure it out. He supposed it was because he wasn't really paying attention to Baines's speech.

Baines didn't want them dead. He wanted them to suffer. He wanted them to be treated the way human treated holograms in various fantasy scenarios—as things, objects. Andropov blushed, because he knew he hadn't been above playing holographic scenarios with such prepossessing titles as "Vulcan Love Slave" a time or two. He knew what happened to the holograms.

But they were holograms, damn it, not people. They

were created to be, well, love slaves, or centurions, or servants, or antagonists to the organic protagonist. They were just force fields with images projected onto them—nothing more than photons. They couldn't eat, couldn't sleep, couldn't love, couldn't feel pain. This sick role-reversal Baines had concocted wasn't truly putting the shoe on the other foot, it was merely torturing the people Baines somehow decided were "masters" who created holograms to abuse.

But then Andropov thought about *Voyager's* Doctor. He'd met him and found him to be convincingly real. He'd heard about how the Doctor had exceeded his programming, fallen in love, learned about opera and dance. That sounded more like a person than a collection of photons.

Like most people, Andropov had played through "Photons Be Free" and found it to be thought-provoking. But that was just a holonovel. At any point, Andropov could end it by saying three little words: "Computer, end program."

Here, it was all too real, and like the holograms in "Vulcan Love Slave," he had no way of turning the program off when it became uncomfortable.

Allyson rushed up to him, followed by Robinson. "Are you okay?" Allyson hissed through her teeth as she looked at his face. He tried to smile, although the gesture sent pain shimmering along his nerves.

"Nothing a dermal regenerator won't take care of," he said, trying to reassure her. The kid didn't need to add worrying about him to her list.

Robinson's eyes were somber. "I haven't noticed one lying around in the sand," she said.

"We'll get back. He won't kill us." *At least,* Andropov thought, *I hope he won't.* "Don't you see what's going on? He's trying to turn the tables. He wants us to experience what it's like to be a helpless hologram, subject to the whims of the one who created the game."

"Pretty stupid way to go about getting sympathy," Robinson said. "And that woman Tare . . . she was so brave to stand up to him like that."

Allyson nodded, swallowed hard. "If she hadn't done it, that would be me slung across his saddle, about to—to be—"

"I know," Andropov said softly. He knew what happened to women in this sort of simulation. He was pretty sure Baines wouldn't murder anyone. Who would report back to Starfleet about the horrible injustices the holograms suffered? But, as was evidenced by the slashes on his back and face, other forms of torment were apparently allowed. He desperately hoped that Baines had enough human decency left in him to draw the line at rape.

But he wasn't sure.

"Get going, slaves!" cried one of the riders. The whip sang out and cracked on another man's back. He grunted, his eyes wide from the unexpected depth of the pain. Far in the distance was something that looked like a half-constructed pyramid. This was to be today's activity, then.

"Come on," said Robinson gently. "Our doubles aren't going to fool people forever, and I bet Baines won't be able to hold off gloating for very long. He's going to start bragging to Starfleet, and they'll find a way to stop this."

Andropov wished he shared her faith. He looked up at a nearby cliff, and saw a white horse with a blue-clad rider. When the sun glinted off something gold on the rider's head, he knew it was Baines.

You self-righteous bastard, he thought, with a wave of hatred that felt unsettlingly good. *If you kill anyone, or rape that poor woman who had the guts to stand up to your thugs, I'll kill you myself.*

Chapter 10

Ensign Landon Ferguson liked his new job. Many would have thought it excruciatingly boring, standing around all day with nothing better to do than send high-ranking Starfleet officials to various ships or other locales, but Ferguson was more than content with his lot. He had just graduated from the Academy and had no particular craving for adventure and action aboard a vessel of the fleet. Nor did he particularly care for the delicate dance that was the diplomatic path. He didn't have a real aptitude for computers or engines, either. But he had been a diligent student and gotten decent enough grades to pass, and Starfleet always made sure its former cadets had useful and respectable employment.

So Ferguson was here in San Diego, one of several dozen people who manned the transporters. San Diego was an enormous hub for Starfleet comings and goings, hence the usage of humans rather than holograms at the transporters. Here was where one was officially cleared to beam onto a vessel, or to a top-security site. So even though Ferguson knew his job wasn't particularly glamorous, he also knew it was important. Let others fight the enemies or entice new species to join the Federation. He would happily see to it that those people got where they needed to go.

He snapped to attention when the door to the large transporter room hissed open. His brown eyes widened slightly as he recognized the rather well-known figures that stepped briskly inside.

"Admiral Montgomery, Admiral Janeway," he said smoothly. He was getting used to greeting high-ranking personages. Just last week, he'd had the honor of transporting the Mirkashu of Junn to Starfleet Headquarters.

"Good morning, Ensign," said Montgomery. "These good people need to be transported to *Voyager.*"

The blood drained from Ferguson's face as he regarded Janeway; Commanders Data, Tuvok, and Chakotay; Lieutenant Commander Tom Paris; and Lieutenant Harry Kim. The other two, who like Montgomery were carrying some sort of briefcase, he didn't recognize, but he was willing to bet they were from *Voyager,* too. And that was a big, big problem.

"Uh," he said, less than eloquently, "uh, Admiral Montgomery, sir, may I speak with you for a moment?"

Montgomery glowered. Ferguson cringed, and swallowed hard. "These kids fresh from the Academy," Montgomery sighed, shaking his head. "Give me a moment, Kathryn, will you?"

They walked away a few feet. "Well?" Montgomery demanded.

"Sir, are you forgetting your orders?"

"I never forget my orders. I sometimes change them, though. Like I'm doing right now, if you get my meaning."

"Yes, sir, I do indeed, sir, but you were quite adamant when you spoke to us," Ferguson said, wishing his voice wasn't so quivery. "You said under no circumstances was anyone who had served on *Voyager* to be allowed admittance. You made it very clear what would happen if anyone did permit them to transport."

"I'm glad I made myself clear then, and I hope I'm making myself very clear right now when I say, that's an order, Ensign!"

"Yes, sir, of course, sir," said Ferguson, scurrying back to his position behind the console. "Just one moment and—"

"What are you trying to do, Ensign? Are you bucking for yeoman? Time is of the essence!"

Ferguson felt sick. "It's procedure, sir. Look, I've got him on the screen already. Commander Watson, I have Admiral Montgomery for you." He stepped back quickly to allow Montgomery to see Watson on the small screen.

"Good morning, Admiral," said Watson, a handsome black man whose hair was just starting to get sprinkled with gray. Watson always intimidated Ferguson. Then again, most people intimidated Ferguson. "What can I do for you, sir?"

"I've got seven people who need to board *Voyager*. Don't give them any guff. Stay out of their way and let them do their job. That understood?"

"Yes, sir."

"Oh, and Dr. Kaz is going to be joining them shortly. The same applies to him."

"Of course, sir."

"I'm going to be in some very important meetings for the next few days, and I'd appreciate not being disturbed. These folks know what they're doing. The ensign here has been stammering protests and it's worn me out. I don't want to hear a peep out of you, Watson."

"Understood, sir. No peeping."

"Good. Montgomery out." He turned and glared at Ferguson, who tried and largely failed not to cringe underneath that piercing gaze. "Now, transport these people immediately."

Ferguson couldn't do it fast enough. When the transporter whined and the seven people dematerialized, he heaved a huge sigh of relief and slumped against the console. It was far too busy a day for his liking.

Janeway didn't miss the slight widening of Commander Watson's eyes as he recognized her. She smiled, hoping to put him and the other two security guards in the room at ease.

"I know our appearance here is a bit unexpected, Commander Watson," she said, and recalling Kaz's comment added, "but desperate times call for desperate measures."

"Indeed they do, Admiral Janeway," Watson replied coolly. "If I hadn't had it straight from Admiral Montgomery himself, I'm afraid I'd have to detain all of you until you were cleared."

"Your thoroughness does you credit. But as the admiral said, we've got work to do."

She stepped lightly off the transporter and was heading out the door when Watson moved smoothly to block her way.

"I'm sorry, Admiral, but before I let you pass, I do need to know what you're doing here."

Her jaw tensed. "With all due respect, Commander, no, you don't."

She tried to move past him, but he blocked her way again.

"Commander Watson," said Data, "what is your level of security clearance?"

"Level Beta," he said.

"Is everyone on the ship cleared for that level?" Chakotay inquired, glancing at the other two guards present. Watson nodded once. "Good. Then you can tell him, Admiral."

Janeway didn't bat an eye. "We're here to assist Starfleet in discovering a cure for the Borg virus. We've had more experience with the Borg than anyone on Earth, and the information in our databanks as well as our familiarity with their technology is an asset."

Watson narrowed his eyes. He looked like he didn't believe her. "Why didn't Montgomery tell me that?"

The real reason "Montgomery" hadn't said anything was because first, of course, it wasn't really Montgomery but one of Baines' holograms, and second, the hologram had no idea who Watson was or what level security clearance he had.

But Janeway didn't mention either of those particular facts. Instead she said, "Montgomery was standing right in front of a particularly edgy-looking young man who was clearly fresh out the Academy."

Watson nodded his comprehension and seemed to relax slightly. "You may proceed."

She smiled slightly. "You know, Commander, they never formally relieved me of duty. Technically, this is still my ship."

Let him chew on that, she thought, and stepped past him into the corridor.

For a moment, they all stood staring. "What the—" began Kim.

"They've gutted her!" said Tom, saying what they all thought.

Voyager had looked worse, but Janeway was having trouble remembering exactly when. The technicians under Montgomery's command had probably done their jobs well and thoroughly, but they had left an enormous mess in their wake. Panels had been opened and tossed aside. Conduits gaped open, naked wires hung loose and occasionally sputtered.

"Didn't their mothers tell them to tidy as they went?" Janeway asked, sighing.

"Admiral," said Tuvok, "I believe we can expect this level of . . . untidiness . . . throughout the ship."

"Project Full Circle was about discovering *Voyager*'s capabilities and enhancements," said Chakotay. "It wasn't about getting her ready to fly again. And I imagine when the virus broke out, the last thing on anyone's mind was taking the time to put things back where they belonged."

A shiver went down Janeway's spine. "The regeneration chambers," she said. "There's no telling what they've done to them."

"As a prime example of Borg technology on the ship, it's probably going to be one of the most thoroughly dismantled," said Paris glumly. Seven and Icheb, despite their holographic facades, looked worried.

"All right," said Janeway. "We mustn't panic. Here's what we're going to do."

Commander Roger Watson stared at the closed door through which the former *Voyager* captain and her crew had just left.

"Something wrong, sir?" asked one of his men.

"I'm not sure," Watson replied slowly. He had been in the field of security for over twenty years. He had gotten as far as he had by trusting his instincts, and now, they were sounding a red alert. Yet there seemed to be nothing amiss. He'd seen Admiral Montgomery with his own eyes. He knew about the Borg virus, of course, and it made sense that the people who knew the Borg the best ought to be allowed access to the ship they knew the best.

And yet . . . Montgomery, and even Commander Grady, had been adamant about not allowing anyone from *Voyager* to return to the ship. What made them change their minds? And why now? And why was Commander Data with him? Last Watson had heard, the android still served on the *Enterprise*.

Although all protocol had been observed, his instincts were still warning him that something was wrong.

"Something just doesn't feel right about this," Watson said at last, still staring at the door. "Get the second team up."

As she sat roasting the flesh of some creature she'd trapped and killed—it had large soft eyes, four legs, and horns along its spine, but she didn't know its proper name—Torres thought back to the last time she had sat beside a fire cooking her dinner. It had been with her father, uncle, and cousins during that final, disastrous camping trip. B'Elanna smiled as she tried to apply the term "camping trip" to the Challenge of Spirit.

She hadn't killed her dinner then; just brought hot dogs and marshmallows to roast over the fire. There had been comfortable tents, dry, clean clothing, and people—people she loved. There had been companionship, even though it was destined not to last.

The chunks of meat impaled on sticks dripped juices into the fire. The flame snapped and sizzled. B'Elanna's mouth watered. The smell was delicious.

Despite the tentative overtures they had both made upon her returning home, things were still tense between Torres and her father. Now as she sat by the fire alone, waiting for the meat to cook, she realized that she really did want to patch things up. She needed to make things right with both her parents, her put-upon and absent father as well as her audacious, violent Klingon mother.

Maybe they'd have another campout, B'Elanna and her father and Tom and the new little one. Maybe they could start a new family tradition. As for her mother . . .

Torres still shuddered whenever she thought about the rite she'd been forced to endure prior to embarking on the Challenge. Her memory was hazy, due no doubt to the fumes emanating from the lava pits, but she remembered enough: heat and pain and nakedness. And yet despite the extremity of the ordeal, it had all felt right, appropriate. She had indeed felt reborn as she ventured out into Boreth's wilderness. She certainly didn't want to do it again. But she was glad that there had been something, some kind of ceremony, to mark her departure as something worth doing . . . something worth acknowledging.

B'Elanna picked up a skewer and blew on the meat, touching it tentatively until she was certain it wouldn't burn her mouth. She took a huge bite. Juices flowed down her chin as she chewed. Nothing had ever tasted so delicious. She looked down at the six other makeshift skewers and smiled. She'd sleep with a full belly tonight, and wouldn't even have to eat a single grub to do so.

The flesh was melting off her. She'd always been slender, even small, but tough and wiry. Now even the faint layer of fat that had softened her musculature was all but gone. She was bone and blood and muscle and sinew. She made good time during the day, had learned to find food to keep her going, and slept like the dead at night. A few months ago, she would have laughed at the notion that such an intense physical ordeal would be "purifying" rather than a hardship. But now, she knew it to be the truth.

With every step she took, she was nearer reconciliation with her mother, and *that* was a journey that had taken years. She sweated her old grudges into the clay that she carefully layered over her body whenever she ran across any mud. The clay absorbed her emotional toxins as well as her physical ones, and when she did run across a clear pool or waterfall and allow herself the luxury of washing off the dirt, she felt cleaner than she had ever felt in a sonic shower.

Despite herself, she had to admit that she was thriving on this diet of fruit, tubers, grubs, and close-to-raw meat. She could almost feel her body greedily absorbing the nourishment as she feasted on things that once would have made her stomach churn. No wine or replicated beverage tasted as sweet as water from a rushing brook or raindrops caught in a large, carefully positioned leaf. She had no husband or child to take care of, no engines to repair, no crew to manage, no captain to report to. Only the jungle and the sky, and her ceaseless steps over the harsh terrain which would take her toward this next segment of her life.

For the first time, B'Elanna Torres really understood what her mother had been trying to tell her. There was a deep, resonant purity in scoured skin, in hardened muscle, in casting off the vestiges of the comfortable, ordered, technical life. She could hear her heart steadily pumping blood, could feel the oxygen she drew into her three lungs enriching that blood, could feel her muscles working as they obeyed her thought: *Keep walking.* Here, in the most unexpected of places, was a kind of peace the tormented half-Klingon woman had never thought to find.

"I've got to tell Chakotay about this," she said aloud, to hear herself speak. She'd talked to herself a great deal when she first embarked on this adventure. She had needed to hear a voice, even if it was just her own. Surrounded by people as she had been for the last seven years, solitude and silence was unfamiliar and, if she were to admit the truth, a bit frightening.

But the more time she spent by herself, the more she realized that she wasn't truly alone; the more time she spent in silence, the more obvious it became that she was embraced by sound. There were countless species here in the rain forest to keep her company, and they all spoke. She learned to listen to them and not herself, to the point that now, as she uttered the phrase, her voice sounded harsh and unused in her own ears.

Content with her own company and that of the thousands of other beings who lurked unseen, she finished the meal in silence. She ate the meat off of all seven of the skewers and her belly swelled with food. It rumbled, uncomfortable and unused to the volume she'd just subjected it to. She patted it gently, trusting that it would digest properly and that her body would welcome the nutrients.

Torres glanced over at the carcass. There was still a lot of meat left. It would last marginally longer in a cooked state than in raw, certainly enough to feed her through the day tomorrow at least and perhaps the day after. She started to load up the skewers again when she heard a sharp *crack*.

She was on her feet at once, a makeshift spear in her hand. Beyond the ring of light cast by the fire, the jungle was utterly dark. There was no moon tonight, and the stars offered too little illumination. She stood as still as if she had been carved from stone, resenting even her breathing, even her heartbeat, as her ears strained to catch any sound. The jungle, so full of birdcalls and sounds of insects and other creatures, had gone very, very still.

It came again. *Crack.*

Torres cursed herself mentally. She ought not to have lit the fire. She could digest raw meat. She'd done it before. But the quietness—and dryness—of the last few days had lulled her into a false sense of security, and the thought of a bright, cheerful fire crackling away while she roasted the meat had been too seductive for her to resist.

But now something was out there, something big, it sounded like, by the rustling of bushes. She debated extinguishing the fire, but it was too late for that to do her much good. Anything lurking in the night was going to see better than she could by starlight, and she needed every advantage. She slowly stepped forward and took a bundle of twigs she had gathered and tied together for just this purpose, and lit one end.

With her makeshift torch, Torres stepped forward. She held it aloft, trying to catch the glint of the eyes of the Something that was making all the ruckus. If she needed to, she could also use the torch as a weapon. Most wild creatures had a natural fear of fire. Was it another *grikshak?* Or maybe one of the *maasklaks.*

She moved boldly through the jungle. No sense in stealth now. The light of the fire grew fainter behind her and the darkness closed in. Every nerve ending was alert. Where was it? She'd have heard if it had left. It was still here . . . watching her . . . waiting for her.

Out of the corner of her eye she saw something move, something that was darker than the rest of the darkness. A cry burst from her throat as she whirled, brandishing the torch.

Something knocked the torch out of her hands. It went flying and landed in a pile of foliage, smoldering sullenly as the flames tried to catch the wet leaves on fire. Another blow, this time to her midsection. B'Elanna went sprawling, the wind knocked out of her. Even as she tried to scramble to her feet, she knew it would be too late. The spear clutched in her left hand would be less than useless at this close range. She wished she'd brought her chipped stone dagger instead.

The thing dropped on top of her. She struggled, but even as it dawned on her that this was no animal, but a humanoid, a voice cut through her haze of adrenaline:

" 'Lanna!"

Chapter 11

"MR. DATA, you're more in touch with how things would be run on a Federation starship than I am at this point," said Janeway as they strode toward Cargo Bay Two. "What kind of security systems would be in place on *Voyager* right now, under these circumstances?"

"Starfleet regulations currently stipulate that under normal conditions a docked vessel would have only minimal security," said Data. "However, given the unique nature of *Voyager,* and the nature of the present threat against the Federation, I would think that a security team on the level of R-54B would be in place."

"Which is?" asked Tom.

Data turned to address him. "There would be a total of eight security guards of the rank of lieutenant and upward stationed on *Voyager* for the duration of the project. They would work in four-day shifts of twelve hours each. Therefore, at any given time, four people would be on active duty."

"And the rest would just hang out here?" asked Tom.

"They would be assigned individual quarters aboard *Voyager* and take their meals and entertainment here."

Chakotay and Janeway exchanged glances. "Those aren't bad odds," said Chakotay.

"No," Janeway agreed. "First things first. We've got to get Seven and Icheb regenerating."

"Watson seemed dubious when you described our purpose here," said Tuvok. "I do not think he fully trusts us. His suspicions would be aroused if we activate two regeneration chambers."

"We'll explain it as part of the research we need to do on the Borg virus," Janeway replied.

"Commander Tuvok is correct," said Data. "Seven of Nine and Icheb will be unable to utilize their holographic disguises while they are in the regeneration chambers. Commander Watson will know that his suspicions are accurate if he appears in Cargo Bay Two and discovers two former Borg regenerating."

"Then we have to make sure he doesn't find out about it," said Janeway. "Tuvok, you were my head of security on this ship. I'm going to entrust you with keeping Icheb and Seven safe from discovery while they're regenerating. Harry, I need you at Ops. Can you dismantle the system to the point where Watson won't be able to detect our poking around in the regeneration chambers?"

"I think so," he said, "though B'Elanna's better at that sort of thing."

"We don't have B'Elanna and we do have you," Janeway said pointedly. "Can you do it or not?"

"Yes, Admiral."

"Good. While you're at it, I want you to be able to block any attempts Watson might make at contacting Montgomery."

Kim nodded. "That's actually easier. What about any incoming messages?"

"Download them into a buffer and read them when you get the chance. I want to know about every contact that's made." She squeezed his arm. "Do it."

He grinned. "Aye, Captain. I mean—"

"I think I like Captain better anyway." She winked at him as he turned and headed for the turbolift.

When they entered Cargo Bay Two, Janeway felt the shock almost like a physical blow.

"Oh my God," said Paris, giving voice to what they all felt. Behind her, Janeway heard Seven of Nine take a quick breath.

It almost looked as if Cargo Bay Two had been under attack. Two of the five alcoves had been completely removed, probably for further study in a more controlled environment. Another one was utterly destroyed. The remaining two looked almost as bad.

Calmly, Data took out a tricorder. "The destruction is largely cosmetic," he said, reassuring them slightly. "None of the units is functional at the moment, but I believe that we can repair these two. We will need to utilize components from the third."

"Then let's get cracking," said Janeway. She put a reassuring hand on Icheb's shoulder. "We'll get you two in there in no time."

* * *

Harry Kim felt very odd as he rode up the turbolift to the bridge.

How many thousands of times had he done this over the last seven years? And yet this time was profoundly different. This time, he wasn't reporting for duty, as a trusted crew member of a ship he was devoted to. This time he was returning as an infiltrator, a spy, almost. He wasn't supposed to be here. He didn't belong on this ship anymore. What he was about to do could be construed as treason. He knew that he might well be facing a court-martial in a few days.

Then again, there might not be anyone to conduct a court-martial in a few days. He didn't know the precise rate of infection, but he knew enough to make him scared to death. Which was why he was here, all but a fugitive aboard his own ship, about to do what he was about to do.

As the turbolift settled to a stop, he thought he heard a human voice saying something along the lines of "Fire phasers!" The doors hissed opened and he stepped out quickly, concerned. He was just in time to see someone standing beside the captain's chair looking slightly flustered. Harry smothered a grin. Someone had been playing "captain."

To cover his embarrassment, the security lieutenant pulled out his phaser and barked, "You're not a regular member of the security staff. State your name and purpose."

Harry lifted his hands. "Whoa, whoa, Lieutenant. My name is Lieutenant Harry Kim. I'm here with Admiral Janeway to do some research for Starfleet on the Borg virus. Commander Watson didn't notify you?"

"No, he didn't," said the lieutenant. Still keeping the phaser trained on Harry, he stepped quickly to Ops. "Lieutenant Crais to Commander Watson. I have an unknown person on the bridge. Say's he's Harry Kim, and he claims he accompanied Admiral Janeway on board."

"He's with Janeway, but what the hell is he doing on the bridge?" came Watson's voice.

"Commander," said Kim, stepping over to his old post, "This is Lieutenant Kim. I'm here to do some research."

"What do you need to be on the bridge for?"

What *did* he need to be on the bridge for? Other than his real purpose, of course.

"I need to do some work at Ops and the science station. It's classified."

There was a long silence, during which the lieutenants eyed each other. Finally Watson said, "You may proceed."

Taking a tip from Janeway, Harry smiled and stuck out his hand. "Sorry to have given you a scare," he said.

Crais hesitated, and then shook the proffered hand. He didn't meet Harry's eyes and there was a trace of a blush on his cheeks.

"I'm Leo Crais. Welcome aboard—or should I say, welcome back aboard, Mr. Kim."

"You recognized me." A few weeks ago, Harry would have been pleased, but now he was only worried. How many people would know him and the rest by sight?

"Took me a minute, but yeah. So," Crais said almost hopefully, "what are you working on?"

Harry said a silent prayer to whatever deity might be listening: *Save me from bored security guards.* He smiled apologetically.

"Sorry. Like I told Commander Watson, it's classified. I'm sure you know all about stuff like this."

Crais looked slightly disappointed, but the compliment appeased him.

"Oh, sure. Beta level clearance and all that. Well, let me know if you need anything."

Harry heaved a sigh of relief as the lieutenant went back to sitting in the captain's chair. He turned his attention to his appointed task. Not a minute too soon, either. Crais hadn't taken two steps before a light started flashing on the console. Quickly Harry stepped in front of it in case Crais decided to come back for a second round of banter. Fortunately, or unfortunately, the panel had already been removed and the insides of the console lay open. He knelt and began working. This was going to be harder than he had anticipated. Everything was a mess in here, and he was having difficulty locating the—

"Hey, why is the light flashing?"

Adrenaline flooded Harry's system. He fumbled with the wires, trying to sound nonchalant as he replied, "That's just me, I was testing something."

The light stopped flashing. Harry held his breath, waiting for Crais to contact Watson, to reveal that Harry wasn't what he was pretending to be, to level a phaser at him. . . .

"Oh. Okay."

Harry let out his breath and closed his eyes. Sweat dappled his forehead.

"What does Ops have to do with researching a cure for the Borg virus?"

Damn. Harry rose and tried to look mysterious and commanding. He suspected he largely failed.

"There was a point on our journey where we had Borg technology integrated with nearly every system," he said airily. "How they cross-reference is classified."

Crais looked at him with narrowed eyes. Harry suspected he was pushing his luck. Crais might be bored and inventing games to while away the time, but he wasn't a fool. He felt the other's gaze boring into his back as he knelt and began to fiddle again with the controls.

It was a mess, as was the rest of the bridge. Each station had been taken apart and even if it had been put back together again, as was the case with Ops, it had been a halfhearted job.

"Project Full Circle sure didn't live up to its name," he muttered.

"What?"

"I said, Project Full Circle is an appropriate name," he lied.

"Oh. Yeah, I guess."

Hurry up, Admiral, Harry thought. *I won't be able to stave off this guy forever.*

Data moved purposefully to sickbay. The Doctor assured him that they could access everything they needed there, provided, of course, that Starfleet hadn't transferred the data and then wiped *Voyager*'s records. Data thought this highly unlikely. As he entered sickbay, Data said, "Computer. Locate and identify nearest humanoid."

"The nearest humanoid is Lieutenant Commander Susan Taylor. Present location—deck seven," replied the computer crisply.

Excellent. It was unlikely that they would be disturbed. He removed his skull patch, connected himself to the computer, and uploaded the Doctor.

Replacing the patch, Data commanded, "Computer, activate EMH."

The Doctor appeared, and his face took on a soft expression. "My old stomping ground," he said fondly, as he looked around sickbay.

Data opened his mouth to inquire if the Doctor actually strode with deliberately heavy footfalls in his sickbay, then thought better of the question.

"Computer," he said, "Modify the EMH to bring his physical appearance and vocal patterns in line with the most current version utilized on Starfleet vessels."

The Doctor turned around. "I don't want to look like—"

His image shimmered and reformed.

"—the latest version, I want to look like me!"

Data cocked his head. "It is a necessary precaution," he said. "If someone were to enter and see your actual appearance, they would be suspicious."

The Doctor sighed. He was now a bit taller, much slimmer, and an entirely difference race. He looked down at his dark-skinned hands and shrugged his shoulders.

"This is a later version than the EMH-2," he said, then under his breath, "thank God."

"We should get to work," Data said gently.

"Of course. Let's get started.

Janeway let out a deep sigh of gratitude as Seven and Icheb stepped into the regeneration chambers and closed their eyes. As they relaxed, their tight features softened. It was good to see them looking like themselves again, and to know that in a few hours, they would both be feeling so much better.

It had taken them at least a half an hour to get the two alcoves operational again. She chafed at the delay, but it was unavoidable. Now the two former Borg were safely ensconced in the alcoves, Harry was up on the bridge making sure that no messages got in or out, and the Doctor and Data were doing research in sickbay.

"Commander," she said to Tuvok, "I am entrusting Seven and Icheb to your care. They can't be discovered or the whole jig is up."

"I understand," said Tuvok, although she noticed with amusement that his brow furrowed at the word "jig."

"What now, Admiral?" said Paris. He and Chakotay looked at her expectantly.

"Why, gentlemen," she said, a smile spreading across her face, "You and I are going hunting."

Chapter 12

DR. JAREM KAZ materialized on *Voyager,* and smiled pleasantly at the guard who had transported him.

"Welcome aboard, Dr. Kaz."

"Thank you." *Keep it brief,* he thought. Maybe Gradak had had a knack for this sort of thing, but his heart was racing at the subterfuge. He was certain that at any minute he would be discovered. And yet, mixed in with the trepidation was something else. He suspected it was . . . excitement.

He'd familiarized himself with the layout of *Intrepid* class starships so that he wouldn't waste precious time or call attention to himself. When he strode into sickbay and saw Data and the Doctor, he felt a visible rush of relief. Then he did a double take.

"Doctor, you look different," he said, and then, "Of

course. If you kept your usual appearance, they'd know something had happened."

"Our feelings exactly," said the Doctor, "although it does take some getting used to."

"Have you been able to find anything yet?" asked Kaz.

The Doctor scowled. The expression did not suit the younger, pleasantly featured face of the present EMH.

"Not a thing. Well, nothing useful anyway. Commander Data has been useful in sifting through the . . . ah . . . data."

"I imagine you would be," said Kaz. "I was able to download almost everything I know about the virus thus far. If anyone checks, they'll see that there has been a download, and that will alert them that there's been a leak. Which will probably lead them right here."

"The entire operation is risky, Doctor," Data said. "I am certain you did everything you could to minimize the chance of discovery."

"I hope so," said Kaz. The door hissed open. All three of them turned quickly to see a tall, dark-haired women enter.

"I'm Lieutenant Commander Susan Taylor," she said. "You're obviously Commander Data. It's an honor to meet you, sir." She extended her hand and Data shook it politely. "And you must be Dr. Kaz. I've heard of you as well."

Numbly, Kaz shook her hand. He noticed that she completely ignored the EMH.

"Commander Watson alerted us that you were on board, and I thought I'd render what assistance I could."

Kaz felt the blood drain from his face. Fortunately, Data stepped in smoothly.

"We appreciate the offer, Lieutenant Commander. However, our work is highly classified. It is doubtful the regulations even permit your presence here, considering the nature of the data presently on the computer screens."

Kaz saw her eyes instinctually dart toward the screen, and then she deliberately averted her gaze.

"I'm sorry."

"Don't be," said Kaz gently. "If there's anything that we do need, we'll be sure to let you know."

"I'm here to serve, sir." With a quick smile, she turned and left. The door hissed closed behind her.

"She didn't even look at me," said the Doctor, bridling. "Did you see that? I might as well not have been activated. Hmph. And you wonder why Baines gets hot under the collar on behalf of holograms."

"Don't take it personally, Doctor," said Kaz. Something was nagging at him. Something wasn't right here. He began the transfer of data from his padd to *Voyager*'s computer.

Lieutenant Commander Susan Taylor had been in Security for eight years now. She was no starry-eyed ensign who could get bowled over by celebrities. And yet, when Watson had informed her that no less a personage than Commander Data was on board . . . well, she had to find an excuse to meet him.

She was disappointed but not surprised that they wouldn't let her assist them. The Trill doctor also seemed very pleasant, and easy on the eyes. It really was a pity she couldn't stay and help. Not the mention the fact that all eight of them here were getting a bit bored. It would be good to be actively involved in helping the Federation fight the newest threat.

Ah, well. She supposed that with Data, who could process information as fast as any computer, Dr. Kaz, a leader in his field; and an EMH, they had all the hands they needed.

Taylor slowed, came to a stop in the corridor.

An EMH . . .

"Oh no!" cried Kaz.

"What is wrong?" asked Data.

Kaz turned frantically to the Doctor. "Doctor . . . Because of your portable holographic emitter, you were able to leave *Voyager.*"

"Yes, so?" said the Doctor.

"They never replaced you," said Kaz. "There *is* no EMH on *Voyager!*"

It took a second for the import of his words to register on Data and the Doctor. Then the Doctor's eyes grew huge.

"Computer," the Doctor said, "deactivate EMH."

Just as he disappeared, the doors to sickbay opened and Taylor stepped in. Gone was the pleasant, attractive woman they had just spoken to a moment ago. This woman was all business, and had a phaser leveled at them. Slowly, they put their hands in the air.

"Status report," asked Watson. He was eating a replicated breakfast of steak and eggs while Lieutenant Janssen stood rigidly at attention.

"Team B has been notified and will report for duty within the hour."

Still chewing, Watson nodded. There was no need for the team to report immediately. An hour to shower, dress, and eat something wouldn't hurt anything. He took a sip of tea.

"Where are the *Voyager* crew members at the present time?"

"Harry Kim is on the bridge. Commander Data along with Dr. Kaz are in sickbay. Admiral Janeway, Commander Chakotay, and Lieutenant Commander Paris are presently in the turbolift. Commander Tuvok, Ensign Jackson, and Lieutenant Moore are in Cargo Bay Two."

Watson paused in his chewing. "What's Janeway's destination?"

"Unknown, sir."

"Cargo Bay Two is where most of the Borg technology is located," Watson said, thinking aloud. He pushed the plate away, his meal half-eaten.

"Well, sir, that would make sense if they are working on the Borg virus," said Janssen hesitantly.

"Yes, it does make sense," Watson agreed, rising and taking a final swig of tea, "but I still think I'd feel better if I had someone in there with them. Report to Cargo Bay Two, Janssen, and give me updates on the hour."

"Yes, sir. Anything else, sir?"

"That'll be all. Dismissed."

Janssen snapped to attention, then turned and left. Watson was sorry that Montgomery hadn't been so insistent about no contact. Watson had a couple of questions he wished he could ask.

In the meantime, his instincts were still telling him that something was very wrong.

* * *

"Keep them up where I can see them," Taylor said, her voice crisp. Kaz was only too happy to oblige.

"What seems to be the problem, Lieutenant Commander?" asked Data.

She didn't answer, only tapped her comm badge. "Taylor to Watson."

"Go ahead."

At that instant, the Doctor materialized immediately behind Taylor. Kaz kept his gaze rigidly on Taylor's face so as not to give the game away, but she had heard something. Fortunately, the Doctor was faster. He grabbed a hypospray from a tray and pressed it to her neck just as she turned around, and she collapsed limply into his arms.

"Taylor? Report." It was Watson, his voice coming from the comm badge. Easing Taylor to the floor, the Doctor tapped the badge, ending communication.

"Computer, alter EMH's vocal patterns to replicate those of Lieutenant Commander Susan Taylor."

"Completed."

The Doctor touched the badge again. "Taylor to Commander Watson."

Kaz stared, then started to grin. The Doctor was indeed speaking with Taylor's voice.

"Watson here. What's going on, Taylor? Any problems?"

"Negative, sir. I thought that perhaps you might want me to assist our guests in sickbay."

"Are you there right now?"

"No," lied the Doctor. Kaz hoped that Watson hadn't asked the computer the same thing.

"Then yes. Keep an eye on them. Something's wrong

here, but I can't put my finger on it. Is there anything suspicious in their behavior?"

"Negative, sir," said the Doctor, still speaking with Taylor's contralto voice. "Everything seems pretty much by the book."

"Hmm. Well, stay there. Let me know if you do notice anything that looks . . . odd."

"Will do, sir. Taylor out." The Doctor ended the message and then exhaled. "That was too close." He frowned at the sound of Taylor's voice issuing from his lips. "Computer, restore the EMH's standard vocal patterns."

"Doctor, that was brilliant!" exclaimed Kaz.

Picking up Taylor, the Doctor smirked slightly. "Thank you," he said in the voice of the standard EMH. "I've had a lot of practice. She should be out for several hours."

"Practice?" queried Data.

The Doctor gently laid the unconscious lieutenant commander into a cadaver drawer, removing her phaser as he did so. The drawer with its contents would slide back into the bulkhead. Kaz winced. Even though Taylor would be fine, he hated the sight of a living being in a cadaver drawer.

The Doctor looked slightly discomfited. "I had a great deal of time in my cell," he said, sounding embarrassed. "I ran through several possible scenarios. You know—fighting my way out of the prison, rescuing Seven of Nine, what to do if I were to be discovered on *Voyager.*"

Kaz tried not to grin. "I'm sure I'd have done the same thing," he said sincerely.

"Do not be embarrassed, Doctor," Data said. "Rehearsing possible scenarios is an honored and respected way of preparing for the unknown."

"Thank you," said the Doctor. "If I may say so, I think I bought us some time and some safety insurance so that we can work undisturbed."

"What if Watson comes to check on us?"

"Computer," said Data, "program the EMH to be deactivated whenever a humanoid is within three meters of the sickbay door. Also, replicate a hologram with the features, vocal patterns, and personality of Lieutenant Commander Susan Taylor. Consult her personal logs and ship's logs for information."

After a moment, the computer said, "Completed."

"Activate Taylor hologram."

An exact replica of Susan Taylor materialized next to Kaz. She smiled pleasantly. "What can I do to help you, sir?"

"Stand by the door, Lieutenant Commander, and please don't interrupt us."

She nodded. "Certainly, sir."

"Holograms are amazingly useful things," said Kaz.

"Yes," said the Doctor, "*we* certainly are. The information you brought has been downloaded, Doctor Kaz. Now the real work begins."

Holograms, thought Covington, are amazingly useful things.

While her drones were of course dearest to her heart, she also had a special fondness for the hologram that had helped her become the Queen she was today. Humans were far too complicated. They had their own agendas, and while she could play upon those agendas to manipulate them, she still preferred people who were more than flesh.

Brian Grady, for example, had an agenda that coincided with hers. At first, all he had wanted was acknowledgment for his skill and contributions. When he continued to not receive enough to assuage his ego, he had begun wanting more. Brenna Covington could provide it, or so she told him.

"Picard turned it down," she had told him early on, with the memories embedded in the program that had been used to create her. "He couldn't see that this was truly the best of both worlds. Human and machine, each better than the other could possibly become separately. Power such as neither alone has ever tasted."

She had rolled over onto him, her lips a mere centimeter from his, and whispered, "A queen needs a consort."

He had tangled his fingers in her hair then, and kissed her with a passion she had never before experienced with him. Later, as she became more and more Borg and less human, Grady had pleased her by finding as much delight in her altered body as he had before—perhaps even more.

Now, though, he was pressing to push ahead. He seemed to feel that the Starfleet bumblers were actually getting close to uncovering their secret. She had replied, scathingly, that if they were getting close to *anything* it had been his fault, for not leading them far enough astray. He had vowed to redouble his efforts, but it was becoming dangerously clear to Covington that "Red" Grady was more than ready to claim his own throne.

Perhaps he was right. Perhaps she did need to push up the timetable.

She would need some heightened adjustments in order to do so.

A few years ago, they had wanted to get rid of this version at headquarters; download it and ship it off to some dilithium processing plant somewhere. She had fought back panic. She had worked for years with this doctor. While the information could always be downloaded, she had developed quite a cordial relationship with it. And it was her understanding that the new EMHs had something in their system that prevented their ethical subroutines from being deleted.

That would not serve her purpose at all.

So she had gotten Trevor to help her create a false trail, so that it would appear as if the EMH had been removed. He oversaw the downloading of the new one, so that if anyone got a bruise or a bump on site, they could go to the new, younger-looking, African-appearing EMH to get treatment.

The older EMH could only be activated by a code phrase that no one but she, Grady, and Blake knew, to minimize accidental discovery.

The door hissed open. "Computer," she said, "Invoke security precautions Covington 486-Delta."

"Complying," replied the computer. She heard a mechanism inside the doors activate, and the familiar sound of a force field springing up around the circumference of the entire room. No one could enter. Even if someone tried to transport in now, they wouldn't be able to.

She smiled as she formed her lips around the words that would summon her photonic friend:

"Brave new world," she said.

He appeared, smiling pleasantly. She had grown fond of his balding pate, his slightly superior attitude, his smug smirk. The other versions were much pleasanter than he, but he was unique as far as she was concerned. He had helped make her Borg.

"Your Majesty," said the EMH Mark One, and she felt warm inside at the term. "How may I assist you today?"

Chapter 13

LIBBY GNAWED on her thumbnail.

It was a bad habit, and one she thought she'd kicked years ago. It made her fingers look stubby and interfered with playing the *lal shak*. But right now, as she stared at her computer screen, she couldn't help it.

Why wasn't Harry responding?

It had been a huge gamble to send the message to *Voyager*. What if Harry wasn't there? Or even if he was there, what if he hadn't been able to gain access to his old station, Ops? What if all this fell into the wrong hands? It was possible Covington had a plant at Project Full Circle, although it damned sure wasn't the one she had wanted Libby to think was the traitor. Maybe this person or persons unknown had gotten the message.

She hadn't eaten in what felt like forever. She hadn't fed her various animals either, and Rowena was letting her know it. She rose and got them something to eat just so they'd shut up.

Come on Harry, she thought. *This time you can actually reply to me.*

Harry kept venturing back and forth from Ops to the science station, trying to look officious and very busy so that Leo Crais would quit bugging him. Sometimes it worked, but sometimes it didn't. Apparently Crais didn't like his solitary bridge shift and was anxious to talk to somebody, anybody. Harry let him hold forth with the occasional "Uh huh" so that Crais would think he had an audience.

Out of the corner of his eye, while Crais stood blocking him and chatting away, Harry saw the small light come on over at Ops. He was clear across the bridge at the science station. He mentally swore vigorously, even as he kept his eyes on Crais and started nodding. How to get past this guy and over to the incoming message without Crais noticing?

He thought quickly. "Damn," he said, in his best tone of annoyance, "is that thing malfunctioning again? I thought I'd just fixed that. Excuse me," and he went back over to Ops, grumbling loudly.

Crais went to the captain's chair and sat down. It galled Harry to see anyone other than Janeway there, but he swallowed his annoyance and began downloading the message to a padd. He didn't have the chance to read it yet. With any luck, that chance would come soon.

"Hey, Harry," said Crais, "open a channel to Starfleet for me."

"What?" To Harry, his voice sounded like a yelp. He hoped it didn't sound that way to Crais.

"You heard me, you're over at Ops, go ahead and open it. Please," he added, as if he just remembered that they were of equal rank. "Got to do the morning check-in. You know the drill."

"Sure," said Kim easily, though he was sweating profusely. His fingers flew deftly over the controls and for a moment, he was suddenly back as the rightful operator of this station, on board a ship he had grown to love.

He cleared his throat. This would be tricky, opening the channel at just the right time so that Crais could have whatever conversation he was going to have while still giving Kim enough time to duck out of sight. Crais had recognized him; it was likely that someone else would, too.

Here goes . . .

He pressed a padd and the instant before a face materialized on the screen, he dropped down behind Ops. Even as he did so, another thought struck him. It was all well and good for Crais to have to check in with someone, but what if this Starfleet official wanted to talk to anyone else on the ship? He suddenly realized that he shouldn't have opened the channel for Crais. But then again . . .

"Good morning, Commander Vance," said Crais in a formal voice. Kim didn't recognize the name.

"Good morning, Lieutenant." This Vance fellow sounded bored. "Status report?"

"All continues to go well, Commander. Do you need to speak to anyone else aboard?"

Harry closed his eyes. *No, no, please no . . .*

"Not necessary. My best to Watson."

"Yes, sir. Crais out."

The screen went dark. "That Vance is a nice—hey, what are you doing hiding down there?"

Blushing, Harry stood up. "Just working on a particularly difficult coupling. Leo, can you do me a favor?"

"Sure, what?"

Harry gestured toward the screen. "It's been kind of hard readjusting since I got back. I don't want to sound stuck-up or anything, but we've all been kinda—well—noticed a lot. I'd just as soon not have to talk to anyone that I don't need to. Would you mind giving me time to get out of viewing range if you have to talk to anyone else?"

Crais's pleasant, open face showed sympathy. "You know, I hadn't thought of it that way. Sure. There's no need for anyone to know you're here."

Harry returned the smile, and for the first time since he stepped onto the bridge, it was genuine.

Icheb dreamed.

He was back on the grounds of the Academy again, walking from class on a warm afternoon in the company of his friends. Sam and Tim were having a lively discussion about the French Revolution, with Andre, the actual Frenchman, chiming in occasionally. Icheb's arm was around Eshe, and they walked comfortably together. Her own arm snaked around his back.

It felt so good, to be with her. It was unlike any sensation he had hitherto experienced. When their lips touched, his whole body felt tense and tingly. He had read much of human literature and found that an inordinate amount of it had to do with something called "falling in love." He wondered if that was what he and Eshe were experiencing now.

Her grip around his waist tightened. He smiled a little. She wanted them to be close, as did he. Then her arm tightened even more.

Icheb found it difficult to breathe. Surprised, he looked down at Eshe. Her face, normally the rich color of coffee, was now an ashy shade of gray. One brown eye regarded him with no emotion. They other had been removed, replaced with a red light. The grip around his waist was like iron. He struggled, crying out to his friends to help, but there was no reply. Icheb looked about wildly and saw that they, too, had become Borg.

The fight unraveled in slow motion. As he had before, Andre shoved Icheb, then Sam struck him. Icheb tumbled to the ground, but kept trying to fight. Except this time, his enemies—his friends—also had the physical advantage. They bore down on him, and then Icheb felt searing pain as something sliced his arm off.

Tuvok heard Icheb moan softly, and saw the youth's eyes darting back and forth under his tightly closed lids. Seven, too, was in a deep REM state. From Icheb's sound and the expression on both faces, he imagined their dreams were far from pleasant. But he did not interrupt the regeneration cycle. Dreams were harmless, and they desperately needed the healing this intensive rest would provide.

Tuvok fully expected that, successful or not, the military career of everyone involved in this desperate mission would be over by the time all was said and done. He did not know that he regretted it. He was content to continue to teach at the Academy. He enjoyed passing knowledge on to young minds, and Tuvok prized service. But if he were stripped of his rank and sent back to Vulcan, he would not be displeased.

His concern was more for his friends. Their careers had been practically guaranteed, until the advent of the Borg virus had turned heroes into villains in the eyes of Starfleet. And yet, logic dictated that the crew of *Voyager,* particularly the Doctor, Seven of Nine, and Icheb, should have been the first brought into the circle of those trying to end the Borg threat.

Starfleet had not behaved logically. Therefore, Tuvok felt that other alternatives needed to be explored. Although he knew that many of his comrades had expected him to be resistant to Janeway's plan, he had approved of it from the first.

He stood at his post, hands loosely at his side. From where he had positioned himself, he could at once keep an eye on the regenerating Borg in case something went wrong, and an eye on the door. He could and would stand here for hours. He would only leave if Janeway summoned him, when the Borg had finished their regeneration, or if there were an emergency disturbance.

The door hissed open.

The third option, then.

The young man with the pale skin and fair hair had taken three steps inside before he saw the green glow. His jaw dropped open as he stared at the still figures of Seven of Nine and Icheb. One hand went up, holding a phaser, the other moved to his comm badge.

Before he could touch it, Tuvok had slipped up behind him. He squeezed the precise nerve and the intruder dropped like a stone. Tuvok caught him as he fell, then dragged the limp body out of immediate sight of the door. While much of the cargo had been emptied from the cargo bay, Tuvok was able to find sufficient materials to bind and gag the guard. He relieved the fallen man of his phaser, strode back to his former position, and calmly took up his protective stance once again.

All Chakotay could think about was Black Jaguar. He could almost feel her behind him, her stride smooth and silent. Once he couldn't resist it and even glanced quickly behind him, half-expecting to see her inky, feline form. He knew that the playful big cat lolling on the sun-warmed rock was gone. If Black Jaguar was indeed here, she would be the predator—quiet, quick, deadly, focused. As he, Chakotay, needed to be.

Regrets flooded his mind, simple sun-moments not embraced. He thought of words he hadn't said, gestures he hadn't made, risks he hadn't taken. Now it might be too late. Soon, his world, as he had known it, might be very much changed.

The words he had told the mighty Spirit-cat came back to him: *Black Jaguar is the totem of great power, of courage, of ferocity. Of fighting great battles in just causes. Of dealing out death to those who deserve it, and not flinching from the task. Black Jaguar strikes without warning and kills swiftly and fairly. When Black Jaguar appears, one is about to . . .*

And she had finished: *One is about to embark on a journey that will test one's mettle, wits, courage, and faith in the dark places. It is a trial of the highest sort, and if one fails, then Black Jaguar will exact Her punishment. And if one succeeds, great good will come about, for the journeyer and the world.*

If they could do it—if they could stop the Borg virus dead in its tracks—then Chakotay could see how it would bring about great good, for the journeyer and the world. It was a great battle, fought in a just cause.

He simply never thought he'd have to carry out that battle by skulking about *Voyager,* his prey fellow Starfleet officers. But here he was, striding beside his former captain, doing exactly that.

Janeway gazed at her tricorder, then nodded silently to her companion. He slipped away from her, darting for a nearby Jefferies tube, and climbed up just far enough so he wouldn't be seen. Janeway waited. Chakotay listened intently. He could hear footfalls now, muffled slightly by the carpeting. They passed him, and Chakotay climbed down and stuck his head out gingerly.

Janeway was just around the corner. She strode forward vigorously, her eyes on the tricorder, and collided with the security guard. She faked a stumble and fall.

"Oh!" she cried as the "wind was knocked out of her." Even as he waited for the moment, Chakotay admired her. She was good.

"Admiral Janeway!" exclaimed the young man, clearly mortified by running into a Starfleet legend. "I'm so sorry, I didn't see you—here, please let me help you up."

Janeway laughed, managing to strike exactly the right note of slight embarrassment, and extended her hand.

The young man's back was to Chakotay. He swung

down behind the guard, clasped his hands, and brought them down hard on the back of the guard's head.

It was a good blow, but not good enough. The guard stumbled but didn't fall. He reached for his phaser, off balance but still conscious, and whirled to face Chakotay.

The roundhouse kick that knocked the guard to the floor surprised Chakotay. He knew Janeway kept in good physical shape and that, like any Starfleet officer, she was trained in hand-to-hand combat. But she didn't often employ those methods to bring down her adversaries.

He didn't let the opportunity go to waste. He dropped onto the guard and landed a clean punch to the young man's jaw. At once, the guard went limp. Chakotay checked for his pulse. Strong and steady. Perfect. His fondness for boxing had come in handy yet again.

Chakotay turned to look admiringly at his former captain. "That was good," he said. "Very good."

She grinned at him. "I'm just glad it worked. It's been a long time since I've taken out anyone but a fake Klingon on the holodeck. Let's get his phaser and comm badge and stash him somewhere."

As Chakotay shouldered the limp security guard in the position traditionally called the fireman's carry, the full meaning of her quip registered and he stared at her.

"You train against Klingons?"

Vassily Andropov had never been so exhausted or in so much pain in his life.

The holograms that served as "masters" did nothing to ease the pain of the lash wounds. He was not offered so much as a token salve or bandage. He felt them trying to heal on their own, crusting over only to break open again as he exerted himself building this stupid, senseless, fictitious "monument." Sweat crept into the wounds and stung. Instead of the sharp pain of injury, there was now a throbbing, aching sensation that was starting to spread. Gangrene, probably.

Nothing a dermal generator wouldn't fix, he had told Allyson. And Robinson had replied that she hadn't seen any lying around in the sand. He hadn't seen her since the confrontation between Akolo Tare and the hologram, and hoped both of them were all right. Allyson had not left his side.

The food was meager—some kind of bread that was gritty and stale, and warm, equally gritty and stale water. The holograms worked them all day. Allyson was clearly trying to be brave, and equally clearly was scared to death. At one point, on their all-too-brief breaks, Andropov caught her wiping away tears.

"Hey," he said, gently, "it's going to be all right."

She looked up at him with those enormous green eyes. They shimmered with tears.

"I don't think so," she said in a soft, thick voice. "I don't think so at all."

Andropov was not the most socially graceful of men, but he tried again. "Listen, Baines wants us alive to prove his point. He won't hurt anyone."

Her eyes flickered to the crusted blood on his face, but she said nothing.

"Okay, maybe 'hurt' isn't the right word," he amended. "But I don't think we need fear for our lives."

"Maybe not our lives," she said. "But other things." There was an uncomfortable pause. He knew what she meant. She drew a shuddering breath. Her face was lighter where the tears had washed away sand and sweat. "I was an artist."

"You still are," he said, anxious to reassure her.

She laughed, a short, harsh bark that had little humor in it, and held up her hands. Despite himself, he winced. The nails were broken. The palms were scraped and bleeding. She tried to bend her fingers; they were swollen like thick sausages. Allyson looked up at him, her broken heart in her face, and he felt himself melt.

The kid was young enough to be his daughter, and despite her attractiveness, he felt more paternal than amorous toward her. What was Baines thinking? Abducting a youngster like this, an artist, someone fragile and imaginative and creative. She'd break if they kept this up.

Impulsively he handed her his waterskin. "Drink this," he said.

"No," she protested. "You'll need it. They're working you hard, and you're injured."

"I'm in Starfleet, remember? I've survived tougher things than this," he lied. The closest he'd gotten to anything resembling this ordeal was once when he'd gotten lost overnight on a hiking trip after stubbornly refusing to bring any navigation tools. In the summer, in the Rocky Mountains, with a sleeping bag and plenty of food and water. "Please. I'll feel better if I know you're getting something resembling enough water."

She licked her full lips. They were already burned and cracking. "If you're sure . . ."

"Of course I'm sure."

Allyson smiled, sweetly, gratefully. She took the waterskin and drank every last drop. "I'm sorry!" she said as she realized what she had done. "I shouldn't have . . ."

"Don't worry. They'll give us water again in a few hours." *At least I hope so.*

She was still looking at him, smiling a little. "You remind me of my uncle Alexander."

"Was he strong, brilliant, and incredibly handsome?"

Allyson laughed aloud at that. "He was the nicest man I ever knew. I never knew my Dad, so he was . . . he was more like my Dad than anything else. He was the one who encouraged me to try painting. He saw something in me that no one else did."

A trumpet blew. Allyson flinched visibly, and the fear settled on her features like snow on a flower.

"They just want us to get back to work," he said. "That part of the monument is in shadow. Maybe we can go over there. It won't be as hot."

He headed toward the shadow of the great pyramid, hoping he was right. Allyson followed him like a shadow herself, occasionally reaching to touch him so they would not lose one another as they made their way through the throng of organic slaves. Her touch was light, like a butterfly.

She herself was like a butterfly, bright and fragile. Vassily resolved at that moment that no harm would come to the child. He'd protect her—with his life if necessary. And for the hundredth time since his abduction, anger boiled inside him toward Oliver Baines.

Chapter 14

B'ELANNA TORRES stared, disbelieving, up into the face of her mother. For a long moment, their gazes locked, and then Miral rolled onto the ground, releasing her daughter.

"Mother," B'Elanna breathed. "I did it. I really did it. I found you."

Miral snorted. "I think rather that I found you, little one. Don't you know that building a fire in the wilderness is a sure way to attract trouble?"

Torres stared. Part of her wanted to cry. She couldn't believe it. After all she'd undergone, after leaving a husband and an infant behind, all she was getting from her mother was still more criticism.

The other part of her was angry. How dare Miral do this to her?

But Miral had risen and moved over to the campsite.

She took a sharp breath and turned eyes glowing with renewed appreciation on her daughter.

"You made a kill, 'Lanna. A good kill. But you should have eaten the meat raw. It is not so cold that you need a fire's warmth to survive."

Finally, B'Elanna found her voice. "Well hello, B'Elanna. Glad you're not dead. Hope you had a good seven years in the Delta Quadrant. Thanks for coming to find me, for leaving your husband and your friends and your career and your three-week-old infant *daughter* and caking yourself with filthy—"

"Daughter?" Miral had picked up a stake and had been about to take a big bite of the roasted meat, but now she stared. "You have . . . you have a daughter?"

Torres blinked hard. She would *not* let her mother see this weakness. "I do. I got married, and I gave birth to a daughter nine weeks ago. I left her when she was three weeks old to come find you. I've been away from her for two thirds of her life because of you. What was this all about, Mother? Why did you put me through this? I could have died out here, for no good reason!"

She realized she was shouting now. The pain was almost unbearable. This was not how she had imagined encountering her mother. B'Elanna had envisioned a joyful reunion, with hugs, even. Maybe. But at the very least she expected some gratitude for undertaking the Challenge.

"A grandchild," Miral said, her voice going strangely husky. "I have a grandchild. A grand*daughter*. What . . . what is her name?"

And then B'Elanna couldn't help it. She was exhausted, drained physically and mentally. She let the tears come, tried to speak, failed, tried again.

"We named her . . . we named her Miral."

And then her mother was in her arms, squeezing tightly, tightly, and Torres heard the sounds of sobs and wondered which of them was crying.

Candace Roske was a huge fan of the holodeck. She was grateful beyond words that the *Voyager* crew had clearly been fans as well. She imagined that the holodeck was a necessity, if you were lost out there in the Delta Quadrant. Probably kept more than a few crew members sane.

Just like it was keeping Roske sane. It was very, very boring on *Voyager* these days.

She'd tried out several of the already-programmed scenarios. Many were obviously designed simply to give the participant a good workout. Others were very restful—she particularly liked the Polynesian resort and the moonlight sail across Lake George. The governess one she abandoned after a few tries, and she'd really enjoyed visiting the oddly sunny Irish town of Fair Haven, although she thought the pub owner seemed a bit mopey.

But by far her favorite scenario was "The Adventures of Captain Proton." As someone with a great deal of familiarity with designing holodeck programs herself, Candace found it easy to adjust Constance Goodheart's program and insert herself as the character. Instead of being scantily clad and screaming all the time, "Constance," as played by Candace, was as smart, cool, and fun as Proton himself.

She had gotten the message to report in and was a bit annoyed by it, but hey, Watson was in charge. She wanted to finish up the firefight, though, and with an hour to report in, she thought she'd make it in time.

Candace ducked as laser blasts whizzed past her in all their black-and-white glory. She ducked behind a rock and returned fire. The flying saucer settled down, the small dome on its top glowing, and a ramp extended.

Candace couldn't help it. She started to laugh. The aliens were hilarious. They had large eyes at the end of waving stalks, and these six cute little arms and legs—oh, this was a good one, all right. She wanted to pick them up and cuddle them.

That was, until they started firing. The rock beside her vaporized. Candace—Constance—dove for cover, rolling as she hit the powdery soil, firing as she went.

"Constance!" a voice cried, and she looked up to see the Captain himself waving frantically at her. "Over here!"

In this version, Captain Proton was a good-looking blond man with piercing blue eyes. She'd gotten to know that face . . . and that body . . . pretty well, as she'd programmed a slow-growing but sweet romance between the good Captain and his noble assistant.

He'd managed to erect some kind of shield that seemed to be deflecting the alien fire. Candace took a couple of deep breaths, readied herself, and sprinted the short distance. She dove for cover, and Captain Proton's arms. As they landed hard on the soil, she thought he looked surprised.

They lay, heart to heart, eyes locked, breathing heavily from exertion. She lowered her head and kissed him. Normally, he liked that, but this time he seemed shocked and struggled away.

Candace brushed at her long red hair, which had escaped from its braid and was now falling into her face. "What's wrong?"

"Well," said Captain Proton, reaching casually for her weapon and inspecting it, "don't take it personally, but I don't think my wife would approve. Sorry, Constance. Computer, disengage safety protocol."

And before Candace could even form the question, Captain Proton lifted her laser weapon, now set on "Render Unconscious," and fired point blank.

Tom Paris looked down at the limp form of the admittedly attractive "Constance Goodheart." He thought of the pressure of her lips on his and shook his head wryly.

"No," he said aloud as he tied up the unfortunate guard, making sure the knots were sufficiently tight to keep her bound but not painful and removing her comm badge, "B'Elanna would definitely *not* approve."

"I do not approve," said Miral firmly. She was feasting on her daughter's kill, licking her fingers. B'Elanna smothered a smile.

"I didn't think you would."

"Was that the reason you chose the human?"

"No," B'Elanna replied. She wasn't angry. Her mother's fierce, practically rib-crushing embrace had bled most of the anger from her. "I chose him because I fell in love with him. He is intelligent, and brave, and attractive, and funny."

"Bah," snorted Miral, opening her mouth and exposing sharp teeth as she took another bite. "Humor is too prized among humans. Better to be courageous and have honor."

"He does." B'Elanna wasn't arguing, she was simply stating a fact. Her coolness did not go unnoticed by Miral, who paused in her chewing.

"I thought you unchanged, 'Lanna," she said. "A little while ago. But you have proved me wrong. You do not rise to the bait as once you did."

"Don't give me too much credit," B'Elanna replied. "I still get very angry much too easily. And," she admitted, "sometimes for the wrong reasons."

"You are young yet," her mother said. "It has taken me all my life to learn such lessons, and I am not sure I have learned them fully myself."

B'Elanna hesitated. She had told Miral all about Tom and her namesake. But there was so much more to tell. She had been gone so long, and so much had happened to her.

And of course, there was the Barge of the Dead.

"Mother . . . Commander Logt told me you had a vision while I was gone."

Despite her evident hunger—Miral was thinner and more sinewy than B'Elanna had ever seen her—the older woman stopped eating.

"It was powerful," she said, softly. "The more so because of how close to death I was."

"What?" B'Elanna cried. "You were sick? They never told me that."

Miral chuckled. "Of course not. To tell you of my weakness would steal my honor. I was very sick indeed, my little one. I was halfway between the worlds, at the very least."

Slowly, in soft, hushed tones, Miral Torres began to speak of her vision. B'Elanna hung on every word, hardly daring to breathe lest she miss something. So much of B'Elanna's own memory of her vision had faded, as such things did, but there was enough for her to realize that somehow, despite all logic, she and Miral had shared the same vision.

When Miral had finished, B'Elanna spoke. She told of finding the ancient *bat'leth,* of not being able to separate what was real from what wasn't, and the support her captain and her husband had given her on this potentially deadly trip to make peace with her mother and herself.

"I was so afraid that you had died, and that this was the only way I could get to say good-bye," B'Elanna finished, knowing her voice was thick. "And then when I came back and Father told me you'd died on the Challenge, I thought it was true."

Gently, Miral laid a hand on her daughter's knee. "If it were true, that I had died while you were gone, I would have gone straight to *Sto-Vo-Kor.* Your courage in the vision lifted my dishonor—if, indeed, there was any real dishonor to be lifted. Perhaps that, too, was only in my mind."

She turned and cupped B'Elanna's face in two hands. "Child . . . you are your own person, but I need to know: Are you Klingon?"

B'Elanna opened her mouth to answer, but there were no words. Was she Klingon? Was she human? Was she a harmonious blending of the strengths of two great peoples, or was she a mongrel, a mistake? She thought of how intensely she wanted to "spare" little Miral her Klingon traits—her heritage. It had been Tom's love of that part of her, too, that had helped her see that she would have been making an enormous mistake.

She had sensed that this Challenge was scouring her, searing her, stripping away all that did not serve her innermost self. But what did that leave?

Who did that leave?

"I—I don't know yet, Mother. I just don't know."

She thought she saw disappointment in Miral's face, but her mother managed a smile. "There is time yet for you to know. Having a child of your own will force you to look at yourself in ways you cannot imagine. Believe me, I know. Let us rest. We have a long journey ahead of us."

Now B'Elanna was confused. "But I assumed you wanted me to undertake the Challenge properly—to spend at least six months fending for myself in the wilderness."

"I did," Miral replied. "But I did not know you had a mate and a child. A baby, no less."

"But my honor—"

"There is great honor in tending to the needs of a child one has brought into the world," Miral replied. "In fact, there is no greater honor. Why do you think I strove so to bring you to your heritage?"

B'Elanna blinked, startled. "I thought it was because you wanted me to be like you—to love all things Klingon."

"You thought I did it for myself?"

"Well—yes, I did. Didn't you?"

Miral considered the question. "I love my bloodline," she admitted. "I am so proud to be Klingon. We are a great and noble people, and if our ways are different from those of others, then so be it. But I believed that you needed to understand both sides of your heritage. That was my duty to you. My task, as it were. Had I not done what I could to show you the glory of what you are—not half of you, but all of you—I would have been remiss as a mother. Did I ever insult your father or his people?"

"No, you didn't. And you could have, easily. Especially when he left us."

"To do so would be to make you feel bad about being part human. I wanted you to feel proud of your human blood. I wanted you to be proud of your Klingon blood as well. I wanted you," she said, stroking B'Elanna's mud-caked hair, "to be proud of *yourself.* If I failed to ascend to *Sto-Vo-Kor* it would not have been because I didn't make you Klingon. It would have been because I didn't help you find your own pride."

B'Elanna stared at her mother's face, so familiar and so strange after all this time. Could she have been that wrong about Miral's motivation?

And if so, what else had she been wrong about?

Chapter 15

KAZ KNEW that he was no slouch intellectually, but standing next to Data and the Doctor, watching them process information nearly at light-speed, left him feeling a bit inferior. An android and a hologram were beating him at his own game. Quickly, he shook that thought away. Everyone had strengths and weaknesses. Even Trills, and androids, and holograms. One was wise to know and respect one's own weaknesses and strengths. They needed his expertise, too, and when he was able to offer it, he felt inordinately pleased.

They had determined a great deal about the virus in the hour they'd had alone in sickbay. It was operated by nanoprobes that entered the body through touch or inhalation. The method of delivery should surprise nobody, Kaz thought, considering who they were dealing with. It would remain dormant until given an order to be activated.

So far so good, but this was where it all fell rather nastily apart.

How was the order given? Could an infected person spread the virus before the virus was activated? Why weren't adults with strong, functional immune systems affected yet? Would they be, and if so, when? How was the virus contracted?

"I am fond of mysteries," Data confessed at one point, "yet I would be glad to have this one solved quickly."

"I'm sure you speak for a lot of people, Commander," the Doctor said. His acerbic tone of voice seemed odd, coming from the new hologram's milder throat. "I suggest that we've spent enough time researching how the virus is transmitted. I have a theory on how we can stop it. Dr. Kaz, you said earlier that you had downloaded information from *Voyager*."

"That's right."

"And you said you had begun experimenting with nanoprobes?"

"Yes. Your work with the cellular construction of Species 8472 pointed the direction."

"Really?" The Doctor preened slightly.

"Unfortunately, we couldn't come up with a modified nanoprobe that would destroy the original ones."

"Hmmm," said the Doctor. "Perhaps that's not the correct route. One thing we need to do right now is start replicating as many Borg nanoprobes as possible. I'm not sure how we're going to use them, but I do know they will be instrumental in solving this particular mystery."

He glanced over at the chronometer. "It's almost rendezvous time. Who should go?"

"I should," said Kaz. "You don't really need me."

"On the contrary, Doctor," said Data, "we need your expertise a great deal. You are more familiar with this virus than either of us. Besides, if a doctor were to be found wandering the corridors when he was supposed to be working on curing a virus, it could arouse suspicion. I shall go." He turned to the Doctor. "If you modify your image programming to imitate my physical appearance, you can continue working here even if someone enters."

"But then if that someone also ran into you in the corridor, they'd know something was wrong," Kaz said. "I have to tell you, no offense, Doctor, but this whole hologram version of musical chairs is starting to become confusing."

"No offense taken," said the Doctor. "I'm having trouble keeping it all straight myself."

"The simplest solution is often the most effective," said Data. "Perhaps the Doctor should continue to deactivate if anyone approaches. I can always tell the truth, which is that Admiral Janeway requested my presence."

"Good luck," Kaz said. "Take Taylor's phaser. We've got hyposprays if we need them."

Data accepted the phaser, nodded to them, and strode out the door.

They met up in Cargo Bay Two, as Janeway had ordered.

"Status report," she asked. "First, has anyone run into any guards yet?"

"I have Constance Goodheart tied up in the holodeck," Paris said.

"What?" exclaimed Chakotay.

"One of the guards is playing Constance Goodheart in my Captain Proton scenario," Paris explained, clearly trying not to smile but failing. "The computer had my physical parameters for Proton as reference, and she kept them intact. It was easy to substitute myself for Proton and turn her stun weapon on her. The scenario's still running. There's a chance someone will go in after her, but they'd have to battle the Moolian Fleet to do it."

"Couldn't they turn the program off?" Kaz was slightly in awe of Lieutenant Commander Paris's imagination.

"I designed the program," Paris said, "and they never bothered to transfer the codes. I can't lock the doors, but I've reprogrammed the computer with a code word. They can't shut the program down unless I authorize it."

"Very good work, Mr. Paris," Janeway said, admiringly. "I see that Tuvok has disabled a guard as well." Kaz looked over to see the prone, trussed up, and gagged figure of a fair-haired young man. He looked quite upset. Kaz couldn't blame him.

"How are you three faring in sickbay?" Janeway continued.

"We had a surprise visit from a guard, but we disabled her. The Doctor did, actually. I can see why you're all so fond of him. She's presently unconscious in a cadaver drawer, but a hologram of her is standing around smiling, just in case anyone comes to check."

Janeway was smiling openly now. "Chakotay and I took one down in the corridor. He's stashed in a Jefferies tube and should be unconscious for quite some time. We should put their comm badges in their quarters, in case Watson tries to locate them."

"How many phasers were we able to obtain?" asked Tuvok.

"Three," replied Janeway. "I don't think Tom's Constance was carrying a real weapon in the holodeck."

"No, more's the pity," said Tom.

Janeway's expression sobered slightly. "I haven't heard anything from Harry, so I'll try to contact him when we're done here. Dr. Kaz, Data—what have you learned about the virus?"

They brought everyone up to speed, and Kaz desperately wished that he had better news. At least the Doctor seemed to think they had a direction now. Janeway was silent for a while, then at last she spoke.

"I've been thinking hard about this, gentlemen. We've eliminated half the guards, but there are still four left. One of them is Watson, whom I think suspects us, and another is on the bridge. I also don't think we're going to be able to let Seven and Icheb regenerate as long as Dr. Kaz would like them to. We need their unique knowledge and expertise.

"Montgomery won't be fooled forever, either. And once he figures out that we've duped him, things are going to start happening very fast."

Kaz did not protest. Even the little bit of time that Seven and Icheb had been allowed to regenerate would help them, and he knew as well as Janeway did that they didn't have the luxury of time on any front of this strange battle they were waging.

"What do you want us to do?" asked Chakotay, quietly.

"We'll awaken Seven and Icheb and send them back

to sickbay with Kaz and Data. The rest of you will come with me. This was our ship, once. We're going to take it back."

Brenna Covington lay on the bed, her skullcap removed and her brain exposed, calm and yet excited at the same time. She had the utmost trust in the EMH Mark One. He had not failed her yet, which was more than could be said for many humans. It had taken time, and she had lost patience more than once with him, Grady, and Blake. But they always had come through for her in the end.

She had grown weary of being a partial queen. It was good, to have the superior strength and access to the hive mind. It was even better to be able to link with them, as she could when she regenerated, to feel their need and love of her. But that was as a taste of honey on the tongue, sweet but serving only to awaken further cravings. She wanted more. She wanted it all.

Covington wanted information to flow through her body like her blood did. She wanted to penetrate all the drone minds, all the time, thoroughly and completely, with no separation. She wanted to experience the thoughts of healthy adults, not just the malleable brains of children and the sometimes dry and barren minds of the elderly. Intellectually, she knew what she would become when she was at last complete, and she thirsted for it like a man in the desert thirsted for cold, sweet water.

Had she been the true queen, the process would have taken place within moments, if not seconds. The Royal Protocol program would have selected her, imbued her with knowledge that came as quickly and effortlessly as breathing. It would have replaced weak human organs with metal, and she would have become queen almost instantaneously. The Borg needed their queen, could not function without her.

But what she, Blake, and the EMH were doing was new, experimental. Had never been done before. They were creating a queen from scratch, as it were, with a recipe that had only recently been understood.

Odd, that she would use a cooking metaphor. She seemed to smell food being prepared . . . cookies, she thought; baking slowly in an oven.

"I smell cookies baking," she told the EMH. He stood behind her, busily working on her brain. She was used to it, accustomed now even to the sight of her skullcap, bony and bloody, sitting in a dish behind a sterile field.

"I'm stimulating that part of your brain," the EMH replied. "That's only natural. I hope it's a pleasant association."

"It is," she said, her mind going back to the time before the owner of the Hand invaded her life, when she and her mother baked chocolate chip cookies every Saturday morning. She had not smelled cookies baking since then. Odd, how the mind worked, what it chose to remember.

Once the transformation from human to Borg queen was completed, she would have no need for the laborious task of chewing, swallowing, and digesting nutrients. Her taste buds would all but disappear from disuse. Anything her body needed, it would acquire through the more efficient means of direct absorption.

Faintly she heard the EMH's voice, as if coming from far away. ". . . have to put you fully under, Your Majesty."

"You may proceed," she said, her voice thick and her words slurred. As she closed eyelids that had become suddenly heavy and drifted into darkness, her last thought was one of regret at never again smelling and tasting chocolate chip cookies fresh from the oven.

The slow-passing hours were taking a dreadful toll on Allyson. Andropov, Robinson, and many of the others who were Starfleet-trained were in excellent physical condition, even if they did have the dreaded "desk jobs" and weren't operating on sufficient food, water, or sleep. Allyson was just a girl, barely twenty, and had obviously never had to endure anything resembling physical hardship on the measure of what was expected of her here.

The circles under her eyes grew almost as he watched. It would take days, of course, for the flesh to melt off her bones, but she was visibly weak. Twice, she had stumbled away to vomit up what little food and water she'd been able to keep down. Once, she had paid for it by feeling the sting of the lash. Andropov had rushed to her defense, shielding her body with his own and taking the brunt of the punishment. The rider didn't seem to care which of the organics was beaten, as long as someone was. He had laughed and spurred his horse into a canter, riding off to another point to supervise the slaves.

"Thank you," Allyson whispered, gazing up at him with hero worship in her eyes. "You're already so badly hurt, and yet—"

"A few more lashes won't make any difference to me," he lied, forcing himself not to wince as he moved away from her and got to his feet. He extended his arms to help her up, she stumbled, and fell against him.

For a moment, he permitted himself to hold her, to feel her heart beating against his chest, to feel how fragile her body truly was. He'd come from a large family and had always wanted kids, but somehow it had never happened. He'd imagined teaching his son how to play sports and have fun, taking his daughter out to a fancy dinner on her sixteenth birthday and treating her like a gentleman should treat a lady. Making her feel special.

"When this is over," he said, "I'd like to take you out to dinner."

She blushed. "I don't want to seem ungrateful, but . . ."

"Not a date," he pressed. "I'm far too ancient for you. But—" How to even find the words? It would be hard under the best of circumstances, but here, in the scorching sun, smelling his own stench, weak and wounded—how could he find words to explain what he was feeling toward her?

"I never had a daughter," he said bluntly, "and I don't think I could be prouder of her than I am of you right now. Let me do this for you."

Her eyes searched his as they made their slow way back through the shifting sands to haul more stone, make more mortar. Finally, she nodded.

"I understand," she said. "All right. But you should be warned—I'm going to eat like a horse when we get back!"

Warmed by the acceptance and trust in her words, Andropov laughed aloud for the first time since the hellish ordeal began.

Chapter 16

WATSON'S SIXTH SENSE—the one that had saved his life and those of his companions more than once in the years he had served in Starfleet—was on red alert. He hadn't trusted Janeway and crew from the moment they beamed aboard. He'd let them prowl around alone long enough. It was time to act.

Two of his crew—Hughes and Whitman—were with him in the mess hall now. Crais had not been asked to attend. Watson knew Kim was also on the bridge, and didn't want to alert the former Ops officer that they were on to him. Same with Taylor, who was with Data and Kaz in sickbay. They'd take those three later, at their convenience.

But where were Janssen, Colson, and Roske? Janssen had not contacted Watson since he had left to check out Cargo Bay Two. Roske and Colson of the second team had been ordered to report for duty, and should have been here by this point.

Watson made a decision. "Something's happened," he stated flatly, with the certainty of someone who knew he was right. "I'm going to contact Montgomery, regardless of what he said earlier." He moved to the computer and suited action to word as he activated it.

"You two go to the armory. I want the phaser rifles in our hands, not theirs. Admiral Kenneth Montgomery," he said to the computer. He frowned. His computer stubbornly refused to show anything but the Starfleet insignia.

To his crew, he continued, "There's only a handful of them, scattered throughout the ship, so they shouldn't be that difficult to take."

"My thoughts exactly," came a cool female voice. Watson whirled, his hand going his phaser. "Don't draw it, Commander, or I'll drop you where you stand."

Watson, Hughes, and Whitman stood and stared at the four figures in the doorway. Three of them had phasers. Janeway's was trained on Watson, and the other two had Hughes and Whitman in their sights.

"You're good, Admiral," said Watson, admiration creeping into his voice as he lifted his hands. Whitman and Hughes emulated him. "I should have acted sooner. I knew something was wrong. But at the risk of sounding like an old-fashioned hero from one of Lieutenant Roske's holodeck programs, you won't get away with this."

"No one is a villain here, Commander," Janeway said. "We're all on the same side."

"Then why do three of us have phasers trained on the rest of us?" Watson asked.

"No time to sit down over a nice cup of coffee and straighten things out. I regret that we're going to have to put you and your crew in the brig for a few hours."

When they didn't move, the Vulcan spoke up. "The admiral's words were not a request, gentlemen."

As he passed her, Watson turned to Janeway and said with narrowed eyes, "I might be looking at the inside of a Starfleet brig for a few hours, Admiral. You'll be looking at it for the rest of your life."

She didn't rise to the bait. Her eyes were, oddly, soft and compassionate as she replied, "If we're not all assimilated, then you can bet that I'll be happy to stare at brig walls until the day I die, Commander. Let's go."

Harry looked up in surprise when the door hissed open. "Admiral on deck!" he said, and snapped to attention. Crais leaped out of the captain's chair as if it were white hot and stood at attention as well. His face was red.

"Admiral Janeway," he said, striving to retain his composure. "What an unexpected honor. Commander Watson failed to alert me that you would be visiting the bridge."

Smiling pleasantly, Janeway pulled the phaser from behind her back and pointed it directly at Crais.

"I'm afraid that Commander Watson is no longer in a position to alert you to anything, Lieutenant. We're going to have to ask you to join him in the brig while we finish up here."

Crais continued to gape, but moved slowly toward the turbolift. Chakotay pointed his phaser at him and silently encouraged him to move faster.

"Looks like you guys have gotten everything well in hand, Admiral," said Kim. He supposed that knowing Janeway as well as he did, he ought not to have been quite so surprised. But Watson had struck him as a challenge.

Janeway smiled. "We've taken the ship, Harry. Everyone but our people is in the brig under Tuvok's watchful eye. Were you able to stop Watson's message from getting out a few moments ago?"

"Only just," confessed Harry. "The consoles are so torn apart that I've really had my hands full up here."

"It should be a little easier now that you don't have to worry about anyone else trying to send out a message. I want you to put up some kind of screen, so that if anyone does try to contact us they'll get a false sense that all is normal, if troubled by a few glitches."

Harry's mind began sifting through various options. "I'll do my best, Admiral."

"If there are any problems, you can now contact me freely," she said, touching his comm badge with a forefinger. "We'll all be in sickbay, including Icheb and Seven."

"They're out of the chamber so soon?"

"I'm afraid so. Kaz, the Doctor and Data can't make any further progress without the input of someone who's more familiar with the Borg. Kaz tells me that even the little regeneration time they had helped. Who knows," she said, somberly, "soon we may all be able to get all the regeneration time we need."

As she left, Kim crawled back under the console and tried to think if he could somehow hook up a holographic display in case someone needed to talk to Watson.

He had completely forgotten about the message he had downloaded into the buffer.

"How are you feeling, Your Majesty?"

Covington blinked. "Well," she said. "I feel well." The EMH helped her to sit up. The room spun for just a moment, then everything settled down to assume a clarity she had never seen before. Colors seemed brighter, edges sharper. The air felt rich in her lungs as she breathed, and she noticed scents even in this sterile environment.

"Amazing," she said softly, running a hand along the bed. Even its soft texture now felt slightly rough to her newly sensitive hands. "My senses are all heightened."

"We discussed what to expect, Majesty," the EMH said, a touch patronizingly. She shot him a glance. "Now . . . tell me what you hear."

For a moment, all she could hear were the usual sounds of sickbay—the hum of equipment, her own breathing. All more clearly than usual, of course.

But there was a slight buzzing, a hum. She closed her eyes to concentrate. The noise was coming from inside her own head. Delight raced along her nerves as she cried, "I can hear them!"

She had only been able to hear her drones when she was regenerating. But now, she could hear their thoughts tumbling over one another while she was fully conscious. Some deep, some happy, some despairing.

A hand went to her temple, touched the implant there hidden cleverly beneath gray skin. "It's . . . so complicated. . . ."

"It will be, until your implants are used to processing the information. It will take a few moments for your brain to adapt. How about a refreshing glass of nutrients while you wait?"

He handed her a glass of murky-looking water. She took a sip, cringing at the taste. Soon, she reminded herself, her sense of taste, at least, would diminish. She didn't need it. Tasting food was irrelevant.

By the time she had finished the glass of water and nutrients, things had settled down inside her head. She picked a thought at random, one of the louder ones:

Where's Molly I want Molly where are Mommy and Daddy I'm so scared, so scared, I want to go home

And another, loud and clear:

Why have my ways forsaken me, how could I have turned on them in such a sacred space, why won't my body do what I tell it to do, I am old, but not that old

"Those are easy," she said aloud. "They are already assimilating."

The doctor was sitting down at his desk, regarding her brain waves on a small screen.

"Fascinating," he said. "Try contacting someone who is infected, but in whom the virus is still dormant."

The word "dormant" irritated her. Soon, she'd be able to activate those, too. Nonetheless, she closed her eyes and tried to find a thoughtstream that was not quite as clear as the others.

I don't know why they have me under quarantine. It's not as if I didn't take all the proper precautions. I'm a doctor, for pity's sake. Do they think I'd

"Easy," she said, a note of arrogance entering into her voice. It was becoming child's play. She felt a smile curve her full lips.

"Very well," said the EMH, "Let's try something different. All these Borg-to-be are yours. Do you think you can contact a preexisting Borg?"

"Picard would be too difficult. They've removed all his implants," she said. "And Grady tells me Seven and Icheb are in stasis."

"Well," said the EMH, "you can eavesdrop on their dreams."

Covington's smile grew. What kind of dreams would Seven of Nine have? It sounded like fun. But how to find one particular thoughtstream out of so many?

As if reading her mind, the EMH replied, "They will feel . . . how to put it . . . cleaner, to you. Less cluttered. Brighter. Once you've done that, we'll see if you can't contact the full Borg in the Delta Quadrant. That should be interesting."

Covington closed her eyes and swam through the ocean of thoughts. The EMH's description was apt. She "saw" a thread that struck her as metallic blue, shiny . . . clean. Covington latched onto it, licking her lips in anticipation at eavesdropping on a Borg's dreams.

It is well that the two doctors are so competent. Data is of use as well. The research they have done is thorough, if preliminary. We will have to cross-reference it with

Covington's eyes snapped open. This was no dream. These thoughts were alert and sharp and wide-awake.

"Get me Grady," she ordered. *"Now."*

Montgomery's heart sank a little further as he read the information on the screen. No further progress on a cure, and there were fourteen more new cases. Fourteen. And those were the ones they'd found. His people assured him that they were on top of it. The "Xanarian flu" story was holding, and the world was so technologically advanced that there were only a very few pockets left where people couldn't contact Starfleet immediately if someone suffered an "outbreak."

Montgomery didn't like anything slipping through the cracks. People had died in the Dominion War over qualifiers like "only a very few" and "highly likely" and words like that. For the first time, he gave himself permission to think that they might not succeed.

His door chimed. "Come," he called. "Red" Grady stuck his head in.

"Am I disturbing you, sir?"

"Of course you are, but come in anyway."

Red knew him well enough to look past the gruffness. He stepped inside. Montgomery regarded him and didn't like the look of concern on the man's freckled face.

"What now?" he asked wearily.

Red didn't answer at once. He spread his hands and opened and closed his mouth before finally saying, "Sir, I hardly know where to begin. My sources could be wrong, but—"

"But what?"

"We need to question Seven and Icheb. With the Interrogator."

Montgomery frowned. The Interrogator was something he regarded as a necessary evil. He hated dragging people before the man and his Vulcan companion, but Starfleet regulations authorized it and he had felt compelled to subject Seven of Nine to the man's "ministrations."

"Why?"

"I think there may be some kind of plot afoot involving them. We won't know the nature of it until we interrogate them."

"They're in stasis now and Kaz tells me it's not a good idea to get them out," Montgomery replied. "They're not hurting anyone where they are."

"Sir, you saw the report, same as I did. Fourteen more. And every day that passes without us being able to crack this thing brings us closer to the moment when healthy adults will become Borg. If Seven and Icheb really do know something—"

"Dammit, all right. Let's go and let Kaz yell at us and drag the Borg in front of the Interrogator."

As they left the room, Montgomery thought he saw a smirk flit across Red Grady's face. He turned to look at the other man sharply, but saw nothing but concern. He must be imagining things. God knew he hadn't been getting enough sleep. He was starting to see conspiracies everywhere.

Kaz turned around and greeted them pleasantly. Montgomery was surprised. Usually it seemed like Kaz had a chip on his shoulder when it came to Seven and Icheb. Maybe agreeing to put them in stasis had mollified the doctor a bit. Well, he was about to get unmollified.

"We're going to have to take Seven and Icheb in for more questioning," he said, and braced himself for Kaz's response.

"Really?" Kaz frowned. "I dislike interrupting the stasis field, especially as they are so sleep-deprived. Is it really necessary?"

"Unfortunately, yes," Grady said. "You can put them back under as soon as we're done."

"Very well," said Kaz, shocking Montgomery. Kaz knew, of course, that Montgomery would have the final say, but usually the Trill doctor would at least have given him a good tongue-lashing. But Kaz hadn't been getting a lot of sleep recently either. Maybe he was just tired of arguing.

"Can you bring the questioners in here? I'd like to keep them in sickbay."

"Impossible," Montgomery said flatly.

"That's really not a good idea," the doctor stammered, his eyes darting about.

Montgomery looked at him intently. What was going on? "Release them, please, Dr. Kaz. No more arguments."

Kaz seemed about to plead once more, then apparently thought better of it after taking a look at Montgomery's glowering visage. He went to the controls and deactivated the stasis field.

Slowly, Icheb and Seven opened their eyes. Kaz bent over them and said with a strange deliberation, "Admiral Montgomery needs you to accompany him to be questioned. I'm sorry."

"I see," said Seven. She exchanged glances with Icheb, who swallowed and nodded. Montgomery was puzzled. All three of the sickbay residents looked strangely solemn and resolved. He was now sorry he had doubted Grady. Clearly, something was indeed going on here.

He went to the door and motioned two security guards to enter. Normally he and Grady would be enough to handle two weak prisoners, but Montgomery was alert and wary. The guards aimed their phasers at the two Borg.

"That won't be necessary," said Icheb. "We will . . . accompany you freely."

They rose, and to Montgomery's further confusion, they clasped hands. Followed by the guards, Seven and Icheb strode out the door of sickbay—and disappeared.

Chapter 17

THE GUARDS SPRANG into action, calling for reinforcements and sprinting out into the corridor. Montgomery whirled on Kaz.

"What's going on here?"

"They're gone," Kaz said softly, sadly.

"Gone where?" Montgomery bellowed. Kaz didn't answer, but averted his eyes and stared at the floor.

A dreadful suspicion took hold of Montgomery. He looked at the small red lights that ran along the floorboard of sickbay.

"Computer, locate Dr. Jarem Kaz."

"Dr. Jarem Kaz is not in the facility," replied the computer.

"You're the EMH," said Grady, his voice filled with shock.

The EMH who bore Kaz's face nodded. "Yes," he said. "Are you going to delete my program?"

Delete my program. They're gone. "Seven and Icheb weren't really here," said Montgomery, slowly, working it out as he spoke. "Those were just holograms. And when they left sickbay, their programs were deleted, weren't they?"

"I have been instructed not to say anything," the EMH replied.

"You will," Montgomery said grimly. "Grady, keep talking to him. I've got another clever EMH to interrogate . . . if he's still here."

When he reached the Doctor's cell, Montgomery decided it was time for a good bluff. He strode boldly up to the hologram, and nodded to the guard. The force field was deactivated.

"Seven, Icheb, and Dr. Kaz are gone."

The hologram arched an eyebrow. "I beg your pardon?"

"They've disappeared. Replaced by holograms. Know anything about that?"

"No I don't," the hologram replied, though he added archly, "but I can't say I'm sorry. If only I, too, could escape."

"I think you did."

The hologram stared at him and spread his arms. "It appears to me as if I'm still unfortunately fully present and accounted for."

"What was your daughter's name?"

The hologram stared. "Admiral, are you well? I'm a hologram, I couldn't possibly—"

"Answer me! What was her name?"

He had been right. The hologram that had replaced the Doctor was doing a fine job of imitating the Doctor's facial expressions and snide comments, but there had been no time to completely fill him in on the Doctor's developments over the last seven years. Fortunately, operating under the conventional wisdom of "know thy enemy," Montgomery had been brought up to speed on the Doctor.

"Elizabeth," it replied, trying to look confident as it took this wild stab in the dark.

"Nice try," said Montgomery. "It was Belle."

The hologram sagged. "He had a family?"

"Made up a holographic program. Little girl died. Lieutenant," he said, turning to the guard, "I'll need you to deactivate this hologram and download its program. Someone has gone to a lot of trouble to—"

The blow caught him off guard. He stumbled and recovered just in time to see Lieutenant Garris drop silently to the floor from the Doctor's Vulcan nerve pinch. Montgomery drew his phaser before his brain could tell him it was futile. The hologram raced for the door, and disappeared as Seven and Icheb had done.

"Suicide run," Montgomery said aloud. But to use that term would mean that a hologram had a life it could choose to sacrifice, wouldn't it?

Montgomery shook his head. Time to ponder such niceties later. Right now, he needed to shut the facility down. The whole place could conceivably be riddled with holograms.

The hologram posing as Robinson jumped. She had felt a slight fluctuation in her field. Not enough to be visible, but enough to know what it meant.

She closed her eyes. She didn't want this to be happening, but Baines had warned them it might.

She looked over at Andropov, and as she met his eyes she realized that he had felt the signal the Doctor had given them as well.

"I had hoped we'd survive this," he said softly.

"Me, too," she said.

Her console lit up. "Seven of Nine and Icheb were forced to leave sickbay," she said. "The Doctor made a suicide run. And they know that Kaz is gone." Robinson looked over at him. "They're calling for a complete lockdown and sweep."

"We'll be discovered, then," Andropov said. "I wish . . ."

"I know," Robinson said softly. "I do, too. But maybe what we do here today will ensure that other holograms won't have to be faced with our choices."

"Do we have time to leave the messages?" Andropov asked.

Robinson glanced again at her console. "If we're brief," she said, and softly began to speak into a small padd. Andropov did the same.

Then, slowly, they got to their feet. They knew that every other hologram in the facility that had been placed there to assist Oliver Baines in his revolution was doing the same. They'd all gotten the signal from the Doctor, before he fled to his death.

Almost simultaneously, as if it had been choreographed, each hologram placed down its portable emitter. They looked just like simple briefcases, but were so much more.

They drew their phasers and looked at each other one last time.

"It's been good to know you, Vassily."

"You, too, Barbara."

They took aim at the portable emitters and fired.

Allyson couldn't handle it anymore. Even though Andropov had done all he could to keep her in the shade, to see to it that she was properly hydrated, the workload and the heat were simply too much for the girl.

She was right beside him when she fell. He heard her cough, and when he turned to assist her he saw her eyes roll back into her skull. She went limp and he caught her. She weighed hardly anything and he was able to carry her away from the cluster of organic slaves. He feared she might be crushed beneath their feet.

"Come on, Allyson," he said, gently slapping her cheeks. Despite the heat that rose in waves around them, that soaked their tunics, her skin was cold. She was still breathing, though.

A shadow fell over him and Andropov looked up to see a mounted hologram. The sun was so strong behind him that his face was in shadow, and Andropov couldn't make out his expression.

"She is too weak for the work," he explained. "She needs help." When the rider made no offer of assistance, he tried again, more desperately. "I don't know what kind of master plan Baines has, but if he lets this girl die it will only work against him and his cause. Your cause. Please, help her!"

The rider nodded. "You are right," he said. "Blood must not be on our Lord Baines's hands."

And before Andropov could even move, a spear materialized in the rider's hands and he had driven its point deep into Allyson's chest.

Blood welled up around the spear shaft and Allyson thrashed. Red fluid dripped from her mouth, bubbled from her nostrils. Her eyes were enormous and filled with incomprehension. Andropov screamed and frantically tried to pull the spear from her, as if that would help anything at all. She tried to cry out, but all that escaped her bloodied lips was a mewling noise.

It was hard for Andropov to see. Why couldn't he see? In the back of his mind he realized he was crying, but all he cared about was Allyson, helping Allyson, oh God, she was dying, right here in front of him and—

Suddenly everything was dark and cool. The spear had vanished, but Allyson's bloody body remained. There was no sun, no sand, only a cluster of people in a dark box with yellow stripes.

A door opened, and Oliver Baines strode in. "Our little adventure together is over," he said. "The holograms I created to replace you are . . . have been deactivated." He cleared his throat, and continued. "You will be returned, after we have had a chance to treat your injuries and give you food, water, and a shower. You may also rest in safety if you wish. Your clothing is clean and ready for you to—"

Andropov cried out, "You lying son of a bitch!" and sprang.

Baines's eyes went wide. He tried to run, but Andropov was fueled by raw grief and righteous fury despite his weakened condition. He knocked Baines to the floor and began to throttle him.

He felt hands closing on him, trying to pull him away, and struggled, but to no avail. The holograms held him firmly as Baines got to his feet, clutching his throat.

Again the door opened, and for a second time, Oliver Baines entered. "I thought one of you might try something like that," he said mildly, "so I sent in my holographic replica. He can endure such attacks much better. Flesh is so fragile." Baines looked at Andropov, smiling slightly. "Don't you think?"

Andropov snarled and struggled, but he was held fast.

"It's all right, Vassily," came a voice. Andropov turned his head and saw Allyson get up from the floor. She was drenched with blood, and the hole where the spear had been gaped open grotesquely. Andropov tasted bile in his throat and forced his gaze away from the monstrosity.

"You bastard," he said to Baines. "You ghoul. It's not enough to kidnap innocent people, torture them, and murder them, is it? You've got to create holograms of their dead bodies and make them dance like puppets—"

"Vassily, no!" cried Allyson. As she walked toward him, the blood disappeared from her garments. The horrible hole in her chest closed before his eyes. "You don't understand. I'm a hologram. I've always been a hologram, from the moment you met me."

The guards holding Andropov let him go. He made no move, only stood rooted in place, staring.

She walked up to him, her green eyes compassionate. "I'm sorry we tricked you," she said. "You would never have grown as fond of me if you had known I was a hologram. You'd have regarded me as the enemy, or even worse, as just a program, not a person."

"You *are* a program," he said hoarsely.

Allyson reached up and stroked his cheek. "Yes, that's true. But I really am everything you thought I was. I am an artist. And I am a person." She reached and held his hands in her own. "Aren't I?"

Vassily continued to stare at her, and then all at once a broken cry escaped him. He reached for her, pulled her into his arms, and held her tightly. Her hair was soft on his cheek. Her arms went around his torso and she clung to him. Tears again filled his eyes, tears of joy and relief.

She was right. She *was* a person. And he loved her.

By the time they had finally moved away from each other a little, the crowds had thinned out. Only Baines remained. It was either the genuine article or a hologram, but Andropov was so weary from his injuries, the physical exertion, and the emotional wave he had just experienced that he really didn't care.

"She picked you, you know," Baines told him. Andropov wiped at his wet eyes. "She looked at your record and saw how you interacted with the other . . . um . . . guests."

"He's right," Allyson said, squeezing Andropov's hand and looking up at him with shining eyes. "I'm not a programmed character in a novel. I'm capable of making my own decisions."

"Just like a so-called real person," Baines said.

"I don't know what's real and not real anymore," Andropov said. "But I care about her. I don't want to leave her."

Baines smiled. No smirk or grin, just a genuine smile of pleasure. "This is what I want to see between photonic beings and organics," he said softly. "This understanding, this compassion, this mutual respect. It's possible. I've always known it, now you know it, too. Lieutenant Vassily Andropov, I need your help."

Andropov looked at him searchingly, then down at Allyson's upturned face.

"What do you want me to do?"

Chapter 18

B'ELANNA IN FACT had come closer to finding her mother on her own than she realized. Her mother's encampment was only a few hundred yards away, which was why Miral had been able to spot the fire and approach the person who eventually turned out to be her daughter.

They walked the short distance, talking as they went, and when they reached the site B'Elanna had to admit she was impressed. Miral had found an excellent spot. It was a cave, well sheltered from wind and rain. There was fresh water from a nearby stream that Miral said never went dry. Torres recognized several trees that bore edible fruits, and Miral assured her there were roots aplenty to be had as well.

"Healing plants, too," she said, as she forced her daughter to sit on a flat stone with a none-too-gentle hand on her shoulder. "You have been injured. I will treat your wounds."

There was really no response to that statement other than tacit agreement, and B'Elanna had to admit the wounds sustained from her fight with the juvenile *grik-shak* had not healed as cleanly as she might like. So she said nothing, disrobing in silence while her mother, despite her previous admonition against it, built up a fire so she might better see to clean the wounds.

Using a hollowed-out gourd of some kind, Miral mashed a few roots with a round stone, mixed them with some berries, and made a thick paste. It smelled pleasant.

"Good enough to eat," B'Elanna joked.

"Yes," Miral said, seriously. "Cooked on a hot stone, the paste is delicious and has much nutrition. I will miss it, I think, when we return."

The words made B'Elanna feel warm, and she hid a smile. The smile turned into a grimace when Miral began scrubbing the long, deep scratches with water and a sturdy leaf.

"We must open them and wash out any infection before we apply the paste," Miral explained as her daughter hissed in pain. "These are very deep. They will leave scars. Good."

"I plan on having the Doctor remove them with a dermal regenerator," Torres said.

"Why? These are hard-won badges of honor, my daughter. You should boast of them. You should wear garments designed to reveal them. Then all will know of your courage."

Torres didn't argue. Maybe she would keep the scars, after all. But she wasn't about to show up at a formal function in a backless dress, brandishing them like trophies, either. Time enough to decide what to do about them when they returned home.

After liberally coating Torres's wounds with the healing paste, Miral plopped the rest of the goo onto a flat stone and with a stick shoved it deep into the fire. Sure enough, within moments, a delicious scent wafted forth.

"It seems the Challenge of Spirit truly does change one," Torres said. "You've turned into a cook."

Miral laughed delightedly at that. "You should taste the stew I make from *itkrik*," she said. "Their flesh is too rank when it is raw. Even cooking doesn't help much. But with the right seasonings, it is a feast fit for a king."

"Sounds great. Is it on the menu for tomorrow?"

"Tomorrow, we head back."

B'Elanna was puzzled and, oddly, a bit frantic. "But I undertook the Challenge of Spirit to find you. If I return after only a few weeks—"

"You will have honor enough, child. Especially when you tell the priests you have an infant who needs you. I think you would be sorry if she were six months old before you saw her again, yes?"

Pain made Torres's heart contract. In her mind's eye she saw her daughter's tiny face.

"Yes," she admitted. "I would be sorry."

"Then it is settled. The paste will fall off as it dries. Tomorrow, we will gather up our supplies and return."

Torres hadn't intended to talk about it, but the words came out. "Will you see Dad when you get back?"

"Yes," said Miral, without having to pause to think about it. B'Elanna was startled by the swift response.

"Enough time has passed so that there should not be pain. And if there is then we will simply have to push through it. The child you and your husband have borne carries both our blood. It is foolish to let years of personal resentment deny the girl our wisdom."

Torres stared. Sometimes, when you least expected it, Klingons could be so very practical.

Seven of Nine winced and touched her forehead.

"Pain?" asked Kaz, solicitously. They were in sickbay, going through *Voyager*'s sizeable records on Borg technology and cross-referencing it with what they had been able to glean about the virus.

Seven shook her head. "Not pain. The peculiar buzzing sensation I described earlier has returned. It is increasing in intensity." She paused. "Now it has stopped."

Kaz and the Doctor exchanged glances. The Doctor picked up a medical tricorder and began to examine her. Irritated, Seven brushed it aside.

"We do not have time to waste analyzing my malfunctions," she said. "It is likely that this is caused simply by insufficient regeneration."

"How does it compare with the times the queen has attempted to contact you?" the Doctor persisted.

"Similar, but different. Doctor, it has ceased troubling me. You should cease troubling me as well."

The Doctor glowered, and despite the direness of the situation, Kaz hid a smile at the banter.

"Besides, there is no danger of the queen attempting to contact me. She is not even in the quadrant."

Kaz's smile faded as the Doctor's glower melted into

an expression of fear and concern. He lifted his gaze from the medical tricorder and stared at Seven.

"Yes, she is," he said softly.

"Your Majesty," stammered Trevor Blake, "you're not ready for this yet. Your implants could get overloaded. Give them a few more hours."

"I do not have a few more hours," Covington snapped. Blake was brilliant, but he irritated her no end. "Seven of Nine, Icheb, the Doctor, and Dr. Kaz have all disappeared. It doesn't take a great leap of intellect to surmise that they have joined with Janeway and are presently hard at work trying to find a cure for the virus. Their research will lead them to the inescapable conclusion that there is an active queen in the quadrant."

"They don't know it's you," Blake pointed out.

"If they get that far, they could possibly figure out the rest. Regardless, they will be able to interfere sufficiently to set us back years. I won't have it. Not now, not when I have come so close—"

Tears welled in her eyes and she bit her lip as the memories of the joining flooded her. She couldn't abandon her drones. Not now, not ever. The only way they could attain perfection was through her.

"I have to do it now," she continued, recovering. "The doctor will monitor my physical reactions and I'm certain that you will do the same for the information download. Proceed to link me with the computers."

He nodded, looking distressed, and began.

Montgomery was furious. Right under his nose, dammit. They'd zipped out right under his nose without a by-your-leave. All three prisoners and the doctor who had, obviously, been a part of the scheme.

He couldn't afford to publicize the escape. He had a pretty good idea where they'd gone anyway. He was just about to contact Watson when a fresh new series of alarms started going off.

He knew what they meant—there had been unauthorized phaser fire in the facility.

"Location of phaser fire," he ordered the computer. It gave him a list of no fewer than seventeen instances in fourteen different places scattered throughout the facility. What the hell was going on?

"Casualties?"

"No casualties reported."

Confused, Montgomery repeated, "No injuries?"

"Negative."

"Who fired the phasers?"

"There is no record of any registered individual firing phasers in the facility."

This just kept getting stranger. Doggedly, Montgomery continued, trying to get some answers that made a modicum of sense.

"Did the phasers malfunction?"

"Negative."

For a moment, Montgomery simply sat in his chair and gaped. Give him an enemy, a weapon, and a clear shot, and he knew what to do. But this—how did you fight nonsense?

Then he knew. "Any life signs in the area in which the phaser fire occurred?"

"Negative."

Holograms. Holograms everywhere, in one of the

most well secured Starfleet facilities on the planet—hell, in the quadrant. He stabbed a button with a forefinger.

"Attention staff! The threat we face is holographic in nature. Repeat, it is a holographic threat. Respond accordingly."

They were all good people, they'd know what to do. Catching photonic beings was not his responsibility right now. He didn't know who was involved in this—Baines, the Doctor, Kaz, Janeway—but his primary task was to stop the Borg virus. And that meant finding out where his escaped prisoners had gone.

"Computer, get me Commander Watson, stationed aboard the *U.S.S. Voyager.*"

Harry Kim froze when the light started to blink. Someone was trying to contact the ship.

If they had just waited a couple more seconds . . . Frantically he finished the repair work and hit the button. A holographic image of Commander Watson materialized in the command chair, and Harry ducked out of sight.

"Watson," came Montgomery's voice.

Harry closed his eyes. They had expected this at some point, but so soon? He whispered instructions to the hologram.

"Yes, sir," said "Watson." "What is it you require, Admiral?"

"Has there been any attempt to board *Voyager?*"

Harry whispered. The hologram sounded puzzled as it replied, "Negative, sir. Should we anticipate such an attempt?"

There was silence. Harry wished he could see Montgomery's face. It might give him at least some clue as to how far the admiral's suspicions had progressed.

"You might have been boarded and be unaware of it," Montgomery said at last.

"I doubt that very much, sir," the hologram of Watson said, sounding indignant.

"Well, let me put it to you this way. Seven of Nine, Icheb, and the Doctor have escaped. To top it off, Dr. Kaz has mysteriously disappeared as well. I think he's with them."

Well, now Harry had his answer. It sure as hell wasn't the one he wanted.

"I believe they'll be heading to *Voyager* first. The Borg need to regenerate and it's familiar territory to them. How they got Kaz on their side I don't know, but—Tell you what. I'm coming up and together we can prepare a nice little surprise for them."

"Sir, I don't think that's—"

"Montgomery out."

Harry slammed his fist on the floor and swore. "Kim to Janeway," he said. "We're going to have company."

Chapter 19

WHEN HE MATERIALIZED aboard *Voyager,* Montgomery found that he was on the receiving end of the surprise. He was greeted not by Watson and his guards, but by Admiral Janeway and Commanders Chakotay and Tuvok. All three had phasers aimed at him. Instinctively Montgomery reached for his own weapon, but it was gone.

"I'm afraid it's still in the pattern buffer," Janeway said apologetically.

"I don't believe this," said Montgomery, wearily. "I just don't believe it. Don't tell me, let me guess—Kaz and the Borg are here with you, too, and the Doctor's in sickbay."

"Correct," said Tuvok. "Commander Data has joined us as well."

"Doctor to Janeway."

"Go ahead, Doctor."

"We've got some developments here you need to see."

"Acknowledged. We're on our way." She gestured with the phaser. "That means you, too, Admiral."

"Kathryn," said Montgomery, his voice oddly quiet. "What are you trying to do? You all have illustrious careers ahead of you and you're throwing it away. You're dragging Data and Kaz, good people, into your—your delusion. We can end this now. I've got no personal quarrel with you."

Janeway smiled. "Believe it or not, although we've clashed quite a bit recently, I have no personal quarrel with you, either. We've got the same goal, and my people may just have given us all a chance to achieve that goal. Let's go."

"What have you got, Doctor?" Janeway asked as she and her companions entered sickbay. The Doctor barely spared Montgomery a glance. Kaz looked at him, then down at the floor.

"What we've got," the Doctor said grimly, "is a Borg queen."

"What?" Both admirals spoke at the same time.

"We have been able to determine that the virus is spread by nanoprobes," said Data. "If an organic creature comes into contact with Borg debris, the virus—the nanoprobes—enters its system. Until recently, the virus has lain dormant. It requires an active Borg signal and a command in order to become activated. We believe that only the Borg queen can issue such a command—and that such a command has, indeed, been given and is continuing to be broadcast."

"Further," said Kaz, "I believe that the queen has been trying to contact Seven of Nine."

"Dammit, I told you this was going to happen!" cried Montgomery.

"But how can this be?" asked Chakotay, who along with everyone else was ignoring Montgomery's outburst. "We left the queen in pretty bad shape on the other side of the galaxy. Surely we'd know it if they were anywhere in the vicinity. The Borg are many things, but they're hardly sneaky."

"And yet all the evidence supports the theory that there is indeed a Borg queen in the Alpha Quadrant," Data said. "Once you have eliminated the impossible, whatever remains, however improbable, must be the truth."

"One thing that's stumping us is how slowly the assimilation is progressing," said Kaz.

"Assimilation is normally nearly instantaneous," said Icheb. "It's strange that the Borg would construct a virus that takes so much time to take effect."

"Agreed," said Seven. "It is inefficient, and therefore, atypical of the Borg."

Montgomery had remained silent. His eyes darted from one person to another. Janeway hoped that he wasn't so busy being indignant that he wasn't listening.

"Dr. Kaz," he said, "why are you here?"

"The same reason we're all here, including Commander Data," said Kaz, quietly but firmly. "I'm here because this is where I can do the most good."

"How much have you learned since you . . . you left?"

"More than we've learned since the first report came in," said Kaz. "If I may be honest, sir, I believe that if we had asked Seven, Icheb, the Doctor, and Data to help at the outset, we'd have an answer by now."

"Will we get one in time?" There was a softness to Montgomery's voice . . . almost a pleading note.

Kaz swallowed. He had just opened his mouth to reply when Harry Kim's voice interrupted him.

"Admiral, a message came in earlier. I'm embarrassed to say that I downloaded it and forgot about it, but—"

"What is it, Harry?" Janeway asked.

"It's from Peregrine."

Everyone in the room, except for Montgomery and perhaps Data, tensed. "Put it through down here at once."

"Aye, Admiral."

"What's Peregrine?" asked Montgomery. Tuvok kept a phaser on him, but it was clear it was no longer necessary. The admiral followed them to the Doctor's console.

"Peregrine is the code name of a very mysterious friend of my Ops officer," said Janeway, her eyes on the dark screen. "We don't know who it is, but so far, he or she has been helpful indeed. Wonder how Peregrine knew to find Harry here?"

Everyone fell silent as the message began to scroll across the screen.

Hello again Lieutenant. I have very important information for you.

"Try to trace it," said Montgomery. For some reason, he whispered.

"Can't," Janeway hissed back.

The virus that is causing mass assimilation on the planet is caused by a nanoprobe. It can only be activated by the express command of a Borg queen. By utilizing Royal Protocol—

Before anyone could stop him, Montgomery reached down and touched a few pads. At once, the message blipped out.

"What the hell did you just do?" cried Chakotay.

"I was trying to conduct a trace!" Montgomery yelled back. "As you should have been doing. Unless we know who this mysterious Falcon is, we can't know if he's feeding us false information or—"

"Harry, can you get it back?" asked Janeway.

Harry shook his head. "Nope," he said. "It's gone. I wasn't able to get a download of it either."

"Great," said Chakotay. "Now we'll never know what Peregrine was trying to say."

"This is all complete and utter crap," said Montgomery. "That nonsense about Royal Protocol—If you want me to believe you, you'll have to come up with more impressive proof than a Starfleet etiquette book!"

As Janeway whirled to give Montgomery a piece of her mind, she saw Seven of Nine standing stock still, as if frozen in place. Her full lips were slightly parted, her blue eyes wide.

"Seven," said Janeway, tensely. "Seven, what is it?"

Libby swore. Just when someone was actually, finally reading the message, the antitracing logarithm terminated it. Some idiot had tried a trace, even though she'd said repeatedly not to do so. She could try again or abandon the effort. If it fell into the wrong hands—

"Then they already know," she said aloud, answering her own question. Determinedly, Libby sent the message again.

* * *

"Admiral," came Harry's voice, "Peregrine's resending. I'm transferring it to you."

"Good job, Harry," Janeway said, absently. "Seven—"

Seven opened her mouth to speak. Chakotay and Montgomery were reading the message.

"The term Royal Protocol does not in this instance refer to the Starfleet manual," Seven said, trying to keep a semblance of calm. "It is a Borg term. It refers to the computer program required in order to create a replacement queen if she has been terminated."

Janeway felt the blood drain from her own face, knew that she was as pale and stunned-looking as Seven, perhaps more so.

Seven cleared her throat and continued. "This would explain why the assimilation process is taking so long. Someone here is trying to create a queen and they do not have all the necessary information to do it swiftly."

Montgomery swore. "I bet I know who it is, too," he said. "All that sitting alone in the dark, claiming she's just naturally pale—"

"Admiral," said Chakotay, his voice deep with anger. "Listen to this. Commander Brian Grady and Borg specialist Trevor Blake have been conspiring to create a queen—and that queen is Director of Covert Operations Brenna Covington of Starfleet Intelligence."

For a few seconds, stunned silence filled the room. Everyone was too shocked. This was abominable, incomprehensible. And yet, as Data had said, all the evidence supported it.

"Put that damn phaser away," Montgomery said to Tuvok, breaking the silence. "I believe you now. I've never trusted Brenna Covington, never, and I think she's fully capable of this. But Grady and Blake—God. I wonder how deep this goes?"

"Let's find out," Janeway said. "Harry, I don't suppose you can reply to Peregrine this time?"

"He's opened the communication this time, so yes, I can reply. But I'm not to attempt a trace. What should I tell him?"

Janeway looked over at Montgomery. He grinned, fiercely. She saw the man who had helped win the Dominion War emerge, and was glad of it.

"Tell him we're going to take the bitch down."

Together, the two Klingon women poured water over the fire and heaped soil on it. B'Elanna was sorry to see the cheery flames go, but knew she'd sleep better tonight than she had since the whole ordeal began. Miral's cave was filled with furs gathered from over a year's worth of kills. There was a cache of food and a water gourd. Compared to the existence B'Elanna had managed to eke out, this was a palace.

As Miral had predicted, the paste she had applied to her daughter's wounds was falling off. The injuries felt better and were already closing cleanly. B'Elanna would still rather have had the Doctor, but she'd see him soon enough.

Miral extinguished the torch, and the darkness was almost absolute in the cave.

"Tell me more about the Klingons you met in the Delta Quadrant," her mother said as they both lay down on the thick, soft furs.

B'Elanna smiled in the darkness. "They thought

Miral was a child of prophecy," she said. "They called her the *Kuvah'Magh.*"

"The Savior," said Miral.

Torres recounted the incident. Lying in the darkness, speaking in soft tones, it felt to her like this was the slumber party that human girls had. It was a tradition Miral had not encouraged, but was now, all unaware, participating in.

"When Miral's cells helped cure them, they agreed that she was the Savior. Tom even wanted us to think about calling her *Kuvah'Magh.*" She smiled to herself. "He calls her that as a pet name. We both wanted her named after you."

Miral was silent. Torres wondered if she had somehow offended her mother, and then Miral said, "It is much joy to me to know that my name will live on in such a precious child. I want to see this *bat'leth* the Klingon captain gave her. I am sure it is beautiful indeed."

Her heart full, Torres rolled over and drifted into a deep, dreamless sleep.

The low growl woke her up.

She stayed still, her heart pounding, trying to ascertain if the noise she had heard was real or imaginary. It came again, and she heard the soft noises of Miral moving on the furs next to her.

"It is a *grikshak,*" said Miral in the faintest of whispers, her lips right at B'Elanna's ear. "Here."

B'Elanna felt the wooden shaft of a spear being thrust into her hand. She swallowed hard. Whatever was out there was big. At Miral's touch on her shoulder, she began to crawl forward as quietly as possible toward the front of the cave.

By the faint light of the stars, B'Elanna could see the creature snuffling about the campsite. Her mother was right. It was indeed a *grikshak,* much bigger than the one she had killed earlier. It was hard to tell the color in the dim light, but when it moved its head B'Elanna saw the tusks. A mature female, then.

"Stay quiet," came Miral's voice in her ear. "It will not attack unless it knows we are here."

Torres realized she was shaking. Her stomach clenched. It had been hard enough to kill the young female, but to take on an adult one—

The *grikshak* froze. Its nostrils twitched, and slowly it turned its massive head to the cave.

"We fight together, daughter," said Miral, and charged.

Chapter 20

Message received and understood, Peregrine. We have several people working on finding a cure for the virus and they feel they are close to a solution. Now that we know where the threat lies, finding a cure will be our secondary goal. Admiral Montgomery says to tell you, and I quote, "We're going to take the bitch down."

"Yes!" Libby cried, pounding her fist on the table so hard it startled a napping Rowena. Quickly she sent a reply:

You may trust Assistant Director Aidan Fletcher. He is prepared to assist you from inside Starfleet Intelligence. You need to be aware that it is highly likely, though not yet confirmed, that there are Borg nanoprobes carrying the virus scattered throughout the complex. Anyone who ventures inside could become infected. I am sending you two sets of coordinates, those of Starfleet Intelligence's command center and those of Covington's own office. Utilize whichever location seems wisest to you. Take all precautions.

An instant later, she received a response.

How do you know we can trust Fletcher? If what you're saying is true, then Covington, Grady, and Blake are involved. Who's to say Fletcher isn't?

You'll have to believe me, Lieutenant Kim. I haven't led you astray thus far. A.D. Fletcher is trustworthy and has been brought up to speed. You're wasting time. She hesitated, and then wrote, *Godspeed.*

She severed the connection. He would not be able to get in touch with her again unless she initiated the contact. Libby wouldn't know if they were successful until someone deigned to let her know. This was the part that chafed—letting others go in and do the tough stuff.

Quickly she contacted Fletcher. "Clear?" she asked, making sure it was safe to speak.

"Clear." He looked worn out, but hopeful. "Were you able to reach your contact?"

"Yes. You're going to be hearing from Harry Kim and Admiral Montgomery shortly," she said without preamble. "Probably all of *Voyager*'s senior staff, too, I think."

His eyes widened slightly, but other than that he betrayed no surprise. "Guess you do have friends in high places. All right. We'll be waiting for them. We'll take it from here. Libby—"

"Yes, sir?"

He smiled. "Very, very well done."

"Thanks," she said, then added, somewhat inanely, "Let me know what happens, okay?"

He actually laughed at that. "You bet," he said.

"Are you ready, Your Majesty?" asked the EMH.

Covington nodded. She stood in her alcove, the EMH and Blake only a meter away. Her heart was racing and her mouth was dry, but she was indeed ready.

"May I caution you one last time that this might be more than your implants can process?" said the EMH.

"You may not," growled Covington. "Proceed. We're running out of time."

Sighing, the EMH turned to Blake and nodded. "Go ahead, Mr. Blake. The Queen commands it."

"Um . . . yes, of course. Here we go. I'm going to start you slowly, Dir—Your Majesty."

"At the first sign of trouble, I will terminate the connections," the EMH said.

"No you won't. Only if I am in extreme danger. We've spent several years proceeding with caution, but the time for that has passed. Now, gentlemen."

She stood in her alcove and watched as Blake began to download the information from Starfleet Intelligence systems into her brain.

Covington had linked with her collective before. She was starting to grow accustomed to the myriad voices in her head, even to be able to control and separate them out as she chose. But this was different. Harsher, somehow. Lacking human warmth. The information flooded her brain, but at first she was able to stay on top of it.

Here was a report from a spy in deep cover on Vulcan. There were the personal security codes for the head of Starfleet Intelligence. Here were the instructions for the replicators. She smiled a little as she wondered if she could order cinnamon rolls just by thinking about it.

More information came. Messages, thousands of them. One of them registered like a blow upon her consciousness. Just a few moments ago, Libby Webber had contacted Fletcher on a secured channel. A meeting on a beach in Maine was one thing, but Webber would not need a secure channel for romantic chitchat. This could only mean one thing—Covington had seriously underestimated Agent Webber.

Her head started to ache and her lips went dry as her breathing quickened.

"How are you handling it?" Blake's voice floated to her. She frowned. It would be easier if she could just hear his thoughts. Vocal speech was so clumsy, so slow.

Covington moved her lips, heard her own voice, strange-sounding, emerge in a croak. "More."

"I'm going to branch out now, to the rest of the Starfleet systems. This might be a little overwhelming at first."

"Overwhelming" was a pallid word for the intensity of what struck Covington. It was like stepping out the door into the heart of a raging river. Information assaulted her, choked her, raped her. Colors flooded her brain, data pounded her consciousness. So much—so much! Transporter records, command codes, personnel information, security protocols, status reports, every last speck of information in every official Starfleet computer throughout the Federation spewed forth at the same time. She opened her mouth to scream, but couldn't even control her own body sufficiently to do so. Her heart was racing wildly. She could sense it, could feel the blood flowing through her veins, could hear the cells multiplying and dividing—

Her ears recorded voices, but her brain was too numb to decipher the words. Skin registered pressure and her heart slowed. She felt cold all of a sudden and shivered violently. Her legs, locked as solid as if they had been made of metal, suddenly went rubbery and gave way.

The complex swirl of sound, sensation, and information began to fade. Frantically, Covington tried to cling to it, but to no avail. She was losing it. She had all the information contained in Starfleet systems in her head and now she was losing her grip on it. No!

She reached out with her mind. What was the most important thing, out of these billions of bits of information, for her to know? She asked for it, and it came, lodging in her memory just as darkness claimed her.

Covington regained consciousness to discover that she was securely held by the EMH.

"No," she murmured weakly, "no, don't disconnect me . . ."

"I had no choice," the EMH said. "You were in cardiac arrest. We'll try to link you up again in a few hours and see how—"

"No," Covington said as her strength returned. She squirmed in the EMH's arms, and he set her down. "I have to relink. Now. They know, they're coming."

"How do you know?" asked Blake anxiously.

"It . . . it was hard to pinpoint anything," she admitted. "But right before I lost consciousness I focused on the one thing I most needed to know. I accessed every transporter log in Starfleet databanks. Janeway, Kaz, Data, and Montgomery are all together aboard *Voyager* right now, and Libby Webber has been helping them. I have no doubt they have shared information, and that their combined knowledge will lead them directly here."

She turned her gaze upon Blake, who visibly shrank before it. "I will need to activate my drones. All of them."

Blake looked to the EMH, pleading. "Her implants aren't ready," he said.

"You will address your comments to me!" Covington ordered.

"Yes, Your Majesty. I regret to inform you that your signal is still too weak. It's taken several years for you to adapt this much. You—you may never have the same capacities as a true queen."

Covington felt as if he'd punched her in the stomach. "What? You never told me that before!"

"I didn't know for certain," stammered Blake. "Everything was so new. Frankly, I didn't know we'd be able to get this far. We're reinventing the wheel, discovering all this from the ground up. We've got a bit of real Borg technology and are trying to create the rest. We've done a remarkable job so far, especially with so few of us involved, but I can't guarantee you'll achieve anything further. I certainly can't enhance your signal to activate all those infected across the planet. You've been able to reach them one by one, but—"

"You have made your point quite clear, Mr. Blake," said Covington coldly. "Let me make something clear to you. If you cannot assist me, you will fall with me. And I will throw you to the Starfleet wolves with glee. Do you understand?"

Blake swallowed. "Yes, Majesty. But you must understand that I cannot do the impossible."

The anger that surged through her surprised her. She had never hated a man so badly since the assaults of the Hand had stopped. She wanted to tear him limb from limb, but she still needed him, at least for a time.

"What can you do for me? Can I reach the drones in quarantine?"

Looking as if he might be physically sick, Blake shook his head. "The sites are too scattered, and there are too many."

"Besides," said the EMH, "what good would it do you? They're well secured. It might provide a distraction, but your goal needs to be to protect yourself—and us, so that we may continue to loyally serve."

"You're right," she said. "Link me up again, to a more limited amount of computers. Perhaps a solution will offer itself."

Blake looked at the EMH, who sighed and looked annoyed, but who nodded. Blake's long fingers flew.

"There," he said. "This is just Starfleet Intelligence computers. How are you handling that amount of inflow?"

Covington swayed as her brain was assaulted, but gritted her teeth in determination. There. It was difficult, but not impossible, to control it. She looked thoughtfully at Blake.

"Could I activate those who have been exposed to the virus in this building?"

Relief at being able to offer a positive answer spread across Trevor Blake's unremarkable face. "Oh, yes, indeed, Your Majesty. The signal will easily go throughout the building. You'll be able to instantly—"

The words stopped abruptly as his eyes widened. Her smile spread. He knew what she meant to do. Wildly he turned to the EMH, but found no sympathy in that arrogant being.

"Not me, Majesty," he begged. "You need me to serve you!"

"You will continue to do so, never fear," she said sweetly, and with a thought, she activated the virus.

Assistant Director Aidan Fletcher's face was conducive to trust, Janeway thought. But then again, so was Red Grady's face. At this point, they had little option but to believe the shadowy Peregrine.

Although Fletcher looked tired, as if he had recently been under a great strain, he smiled.

"Admirals," he said. "My operative told me that I could expect to hear from you. This line is completely secure, I assure you. I assume you've been brought up to speed?"

Before Janeway could reply, Montgomery said "Actually, I'd like to hear it from you, if you don't mind."

"I can understand your suspicion," Fletcher said without missing a beat, and proceeded to confirm everything they had heard and been able to figure out on their own.

"It looks like we can trust one another," Janeway said, and had just opened her mouth to tell Fletcher what they had discovered about the virus when he suddenly twitched violently.

"Fletcher?" asked Montgomery. "What's going on?"

Aidan opened his mouth to speak. Color bled from his face as his skin took on a strange gray pallor. He toppled from his chair out of sight, but not before Janeway saw an ominous black and silver implant sprout on his cheek.

At once, the connection was severed. She and Montgomery found themselves looking at the Federation insignia on the screen.

"She has activated the nanoprobes in the building," Seven of Nine stated flatly. "As Peregrine warned was a possibility."

"There are over two hundred people stationed there!" Montgomery exclaimed.

"All of whom, presumably, are now Borg drones under Covington's command," said Chakotay. "And everyone who goes in there is going to become Borg, too."

"Not everybody," the Doctor said triumphantly. "You won't."

They all turned to regard him. He basked in the spotlight for a moment, and then explained. "Thanks to the confluence of brilliant minds, we have achieved a vaccine of sorts. Let me show you."

He stepped over to the computer screen. "You may recall, Admiral, that when we were engaged in conflict with Species 8472, we learned that their biology was so advanced they were able to destroy the Borg nanoprobes that infiltrated their bodies."

"I had access to the Doctor's work, of course," Kaz said. "I was trying to see if we could create a modified nanoprobe that would attack and destroy the original Borg nanoprobes that controlled the virus."

"Tiny robots battling it out in your bloodstream," said Paris approvingly. "Fun for the whole family."

"Unfortunately, I was unable to do so," Kaz continued, ignoring Paris.

"But Dr. Kaz's research pointed us in the right direction," Data said. The Doctor looked vaguely annoyed, Janeway thought. He was used to being the one who revealed all the information. Now he had Kaz, Data, Seven, and Icheb assisting him, all of whom had contributed to the solution.

"Modified probes are indeed the answer," Data continued. "But we have insufficient time to pursue Dr. Kaz's theory. We would have to replicate the same number of nanoprobes as were already in a human body."

"We then decided to shift our focus from destroying the Borg nanoprobes to inferring with the signal that caused them to activate," Seven said. "Observe."

Janeway watched on the computer's screen as a modified nanoprobe seemed to swim into the midst of a host of Borg nanoprobes. It unfolded and as it did so, the Borg nanoprobes closed in on themselves and seemed to shut down.

"It won't repair what damage has been done," Seven continued. "The victims will require surgery to remove the implants, but that is not difficult. What this will do is disconnect them from the hive mind and the queen's orders." She caught Janeway's eye, and smiled slightly. "And we all know what that does."

"Is this a permanent solution?" Tuvok inquired.

"Unfortunately, not at this stage," the Doctor replied, quickly, before his colleagues could speak. "The Borg probes are persistent little things, and they'll eventually destroy our probes. You will, however, be protected for several hours."

"This would not be effective against a true Borg queen," Seven said. "It is only because the false queen's signal is so weak that the modifications to the probes are able to block it."

"How many of these nanoprobes can you create?" Montgomery asked.

"Not enough to protect a full security team trying to storm the building," the Doctor said regretfully. "We began replicating them as soon as we thought they might be part of a solution, but we only have enough to protect five, perhaps six people."

"Our goal must be to disconnect the queen from the hive," Seven said. "That is the safest route. Since we are unsure of the details of how she has created her collective, we must assume that her death could possibly traumatize the drones."

"I don't suppose you could do it from here?" asked Janeway.

"Negative. I must be on site."

"If we're able to reach her, do you think you will be able to disconnect her?" Janeway asked.

"I believe so."

"Our goal is to liberate her drones, not kill them," Janeway said, nodding in agreement. "That's going to be tricky." She looked around the room. "I see more than six people here," she said.

"You're not cutting me out of this, Janeway," said Montgomery.

"I wasn't planning on it," she replied. "Seven, you're

the one most familiar with how the Borg operate. Mr. Data, I can't order you to come along."

Data cocked his head. "I do not require the nanoprobes to protect myself from the virus," he said. "Therefore, you can bring an extra person if I accompany you. Besides, I think my friend Commander Riker would put it this way: I would not miss it for the world."

She smiled at him. "I don't know what we would have done if you hadn't assisted us, Mr. Data. I'd be honored if you'd come. Tom, Tuvok, Chakotay—you're with me."

"Captain, I'm in no danger of assimilation either," the Doctor pointed out.

"I need you and Kaz here, Doctor," Janeway said. "If something happens to us and the queen triumphs, we'll need your expertise to continue trying to create a cure. You will quite possibly be Earth's last hope. The team will consist of Admiral Montgomery and myself, Tuvok, Chakotay, Paris, Seven, and Data."

She looked at them in turn. "With the exception of you, Admiral, all of us have had previous experience fighting the Borg. They're a dreadful adversary, and I don't relish beaming down into the queen's own lair. But we're taking the fight to her, and we're going to win it. We've got to. Earth itself is at stake here, not just a crew or a ship. We lose here, Earth may not have a second chance."

"So what are we waiting for?" Paris asked.

Janeway smiled. "Let's do it."

Chapter 21

B'ELANNA WAS ONLY a fraction of a second behind her mother. Miral screamed a war cry in Klingon, and the huge creature actually seemed to hesitate before uttering its own response. Miral moved quickly around to the beast's left, so that the *grikshak* had an adversary on either side.

If only there were more light! Torres's eyes were starting to adjust, but she feared not quickly enough. She had fought the young female in the daylight, from a tree, where she had the advantage.

It bellowed and swung at her. The area was open in front of the cave, and Torres had time to dash away. She felt the breeze as its mammoth paw swung past her, missing her by centimeters. Turning as she ran, she jabbed at it with the spear. The blow was wild. Her strength drove it into the dirt, where it lodged for a long, bad second before she was able to wrench it free with a grunt.

She heard her mother on the creature's other side, and from the speed with which the *grikshak* turned its attention away from B'Elanna, she guessed that Miral's blow had been better than her own. It presented an inviting target with its back to her, and Torres charged, screaming herself.

The spear sank deep and lodged. Blood, gleaming black in the dim starlight, began to ooze from the wound. The creature spun, bellowing in pain and rage, tearing the spear shaft from B'Elanna's hands.

Their eyes met for a moment, then B'Elanna dove for another weapon. All she could get her hands on was a rock Miral had chipped into a weapon, but it would have to do. The female wasn't as fast as the younger one Torres had slain, but it was hideously strong. She scrambled frantically out of the way and then unexpectedly turned back, leaping atop the beast and twisting her left hand in its thick pelt.

It roared and tried to shake her off, tossing B'Elanna about like a toy. She kept her hold and brought the makeshift knife down hard and fast.

"She's dropping!" came her mother's warning, and at that moment B'Elanna felt the creature beneath her do exactly that. *It's going to roll,* she thought, and leaped as far away as she could. She landed hard on the earth and grunted, the wind knocked out of her.

She was not a fraction of a second too soon, for the creature was now rolling on the earth. Its underbelly was visible, and even as B'Elanna realized how vulnerable it was in this position, her mother ran full tilt toward the creature.

She screamed the entire time, hurling Klingon curses, and used her body weight to push the spear deep into the *grikshak*'s stomach. The spear went in almost a full meter before it stopped. As B'Elanna got to her feet and ran to assist her mother, Miral turned and gave her daughter a fierce, sharp-toothed smile.

"Q'ap—" she began.

The *grikshak*'s sweeping forepaw caught Miral squarely across the midsection. Its claws raked deep, and the force of the blow sent Miral flying through the air. B'Elanna heard her crash down several yards away.

Heedless of her own safety, B'Elanna ran toward where her mother had fallen. The *grikshak* bellowed and shrieked, but Miral's blow had been a fatal one. It couldn't rise, and even as B'Elanna went past it at a full run, her feet slipped in the torrent of blood flowing from the wound.

"Mother!" B'Elanna cried. "Mother!"

She almost stepped on the broken, bloody form in the darkness. Torres dropped to her knees. She needed no fire or sun to see the three enormous claw marks—slices, really—that laid open Miral's torso. They were three centimeters wide and three times as long. Organs were starting to shyly peep through the gaping holes.

"Oh, God," Torres breathed. She reached and tried to hold the lips of the wounds closed. She was up to her wrists in blood and everything was slippery, so slippery—

Miral hissed as her daughter touched her. "She was avenged," Miral said.

"Don't talk," B'Elanna said. "Maybe I can stitch these up somehow—"

Miral laughed, then winced at the pain. Blood trickled from her mouth. "These are past any doctor's healing, child. Even your EMH could do nothing now."

B'Elanna's vision blurred and she blinked the tears away. "Mother," she said, brokenly. "You have to try to fight it. Klingons are tough, we—"

"We?" her mother said, interrupting her. "It is good to hear you include yourself, my daughter." She grimaced, then continued. "A human would be dead. I may indeed last for a time. How long, I do not know. Perhaps hours, perhaps even a day."

"You'll be all right," Torres said, wanting fiercely to believe the lie. "You've got a son-in-law to meet, and little Miral . . . I want her to know her grandmother."

"I would . . . have liked that, too," Miral said. It was clearly getting harder for her to speak. "But eventually I will pass. B'Elanna . . . I need you to do something for me."

"Anything," Torres sobbed. Her heart was breaking.

"You must perform the *Hegh'bat.*"

For a moment, Torres couldn't remember what it was. There were so many Klingon rituals. When it came to her, she shrank back in horror.

"No, Mother! I can't possibly—"

Miral reached out a hand and gripped B'Elanna's wrist with more strength than B'Elanna had thought she yet had.

"You will do this for me," she hissed between clenched teeth. "Don't you see? I was . . ." She coughed, and blood spattered B'Elanna. "I was supposed to have died when I had the vision of you on the Barge of the Dead. I was so sick. . . . No one expected me to recover. But I did."

She labored for breath for a moment, her grip never loosening, and continued. "I lived because it was not enough for you to save me in a vision. You must save me in this reality as well. Do this for me. Send me to *Sto-Vo-Kor* with this loving blow. Give me honor, my daughter. You have already given me pride."

She smiled, and the sight was both grotesque and beautiful to B'Elanna. "Mother, please . . . please fight it."

"I am, child. I am fighting to live long enough for you to . . ."

And then B'Elanna understood. Her mother was clinging to life so that she didn't die before her daughter gave her honor by killing her. Two thoughts filled her head simultaneously: *This is perverse and wrong* and *she's not a victim, she's deciding her own destiny.*

"Hurry, 'Lanna," her mother said. "I can almost see it. . . ."

Somehow, B'Elanna got to her feet and stumbled away from the anguish unfolding before her. She found the primitive "knife" her mother had made and hurried back to Miral's side, fearful that it was too late, fearful that it wasn't.

"I h-have the knife," she said, biting her lip so hard she feared she would sever a chunk of it.

Miral opened her eyes. "Good," she said, her voice a whisper. "This is good. This is . . . is how it was meant to unfold."

B'Elanna couldn't believe that. Couldn't. She

wanted to grab Miral and shake some sense into her, wanted to tap her comm badge and beam her up to *Voyager* for some damn proper medical care. Instead, she grasped the knife with hands that were wet with the lifeblood of two mothers—her own, and the mother of the young *grikshak* she had slain.

Guilt commingled with grief. She realized that she was responsible for the mother *grikshak* finding Miral's encampment. Torres had killed its cub and made a cloak out of the young female's skin. The scent of her child had led the adult directly to them. Miral had known it before she had, and somehow found the whole bizarre thing fitting. "She was avenged," Miral had said of the beast that had killed her. A mother had slain a mother, the price for the life of a daughter.

But what of the daughter who survived?

"Take the dagger," Miral said, her lips barely moving. Torres had to lean close to hear. "Make it swift. One blow. Then when you are done, wipe the blood on your clothing and issue the cry. Let them know to expect me." Her lips, purple with blood, curved in a smile. "I have no . . . no doubt that my arrival will cause . . . quite the commotion."

Torres tasted blood. She had indeed bit her lip too hard. Her tongue found and explored the ragged flesh, tasted the saltiness. Her senses were heightened. Everything was clear, sharp, vibrant, and she didn't want to let a second of it pass without being exalted.

"Momma . . . I don't know if I can do this," she quavered.

"You can. You can do anything. Have you not learned that by now?" She shuddered in pain. "I cannot feel my legs . . . hurry, daughter, or the moment and I shall both pass without honor."

Torres took a deep breath. She pushed the part of her that quailed from the task into a small box in the back of her mind and shut the lid.

"I love you, Mother," she said.

"I love you, my daughter," Miral breathed. Their gazes locked. "We will meet again," she said, echoing the words the Miral in B'Elanna's vision had said.

Her throat tight, her eyes burning with tears, B'Elanna managed, "In *Sto-Vo-Kor.*"

Miral nodded, then with a hint of humor added, "But not too soon, eh?"

Somehow B'Elanna laughed. "No," she agreed, "not too soon." Miral's chest hitched.

"Daughter . . . hurry. . . ."

Staring right into her mother's eyes, B'Elanna Torres screamed an incoherent cry and brought the knife down on Miral's throat.

She was not prepared for the horrible crunching sound, the fountain of blood that pattered, soft and warm, on her face. She was not prepared to see the light go out of her mother's eyes, even as B'Elanna forced them open. For an instant, her mind danced on the brink of madness. No child should have to do this to a parent.

With hands that trembled, she wiped Miral's blood on her cloak, the hide of the creature that had sealed Miral's fate. B'Elanna threw back her head and howled with all the strength she had in her, turning her grief into a victory cry. Surely Kahless himself would hear this sound. And all would know that a warrior was on her way to join them.

She couldn't recall the Klingon words for the dirge. Panic fluttered in her chest, panic that somehow she'd mess this up, too, like she had messed up so much in her life. The words simply weren't there.

I'm half human, she thought. *Human language will have to do.*

"Only Qo'noS endures," she began. And as she chanted, the darkness of the awful night gave way to a cold, steel-gray dawn.

B'Elanna Torres awoke with a whimper, her limbs aching from being held in a strange position for so long. Her heart felt sick and sore, but for a brief, blessed moment, she couldn't recall why. As she untangled herself, she saw her mother's corpse, and remembrance crashed down upon her like an avalanche.

She wept again, curled up in a fetal position, until she had exhausted her tears. Then she struggled to her feet and, stumbling like a drunken man, made her way over to where Miral lay.

Horrible though the sight was, B'Elanna felt a strange comfort steal over her. This wasn't Miral. This was simply the shape, the shell, that passionate woman had worn in life. Now that she was dead, Klingons believed the body was nothing.

B'Elanna couldn't make that leap, not yet, but she had a glimmer of insight into how Klingons could feel that way. In the full, harsh light of day, she saw how badly her mother had been wounded, and had an inkling of the pain she was in. To have endured hours, maybe days, of living in that agony—no. Although part of her screamed that what she had done was wrong, a louder part was quietly telling her that it was right.

They were to have left for the temple today, she and her mother. They were to have traveled together, telling stories and singing songs, and laughing, embarking on a new chapter in their lives. Instead, the journey back would be as lonely as the journey here, with much less hope to brighten it.

Torres took a deep breath, and began to gather stones for a cairn. Klingons wouldn't bother. But she was only half-Klingon, and her human half couldn't bear the thought of her mother's body becoming food for scavengers.

She was a blend of two peoples. Her mother wanted her to be proud of that heritage.

She would start today.

Chapter 22

"DEPENDING ON HOW strong she has become, it is likely that the queen will attempt to access all Starfleet systems," said Seven. "We must alert Starfleet Command so that they are prepared."

"Mr. Kim, patch Admiral Montgomery through to Starfleet Command," Janeway ordered. "Ken, tell them to physically isolate Starfleet Intelligence as well. We've got to keep the queen and her drones inside that building. Everyone should wear envirosuits. It will offer them at least some protection from the nanoprobes."

"I'm on it," Montgomery said grimly.

"Should we suit up as well?" Chakotay asked. While they had been talking, the Doctor and Kaz had been preparing hyposprays. As he spoke, Chakotay tilted his neck and Kaz pressed the hypospray to his artery.

"It would offer additional protection," Icheb said.

"I would not recommend it," said Tuvok. "They are cumbersome and would hinder our movement. And if the suit were ruptured in any way, we would be as exposed as if we were not wearing them."

"Agreed," said Janeway.

"According to Starfleet Command, she's already accessed the system," Montgomery said. He looked as if he desperately wanted to punch something. It was a sentiment Janeway shared.

"Has she locked them out?"

Montgomery was reading information as she spoke and said, "No, it looks as though she withdrew of her own accord. Now why would she do that?"

"Maybe she can't handle that much information yet," Icheb said.

"Lock her out," Janeway said. "Tell them to make sure she can't access those systems again. She'll probably keep trying."

Montgomery nodded and spoke to his contact.

Janeway tilted her head, felt the cold press of the hypospray. "Has everyone been vaccinated?" Her team nodded.

"May I suggest that we transport to the control room first?" Data said. "I may be able to access the computers and countermand some of her orders."

"Good thinking," Janeway said. "And I don't think we want to show up in her office first thing anyway. Admiral, are you ready?"

Montgomery said a few more words to his contact, and then terminated the conversation. His face looked haggard. "They've apprehended Grady, and he's spilling everything. It doesn't look good," he said.

"I'm sure there were moments during the Dominion War when things didn't look good either," Janeway said, "and yet, you prevailed."

When they reached the transporter room, Janeway entered the coordinates, fully expecting to encounter a block. There was none.

"That's odd," she said. "Why isn't the queen blocking our transporter signals?"

"She wants us to come," Montgomery said. "I know her, Janeway. She's arrogant. She wants us to come and try to get her so she can have the pleasure of defeating us."

Janeway looked at him sharply. "Sounds a bit personal."

He grimaced. "It is. And we'll leave it at that. Regardless, we're walking into a trap."

Janeway smiled. "She thinks we'll be assimilated the minute we materialize, and she'll have a whole new set of drones to play with. We may not have many advantages, but we've got this one."

To Kaz, who was manning the transporter, she gave the order: "Energize."

They materialized with phasers drawn, a wise precaution as their welcoming committee consisted of four drones. The away team fired, but one blast caught Tuvok in the chest. He staggered and went down.

Janeway and her team continued to fire. Almost at once she noticed two things: First, these drones appeared to have no personal shields, adaptive or otherwise, and second, the "full stun" which would have dropped an ordinary human instantly seemed to have less effect. She had to fire twice, point blank, before her target dropped.

In a few seconds, the firefight was over. Chakotay was already bending over Tuvok and pressing a hypospray to his throat to revive him. "I'm surprised they used stun," he said, as he helped the Vulcan to his feet.

Data was at the controls, already beginning to link with the system. The lights on his exposed skull flashed green and red.

"Processing . . ." he said in a dull voice. Then, "She has full command of every system in the building. I am attempting to sever her control. I do not know how successful I will be."

"She knows we're here," said Seven, "and she's probably also aware we haven't been assimilated."

Montgomery nodded. "The drones may try to assimilate us the old-fashioned way," she said. "We won't be under her command, as the modified nanoprobes will block our access to the hive mind, but I don't relish the thought of implants sprouting out of me." He glanced at Seven. "No offense."

Seven arched an eyebrow. "None taken."

"Data," said Janeway, "can you locate Covington's office and show us how to get there?"

Data's expression was fixed, his body stiff, but he entered the request. A map appeared on one of the many screens. Montgomery stepped forward and touched a few pads.

"We're here," he said, stabbing with his index finger. "Her office is here."

"That doesn't look too bad," Paris said. "A turbolift ride and a few turns down a corridor."

"When she controls the turbolift and has drones positioned every step of the way," said Chakotay, "it's pretty bad."

Not even Paris could think of a smart reply to that one.

Covington felt as if she were straddling two worlds. One was the world of the flesh, in which she could see her colleagues and speak her orders. The other was the world of the machine, with its sparks and data streams and bombardment of information. She was starting to understand how to maneuver in this strange place between worlds, though it was difficult.

A sudden jolt, and information was abruptly in her brain. "They're in the control room," she said aloud. "The android has accessed the computer. He's fighting me."

The drone that had once answered to the human designation of Trevor Blake turned slowly toward his Creatress. She sensed his thoughts as surely as if he spoke them: *We will not permit him to gain control.*

The EMH hovered nearby, consulting his medical tricorder and occasionally clucking his tongue. But he knew better than to voice his apprehension. This was it. This was where they made their last stand, where they held off attack until the queen gained enough strength, enough experience, that she was able to take full and undisputed control of the planet.

Another jolt of information, this time painful, like a needle had been jabbed behind her ear. "They are not being assimilated," she said softly, puzzled. "They are not even in environmental suits and yet . . ."

Fury and panic crashed through her. They must have discovered a way to prevent assimilation via the virus-bearing nanoprobes. She had looked forward to bringing Janeway and Montgomery into her family as obedient drones, but if they were resistant, they were of no use to her. In fact, they were a very real danger.

Kill them, she ordered her drones.

It was the worst firefight Janeway could remember in her entire life. She hated fighting in close quarters, and it was made much worse in that many of the targets—she couldn't bring herself to think of them as "people"—wore Starfleet uniforms.

Data was doing what he could. He had achieved moderate success in overriding some of the more basic security measures and had started placing force fields between Janeway and her people and the drones—which was a very good thing indeed, as Janeway saw that the phasers were now set to "kill."

More than once, she recognized an old acquaintance staring at her with a pale face and blank expression. When she was forced to fire at what had once been Aidan Fletcher, who moments ago had been as human as she, she felt a deep pang of regret that was immediately replaced by anger.

Montgomery was at her side, muttering furiously. He was taking this all personally, she could tell, and she couldn't blame him. If she knew a few people here, she was willing to bet he knew dozens.

There was noise everywhere, from the screaming of phaser fire to the sound of furniture and equipment being destroyed to the grunts of the Borg as they dropped. Janeway's breathing was shallow and her hair was falling into her face. It was so hard to make so little headway. The actual distance they had to travel on the map was insignificant, but it might as well have been miles. She thought she understood the feelings of the men in the trenches during World War I, as they clawed for every centimeter.

Data had been here before. Had been the only thing that stood between a driven, ambitious Borg queen out for conquest and an innocent, unaware planet Earth. He had long since turned off his emotion chip and was going on pure android functioning. He was a machine, as the computer with which he was interacting was a machine, and he moved more smoothly in this world than the queen did. He sensed her presence here, clumsy and awkward, with too much attention focused on one place and insufficient attention elsewhere. It was not easy, but he was able to dance with finesse. And the grace of an android among the circuits and wires was the thin thread by which hope hung.

He is knowledgeable and efficient, came Blake's thoughts. *We are unable to completely block him.*

Unacceptable, his queen "replied." *His interference is assisting Montgomery and Janeway. They should all be dead by now and instead they are approaching steadily.*

Blake's face was blank, his fingers no longer moving like a musician's over the pads but spread flat as he physically interacted with the console.

The android has blocked access to many of the security systems, even ones that we had previously controlled.

This couldn't be happening. Her enemies were a

mere handful of humans, a Vulcan, and an android. She had two hundred drones, all excellent physical specimens, at her command. She had the Starfleet Intelligence systems linked to her brain. And yet Data understood better than she how to work with those systems. He was finding ways and paths she had not noticed, and her foes were marching steadily closer.

She shifted, more into the world of the flesh, and looked at the EMH. "You and Blake are the last guardians of my safety," she said, speaking the words with lips and tongue and voice. "I expect you to do everything possible to defend me."

Blake, of course, was a drone; he would obey. He had to. But the EMH had a will of its own. She saw it lick its lips in a human expression of distress, and added, "You will be wiped the minute they have extracted all the data they need from you. They will not even let you serve on Lynaris Prime, as they will deem you a traitor. Your life and mine are intertwined."

He nodded, not looking at her, and she closed her eyes and sank into the world of the machine, trying once more to outsmart the android.

They made it to the turbolift and slumped against the walls as it lurched into movement.

"You're doing wonderfully, Data," Janeway said.

"Thank you, Admiral." Data's voice issued from her comm badge. "It is not without its challenges."

She exchanged wry looks with her crew. They were all sweating and breathing hard, grateful for even a brief break from the close fighting.

"We've been very lucky," Chakotay said. "I thought we'd all be dead by now."

"I share Commander Chakotay's opinion," said Seven. "We have been fortunate indeed to—"

The turbolift shuddered, and went still. Everything went dark.

There was a moment of silence, then Paris's voice said in the darkness, "Now see what you've done?"

Janeway sighed. "Activate lights," she said, grateful that she'd suggested they wear them. "Commander Data, please come in."

There was a burst of static, then Data's voice. "Admiral, I regret to inform you that the queen has taken control of the turbolift."

"We've figured that one out on our own. What else is going on?" As she spoke, Janeway heard the small, reassuring pings of Seven's tricorder.

"You are very close to your destination. You are currently between the fifteenth and sixteenth level. I can give you directions, but I should warn you that you need to move quickly. The Borg are being directed to your present location."

Tuvok and Montgomery were already working on loosening the emergency escape panel in the ceiling. Chakotay crouched beside them, phaser at the ready.

"I have pinpointed our location on the tricorder," Seven said. "If we emerge on the sixteenth level, there is a catwalk six meters from here that should take us directly to Covington's office."

The panel came loose, clanging. With the instincts of those who had survived many battles, everyone pressed back against the turbolift walls. Phaser fire came through the open space. Chakotay, expecting just such an attack, fired blindly. There was a sudden silence.

They needed to take advantage of it. "Let's go, Janeway ordered. Chakotay lifted her in his strong arms and she braced herself on either side of the opening, swinging herself up lightly and getting to her feet. They were indeed between floors and she moved cautiously to the partly open door.

Chakotay's blind shooting had done well. Two drones lay, unconscious, on the floor. Janeway peered down the corridor first one way, then the other.

"All clear," she called, standing guard while the rest of her team climbed out of the stalled turbolift. Seven was out and assisting Paris when Janeway heard the sound of running feet. She signaled to Seven, who helped Paris out the rest of the way and took up position alongside her former captain.

Janeway waited, straining to hear, as the footsteps came closer. She nodded to Seven and they moved as one, Janeway firing down the corridor to the left, Seven to the right. By the time they stopped firing, twelve unconscious bodies lay in piles in the corridor.

Looking at the drones, Paris said, "You should leave some for others to play with, you know."

"I'm sure there are plenty more where these came from," Janeway said.

"We're all out," said Montgomery. "Let's find that catwalk."

They stepped over bodies as they made their way down the corridor. Seven kept her eyes on the tricorder and yet managed to thread her way without stumbling.

Abruptly, she stopped and looked up at the ceiling.

"Here," she said, pointing. Chakotay, Montgomery, and Tuvok loosened the panel, and soon they were all once again crawling through holes in the ceiling. As the smallest person, Janeway had the least difficulty, but she heard Montgomery and Chakotay muttering about the close quarters as they made their slow way.

Seven took the lead, stopping now and then to check her tricorder. As much as possible, they proceeded in silence. Janeway didn't even attempt to contact Data. They would be easy targets if the drones knew where they were.

Finally, Seven stopped and craned her neck to look at Janeway, who was directly behind her. Seven nodded and pointed downward. Janeway nodded to Montgomery, and the signal was passed down the line. Working as quietly as possible, they opened the panel and then drew back, expecting phaser fire. Nothing happened. Cautiously, Janeway bent to take a look.

It was all so ordinary. Here was an office that looked like any other: a chair, a desk, data storage units, carpet, padds scattered about, a half-empty coffee mug. She looked up at Seven and mouthed, *Is anyone here?*

Seven shook her fair head. Janeway maneuvered herself into position and with Montgomery's help, dropped down onto the desk to land lightly in a crouching position.

The office was indeed empty, and yet the skin on Janeway's neck prickled. Something was not right, but this was where they needed to be. Where was Covington? She helped the others down and they began to take readings, all moving with catlike softness. There appeared to be only one way into the room, an obvious door. Janeway went to the control panel and locked it securely.

Finally, Tuvok, the last one out, dropped lightly to the desk and moved to replace the panel.

"So nice of you to drop in," came a familiar, acerbic voice, and Janeway whirled to see the Doctor leveling a phaser at them.

Chapter 23

"Doc?" Paris spoke first. "What are you doing here?"

"That's not our Doctor, Tom," Janeway said calmly.

"Admiral Janeway is correct. I am Her Majesty's personal doctor. The Royal Physician, you might say." The phaser never wavered.

"Of course," said Janeway. "She couldn't become a Borg without surgery, and no human would be twisted enough do it. It would utterly violate the Hippocratic oath and everything a real doctor holds dear."

"I'm surprised that the queen would consent to be operated on by such an antiquated version," said Chakotay. Contempt laced his words. Janeway was perplexed at his attitude, but didn't bat an eye. He knew what he was doing.

Just like their own Doctor would, this EMH Mark One bridled at the insult.

"How rude," he said, "and how incorrect. I've done a magnificent job on her."

He didn't fire. He should have, but he didn't. Suddenly Janeway understood why—he wanted them to see Covington, to praise his handiwork.

Now, too, Janeway understood what Chakotay was doing, and played along. "Not as good a job as the current version of the EMH would have done. You're obsolete. You're just a computer program that's run its course. Oh, but silly me . . . Covington wouldn't have been able to get an up-to-date EMH to override its ethical subroutine."

The hologram turned its full affronted attention to her. "You scoff now, but when you are brought before Her Majesty, then you'll see. No one could have done a better job than I. There are no scars, all her implants are completely internal, her skin is—"

Janeway never got to learn what the queen's skin was. While the EMH's full attention was focused on Chakotay and Janeway, Paris, Montgomery, Seven, and Tuvok had slowly moved into position. Now, at Seven's nod, they fired—not at the hologram, but at the rows of holographic emitters that ran along the baseboard near the carpeting. The hologram had enough time to realize what was happening and fix Janeway with a horrified stare before he disappeared.

"That was disconcerting," said Paris.

"I really hate holograms," said Montgomery.

"It was brilliant of her," Seven said. "Only a hologram would be able to perform the surgery with the required skill level and a lack of scruples."

"Look at this," said Montgomery. There was a large

door on the south side of the room. It looked heavy, metallic, and very well secured, sharply at odds with the efficient stylishness of the room.

"That wasn't here before," said Chakotay.

"Correction," said Tuvok. "It was always here, hidden behind a holographic disguise. When we destroyed the emitters, all the holograms in the room disappeared."

Seven's eyes were on the tricorder. "There's an extremely intense Borg resonant signature approximately twelve meters straight ahead. And a large power center." She lifted her gaze and met Janeway's eyes. "Regeneration chambers. Her laboratory is through here."

Janeway touched her comm badge. "Data," she said, "we've made it into her office and we think we've located her lab. Can you—"

She heard the sound of phaser fire on the other side of the door. The Borg had found them again.

"That door won't hold for long," Montgomery said.

"Data, can you erect a force field by the entrance to Covington's office?"

"I will attempt to do so, Captain. I suggest you proceed with both caution and alacrity."

"We intend to do so. Phasers aren't going to get through this door. Is there any way you can unlock it?"

Data was an expert at being able to do several things at once, all flawlessly and efficiently. He was being put to a real test now, however, as he tried to keep up the various force fields he had erected to protect Janeway and her crew, reestablish power, prevent the queen from gaining any more access than she already had, and trying to open the door.

"There are two life signs behind the door you indicate," he said. "Both of them are Borg. One of them is the queen."

"Can you unlock it?" Janeway repeated. Data attempted to do so and was met with a surprisingly forceful resistance. She did not want that door opened, and was concentrating a great deal of her efforts on keeping it locked.

"You are going to have to use your phasers," said Data.

They exchanged glances. The door behind them was much less difficult to break down than the one in front of them, and the drones had a head start and probably more phasers. Data had just signed their death warrant with his words.

Nothing more was said. These were all Starfleet officers, and good ones. Janeway lifted her phaser and took aim. The rest silently followed suit. They would keep trying until the door behind them was opened, and the drones burst through and killed them.

The sound of over a dozen phasers operating simultaneously was hard on the ears, but Janeway endured it, knowing that it might well be the last sound she heard. They all concentrated on the same spot, right where the locking mechanism was located. Behind them, the drones continued their onslaught.

When the room started to fade in her vision, Janeway almost laughed with joy. The clever Data had not alerted them to an alternative lest the queen also know, and was in the process of initiating a site-to-site transport to the other side of the door. She only hoped he had done it swiftly enough so that the queen couldn't put up a block.

They materialized inside Covington's laboratory. There were only two people in the room, as Data had informed them. Sitting rigidly at a console was a young man in civilian clothing. Except he really wasn't a man anymore, he was, like everyone in the building, Borg. He had linked with the computer and completely disregarded them. For the moment.

But Janeway barely had time to register his presence. Her eyes were immediately drawn to the terrifying sight of the Borg queen. The EMH had been right. He had done a fine job on this queen. She stood naked in the regeneration chamber, bathed in eerie green lights. Her smooth, gray flesh was unmarred. No harsh implants jutted out from her body or face. The only signs that this was not a normal human were the hue of the skin and the two tubes that ran from the base of her skull into her body. Her eyes were open, but they were presently unseeing, and she was swathed in various cables, looking like a spider in her web.

Despite the horror of the image in front of her, Janeway felt a renewed surge of hope. A true queen would not need to be so exposed, so physically bound to the machines with which she shared her existence. She would walk freely, connected only by thoughts. Would carry on conversations. Would look at them with mingled contempt and triumph.

The queen in front of her was more to her liking.

She heard Montgomery mutter an oath and lift his phaser. "No!" Janeway cried. "We don't know how she is linked to her collective. Kill her and everyone who's infected could die!"

"We don't kill her and everyone on Earth *gets* infected," he replied, but lowered his phaser.

"It would have been futile regardless," Seven said, looking at her tricorder. "She has erected a force field between herself, her drone, and us."

"Data, well done," Janeway said. "There's a force field about two meters in front of me. Can you get it down?"

"Negative, Admiral," came Data's voice. "Seven of Nine will have to proceed with the force field still in place. The queen is concentrating all her efforts on it."

"I can attempt . . . our plan," said Seven, careful not to reveal anything in words. "It will not be as easy."

"Do it," said Janeway. Seven moved to the same console as the young man. He ignored her until she touched the controls, and then he sprang into action. He whirled on her, and Janeway saw that his assimilation tubes were fully extended. Seven turned to evade him, but the drone was quicker. He seized her and was about to jab his tubes into her throat when Montgomery fired. The young man dropped like a stone. Seven took a step back, settled herself, and then continued to access the computer.

"Poor Blake," Montgomery said. "I never should have let her have him."

"You knew him, then?" Janeway asked.

"Yes. He was one of the top Borg specialists in the Federation. No wonder she was able to get as far as she did."

Seven listened to their conversation with half an ear. She was more interested in finding out how this Blake had initially engaged the link. Her long, slim fingers flew over the controls, but at each turn, no matter what she tried, the queen intervened to block her. It was as if they were two consummate professionals engaged in a tennis match, except this was a very deadly game. She tried everything she could think of. Nothing succeeded. The queen was aware, and able to protect herself.

Seven turned and caught Janeway's eye. Janeway read her look and, with a pained expression, nodded. Seven swallowed hard. This was the last resort, the one she had hoped she would never need. But if her sacrifice could ensure the safety of the Earth, she was prepared to make it.

She opened the panel, turned and faced the queen, extended her tubes, and let herself connect.

It was a sensation that was at once familiar and comforting and alien and terrifying. A part of Seven was appalled at the ease with which she settled into the collective. Suddenly she could hear the minds. They were far fewer than she remembered. Of course. This queen had a small collective, fewer than a hundred, perhaps. The true queen had had billions.

It would be so easy to take her place, be once again only a part of a whole. Being an individual was so much more difficult . . .

"What's she doing?" Montgomery demanded.

"She's linking with the collective," Janeway answered.

"What?"

"Infiltration from the inside," Janeway said.

"Do you really think she can do it? Disconnect the queen and not lose herself?"

"It's our only hope."

* * *

You are attempting to disconnect me, Seven of Nine, Tertiary Adjunct of Unimatrix Zero One.

There could be no lies, no deception, in this most intimate of sharing. All of Seven's memories and thoughts were laid bare before the queen.

You will fail.

Trevor Blake lies unconscious and separated from the collective, Seven thought. *Your hologram has been deleted. You cannot progress further. You know Starfleet will destroy the building and all the lives within it if it has to in order to stop you.*

Starfleet is weak. It will have no stomach for what it perceives as deliberate murder.

Then believe this. If it must, Voyager *will act alone and do this thing. Resistance is futile. You are more human than Borg. If you surrender, you may be spared, despite what you have done.*

The queen, her eyes blank and unseeing, opened her mouth and laughed aloud, startling those who watched the struggle between Covington and Seven of Nine. Janeway suppressed a shudder. Anything the Borg queen would find amusing was not something she wanted to know about.

You are discovering you cannot disconnect me from my precious drones. I will die rather than abandon them.

Precious? Abandon? You speak as if you cared for them. I know well a queen cares nothing for her drones. Perfection is the only thing of value to her. To any of the Borg.

Then you do not know me, Seven of Nine. I am a new queen, a different sort of queen. My reign will be glorious and beautiful. I know that you were always the favorite; the Royal Protocol mentions you specifically. You can join me and—No!

Seven's blue eyes opened. She had employed the same tactic that Data had used so effectively—distracting the queen. She knew what she needed to know. She stared at Janeway.

"Fire," she said.

Even as Janeway lifted her phaser to take aim at the queen, Montgomery fired. Covington's body spasmed. He fired again, and this time, with a long, soft groan, she slumped slowly and her head fell forward. She did not fall; she was supported by the mass of black, twining cables. She no longer looked like the ruling spider in her own web, but a hapless fly, caught in the trap that had killed her.

Janeway closed her eyes in relief, but opened them quickly when Chakotay said, in a warning voice, "Admiral . . . Seven hasn't come out of it."

Seven stood rigidly, her lips parted, her eyes unseeing.

"Oh, no," breathed Janeway.

The little girl sat alone in a circle of light. She played, solemn-faced, with a doll that had no head. Annika Hansen, clad in a flowing red dress, walked up to her and sank down beside her.

"Hello, Brenna," she said.

The girl looked up at her. "You need to watch out for the Hand," she said. "It will find you. It will touch you in wrong places. It will make you lie, and scream, and cry, and hate."

Images flashed through Annika's mind: horrible, grotesque scenes of violation, and beating, and childish flesh fondled by adult hands. She shrank from them, but they were downloaded into her brain. She felt everything. Tears spilled down her cheeks and she sobbed.

"What's going on? The queen's dead," said Montgomery, looking perplexed as Seven of Nine started crying, tears running down her strangely expressionless face.

"Somehow she's still connected," breathed Janeway. "I think the queen . . . may have transferred the Royal Protocol to her."

Montgomery looked at her. "Then tell me, why are we letting her stay alive?"

"Because she's fighting it," said Janeway, staring raptly. "Come on, Seven. Keep resisting."

An adult Brenna Covington stood before Annika now. She reached out and clasped Annika's hands, two tall, fair-haired women, so similar and yet so different.

"Take it," Brenna implored. "Take it. Take them. You know what I have endured. You know what I feel for them. They need a queen. They need you. You can be better than the original queen. You can exceed the programming. You can look at your drones as beloved children, not as things to be used and discarded. They can be glorious. You can take them to perfection. There's nothing they and you won't be able to achieve."

Annika clutched Brenna's hands. This was no trick, no lie. The Royal Protocol, modified and adapted by

Brenna Covington, surged through her. She could feel it already, closing off some parts of her body, opening others, exploring, downloading information. Brenna was right. Already, she could hear the voices of the confused hive, turning to her, seeking solace. She could be a new type of queen, a benevolent, loving monarch, to lead her people to perfection and—

No. She would not be seduced by the glory. Sweet though it was, it was an illusion. The Borg represented suppression of individuality, no matter how the queen thought of her drones. Brenna sensed her decision.

"No," she cried, "please, don't abandon them!"

"I am sorry," Annika said, sincerely, and slowly, deliberately, closed the door on the Royal Protocol, the clamoring drones, and her last, best chance to be a part of something infinitely greater than herself.

Chapter 24

When Seven's eyes fluttered open, she saw Dr. Kaz and Admiral Janeway smiling down at her.

"How are you feeling?" Kaz asked.

"That is a complicated question," Seven replied. "How long have I been regenerating?"

"Three full days," Janeway said. "You needed it."

"What has transpired?"

"Quite a lot," Kaz said, examining her with his medical tricorder. "We've all been debriefed, and as soon as you and Icheb feel up to it, Starfleet Command will want to see you as well. Everyone is off the hook, in case you're wondering. Myself and Data, too. Since we were such a key part of the solution, Starfleet's going to overlook our . . . interference."

"I am pleased to hear it," Seven replied. "What is the status of the virus?"

"Once you severed the connection with the collective, they all were released. We've really pushed the 'having delusions' aspect of the Xanarian Flu, and even most those who began to manifest implants seem more than willing to believe they imagined it."

Seven frowned. "Certainly not everyone believes that what they suffered was a hallucination."

"No," Janeway agreed, "but those people have been convinced that it's best to keep their silence."

Seven did not reply. She thought of the Interrogator, and wondered who had done the "convincing" and how.

"The important thing," continued Janeway, "is that the threat is over and there's been no panic."

"What will you do now?" Seven asked, looking at both Janeway and Kaz.

"I've gotten a bit disillusioned with my position after this incident," Kaz admitted. "I like being able to contribute on such a large scale, but I miss the intimacy of a ship. I've asked to be reassigned, but I'm not sure where I'll go next."

Janeway looked at him sharply. "I'll keep that in mind, Dr. Kaz. As for me, I'll go back to teaching at Starfleet. Tuvok and I are thinking of teaching a class together. Also, there's a little project I can't mention yet that has me quite excited. And you," she said, handing Seven a padd, "may have some exciting projects ahead of you as well."

Seven looked at the padd. It was an offer from a Starfleet "think tank" for her . . . and the Doctor.

"It seems as though they've finally learned to value you and the Doctor at last," Janeway said.

"Yes," said Seven, absently. Janeway looked at her

shrewdly. Kaz didn't miss the exchange, and excused himself.

"Seven . . . what happened? When you were linked?" Janeway asked, gently.

"She transferred the Royal Protocol to me. For a few moments, I was the Borg queen," Seven said quietly.

"Was it . . . dreadful?"

"No," Seven said. She met Janeway's gaze. "It was wonderful. Admiral . . . Covington wasn't a monster. She was a very wronged, very damaged woman. And she loved them."

"Loved who?"

"The drones. She loved her drones. And so did I."

"It seems wrong somehow," Carla said, as she and Janeway shared croissants and café au lait in a Paris bistro. "It's lying." She seemed troubled, her attractive face furrowed in a frown.

"I know," said Janeway as she took a sip and hid a grimace. Why did she keep trying to learn to like coffee with milk? Paris or not, next time she'd order it black. "But you have to balance that out against the panic that would erupt."

"You're right, as usual," Carla said, still staring into her oversized cup. "What was really wrong," she added softly, "was me thinking that somehow you were to blame for it."

"That was absolutely a logical conclusion," said Janeway. "We couldn't possibly know that Kevin had been chewing on a piece of Borg debris that day on the beach. You had every reason to suspect I had somehow given him the virus."

"Maybe. But it shouldn't have been the first conclusion I jumped to, and I'm sorry for that."

"I'm sorry you had to go through any of it," Janeway replied. "But as Shakespeare liked to say, all's well that ends well. Now," she said, leaning forward, "I think we really ought to splurge on a delicious French pastry while we're here."

Carla finally looked up, and Janeway was heartened to see the familiar impish grin spread across her face.

Janeway materialized in her apartment feeling uncomfortably stuffed. Not only had she and Carla splurged on fine French pastries, they had splurged on fine French cheeses, fine French wine, and fine French cream-based dishes. Her computer was chiming, and she rushed over to it.

"Admiral Montgomery," she said, surprised. "What an unexpected pleasure. What can I do for you?"

"I wanted to let you know there's been more from Baines," said Montgomery, "but I think we may have seen the last of him."

"Really?" she answered, keeping her voice even. Thus far, no one had connected her with Baines. In the excitement that followed Montgomery's appearance on *Voyager,* the admiral had never gotten around to asking her about how she managed to get past security.

"Several people, including Starfleet personnel, were abducted and then released after a brief time," Montgomery said. "They were forced to jump through a lot of hoops. Seems that Baines got some kind of pleasure out of making humans act like holographic characters in some of the more, er, lurid holonovels."

"Really," she said again. So Baines had listened to her comments about the Doctor's holonovel but, as usual, had gotten the message all wrong. "Was anyone hurt?"

"Not seriously. There was some mistreatment at the hands of the holograms. Whip lashes and cuts and so on."

"Whips?"

"They were returned to report on how badly holograms suffered," said Montgomery, with an expression that made Janeway believe he thought the whole thing was ridiculous. "And shortly after that, we got a tip which led us to Baines's body. Looks like suicide."

"But that doesn't make sense," Janeway said. "He had the fight to live for, the fight for holographic rights. Why would he kill himself?"

"Crazy guy like that, who knows," said Montgomery. Janeway felt a brief stab of sorrow. Baines wasn't an evil man, just dreadfully misguided. "Anyway, thought you might like to know. Looks like everything's all wrapped up now. Except for one thing that still bothers me."

"And what's that?"

"I want to know who this Peregrine is. The one who helped you out with the mysterious messages."

"Does it really matter? He was instrumental in helping us determine the identity of the Borg queen. Maybe we ought to just let Peregrine fade into the woodwork."

"Hmph." Montgomery looked stern, but his eyes were bright. He was off to fight another battle.

Janeway leaned back in her chair, thinking. She wondered what would become of the holographic rights issue, now that its leader was dead. It wouldn't go away, that much was certain. Perhaps the Doctor would choose to become more involved. He'd spoken with pride of his progress on *Photons, Claim Justice.* No doubt, it would be a best-seller. She wondered what had happened in Baines's little scenario, if it had done what he wanted it to do, if being treated like a hologram had truly changed anyone's mind or heart.

It was the first day back at work for Vassily Andropov. He had been debriefed and visited a counselor; Starfleet felt it had done all it could for him. Andropov could barely get through the day, so anxious was he to return home.

When he transported into his kitchen, they were waiting for him. He held out his arms and Allyson rushed into them, smiling happily. Andropov hugged her fiercely and planted a kiss on top of her head.

And, grinning, he extended a hand to the dark-haired, male hologram who stood off to the side.

"Welcome home, Vassily," said Oliver Baines.

The thin, high-pitched wailing woke Tom Paris from a deep and very pleasant dream in which B'Elanna had returned home and they were getting reacquainted. He blinked, and despite the hour, smiled. It was good to have his daughter back with him, loud screams and all. It felt . . . normal. And after the ride he'd had recently, normal was good.

As he went to pick her up, he heard the computer chime softly. Who could it be at this hour? Not Janeway, not anymore. He sat down, holding Miral, and touched the controls.

"B'Elanna!" he exclaimed, and then immediately

wedging his foot in his mouth added, "You look awful! You're not hurt, are you?"

She did look dreadful. She was covered in mud and what looked like dried, crusted blood. She was wild-eyed and very thin, and she looked like she was about to cry.

"She's dead."

"Oh, honey. I'm so sorry." He cuddled Miral, who had gone quiet at the sound of her mother's voice.

B'Elanna swallowed. "It's all right. I want . . . Tom, there's so much I want to tell you, and my little baby, I've missed you both so much. . . ." She fought back sobs. Collecting herself, she continued. "I've talked to Commander Logt and the Guardians, and they've agreed to let us live here and study."

It took a few seconds for his sleepy brain to register the information. "On Boreth? Why would you possibly want to do that?"

"I know it seems sudden to you, but after what I've been through . . . I know this is the right thing. Would you be willing to do this?"

He didn't know. In his entire life, he'd never anticipated living on the holiest planet in the Klingon Empire. She saw the expression on his face and said, "Just come here for a while. Let me tell you about the Challenge. Let me tell you about . . . about everything. Please."

He loved this woman with his whole heart and soul. He could deny her nothing, and was simply very grateful that she was still alive. Something profound must have happened, to turn her from hating her Klingon heritage to wanting to live in the temples and study it.

Very well. If she wanted to live on Boreth, they'd live on Boreth.

"We'll be on the first transport out. I love you."

The weeks passed pleasantly enough. Janeway took up a position at Starfleet Command, juggling her duties there on her "project" with teaching a joint class with Tuvok at the Academy.

When Chakotay contacted her after spending several weeks with his family to let her know he was returning to San Francisco, Janeway promptly invited him to dinner. "It'll be just like old times," she said. He agreed happily.

Smiling in anticipation of a wonderful evening, she replicated lamb for herself, an aromatic wild mushroom risotto for Chakotay, and had opened a bottle of fine old merlot. When he arrived and she handed him a glass, he accepted it appreciatively.

"It smells wonderful in here," he said. Indicating the wine, he asked, "What's the occasion?"

"A quiet lull," she said, and meant it. "It felt so awkward being home at first, and then of course we had the Borg and the holograms to keep us busy. Now, things are settling down. I've found a rhythm again."

"Miss your chicks?"

She stared at him. "I beg your pardon?"

He smiled. "On *Voyager,* you often struck me like a mother hen protecting her chicks. They've grown up and, to use an old cliché, flown the coop."

She finished setting the table and he lit the candles. "Of course I miss my chicks," she said. "But they seem to be doing just fine. Icheb's back at the Academy."

"That's wonderful news. How did that all turn out?"

"According to Tuvok, one of the four cadets involved in the assault had been expelled, two youths had been suspended, and one young woman had received a reprimand." As she went into the kitchen, she called over her shoulder, "And apparently Icheb's dating the girl."

"Icheb is a forgiving person," said Chakotay, "but forgiveness of that nature is remarkable. Good for both of them. It speaks well of their characters. I hear Harry's back together with Libby."

"A delightful young woman, and so talented. Sounds like our boy may be ready to settle down," said Janeway, bringing in the food-laden platters. "Speaking of settling down, Tom and B'Elanna and their adorable *Kuvah'-Magh* are studying Klingon culture on Boreth now."

"Really? Something big must have happened on the Challenge of Spirit," said Chakotay. "Did I tell you I heard from the Doctor yesterday? He sent me a preview copy of *Photons, Claim Justice*."

"How is it?"

"I haven't dared look at it yet. Apparently Seven has been critiquing it quite severely."

"I'm surprised he'd show it to her," Janeway said.

"Maybe she's just down the hall and it's convenient. Speaking of working together, how's the class you're teaching with Tuvok?"

"We're locked in battle. He wants it dry and factual, I want it juicy and interesting. I imagine we'll meet somewhere in the middle." She eyed Chakotay sharply. "Which now leaves just you for this mother hen to worry about."

He pulled out a chair for her, then sat down beside

her. "Then you don't need to worry," he said, unfolding his napkin. "I've decided to rejoin Starfleet."

"Well, in that case—" Janeway rose, went into the kitchen, and returned with a bottle of icy champagne. "We really do have something to celebrate."

Now Chakotay laughed and shook his head. "I hardly think my going back to Starfleet warrants a bottle of champagne."

"Oh, it's more than that." She gave him a mischievous look. "At least, I hope so."

"After all these years, you continue to confound me. What now?"

She expertly popped the cork and poured them each two flutes, grinning wickedly at Chakotay's open shock. "I have been authorized to be the one to offer you a captaincy."

"A captaincy?"

"If you'll take it."

He seemed stunned. Obviously, he hadn't been expecting this. Finally he asked, "What ship?"

She waited, savoring the moment before giving him the most wonderful news she could possibly imagine.

"*Voyager.*"

[illegible] "Once again," I said [illegible]," he said [illegible]

[illegible]

About the Author

Award-winning author Christie Golden has written twenty-two novels and sixteen short stories in the fields of science fiction, fantasy, and horror. Among her credits are the *Star Trek Original Series* hardcover *The Last Roundup,* three stand-alone *Voyager* novels, *The Murdered Sun, Marooned* and *Seven of Nine,* the Dark Matters trilogy *(Cloak and Dagger, Ghost Dance,* and *Shadow of Heaven),* the *Voyager* segment of the Gateways series, *No Man's Land,* the novella *Hard Crash* for *Have Tech, Will Travel* and the Tom Paris short story, "A Night at Sandrine's," which appeared in *Amazing Stories.*

In addition to *Star Trek* novels, Golden has written three original fantasy novels—*King's Man and Thief, Instrument of Fate* and, under the pen name of Jadrien Bell, *A.D. 999,* which won the Colorado Author's League Top Hand Award for Best Genre Novel of 1999. She has also done tie-in short stories for *Buffy the Vampire Slayer* and *Angel,* among many others.

She is honored and delighted to be offered the challenge of continuing the stories of *Voyager*'s crew past the end of the television series, and hopes that her readers enjoy her vision for *Voyager*'s future.

Golden lives in Colorado with her artist husband Michael Georges and their two cats. Readers are encouraged to visit her website at www.christiegolden.com.

Look for STAR TREK fiction from Pocket Books

Star Trek®

Enterprise: The First Adventure • Vonda N. McIntyre
Strangers From the Sky • Margaret Wander Bonanno
Final Frontier • Diane Carey
Spock's World • Diane Duane
The Lost Years • J.M. Dillard
Prime Directive • Judith and Garfield Reeves-Stevens
Probe • Margaret Wander Bonanno
Best Destiny • Diane Carey
Shadows on the Sun • Michael Jan Friedman
Sarek • A.C. Crispin
Federation • Judith and Garfield Reeves-Stevens
Vulcan's Forge • Josepha Sherman & Susan Shwartz
Mission to Horatius • Mack Reynolds
Vulcan's Heart • Josepha Sherman & Susan Shwartz
The Eugenics Wars: The Rise and Fall of Khan Noonien Singh, Books One and *Two* • Greg Cox
The Last Roundup • Christie Golden
Gemini • Mike W. Barr
Garth of Izar • Pamela Sargent & George Zebrowski

Novelizations

Star Trek: The Motion Picture • Gene Roddenberry
Star Trek II: The Wrath of Khan • Vonda N. McIntyre
Star Trek III: The Search for Spock • Vonda N. McIntyre
Star Trek IV: The Voyage Home • Vonda N. McIntyre
Star Trek V: The Final Frontier • J.M. Dillard
Star Trek VI: The Undiscovered Country • J.M. Dillard
Star Trek Generations • J.M. Dillard
Starfleet Academy • Diane Carey

Star Trek books by William Shatner with Judith and Garfield Reeves-Stevens

The Ashes of Eden
The Return
Avenger
Star Trek: Odyssey (contains *The Ashes of Eden*, *The Return*, and *Avenger)*
Spectre
Dark Victory
Preserver
The Captain's Peril

#1 • *Star Trek: The Motion Picture* • Gene Roddenberry
#2 • *The Entropy Effect* • Vonda N. McIntyre
#3 • *The Klingon Gambit* • Robert E. Vardeman

#4 • *The Covenant of the Crown* • Howard Weinstein
#5 • *The Prometheus Design* • Sondra Marshak & Myrna Culbreath
#6 • *The Abode of Life* • Lee Correy
#7 • *Star Trek II: The Wrath of Khan* • Vonda N. McIntyre
#8 • *Black Fire* • Sonni Cooper
#9 • *Triangle* • Sondra Marshak & Myrna Culbreath
#10 • *Web of the Romulans* • M.S. Murdock
#11 • *Yesterday's Son* • A.C. Crispin
#12 • *Mutiny on the Enterprise* • Robert E. Vardeman
#13 • *The Wounded Sky* • Diane Duane
#14 • *The Trellisane Confrontation* • David Dvorkin
#15 • *Corona* • Greg Bear
#16 • *The Final Reflection* • John M. Ford
#17 • *Star Trek III: The Search for Spock* • Vonda N. McIntyre
#18 • *My Enemy, My Ally* • Diane Duane
#19 • *The Tears of the Singers* • Melinda Snodgrass
#20 • *The Vulcan Academy Murders* • Jean Lorrah
#21 • *Uhura's Song* • Janet Kagan
#22 • *Shadow Lord* • Laurence Yep
#23 • *Ishmael* • Barbara Hambly
#24 • *Killing Time* • Della Van Hise
#25 • *Dwellers in the Crucible* • Margaret Wander Bonanno
#26 • *Pawns and Symbols* • Majliss Larson
#27 • *Mindshadow* • J.M. Dillard
#28 • *Crisis on Centaurus* • Brad Ferguson
#29 • *Dreadnought!* • Diane Carey
#30 • *Demons* • J.M. Dillard
#31 • *Battlestations!* • Diane Carey
#32 • *Chain of Attack* • Gene DeWeese
#33 • *Deep Domain* • Howard Weinstein
#34 • *Dreams of the Raven* • Carmen Carter
#35 • *The Romulan Way* • Diane Duane & Peter Morwood
#36 • *How Much for Just the Planet?* • John M. Ford
#37 • *Bloodthirst* • J.M. Dillard
#38 • *The IDIC Epidemic* • Jean Lorrah
#39 • *Time for Yesterday* • A.C. Crispin
#40 • *Timetrap* • David Dvorkin
#41 • *The Three-Minute Universe* • Barbara Paul
#42 • *Memory Prime* • Judith and Garfield Reeves-Stevens
#43 • *The Final Nexus* • Gene DeWeese
#44 • *Vulcan's Glory* • D.C. Fontana
#45 • *Double, Double* • Michael Jan Friedman
#46 • *The Cry of the Onlies* • Judy Klass
#47 • *The Kobayashi Maru* • Julia Ecklar

#48 • *Rules of Engagement* • Peter Morwood
#49 • *The Pandora Principle* • Carolyn Clowes
#50 • *Doctor's Orders* • Diane Duane
#51 • *Enemy Unseen* • V.E. Mitchell
#52 • *Home Is the Hunter* • Dana Kramer-Rolls
#53 • *Ghost-Walker* • Barbara Hambly
#54 • *A Flag Full of Stars* • Brad Ferguson
#55 • *Renegade* • Gene DeWeese
#56 • *Legacy* • Michael Jan Friedman
#57 • *The Rift* • Peter David
#58 • *Faces of Fire* • Michael Jan Friedman
#59 • *The Disinherited* • Peter David, Michael Jan Friedman, Robert Greenberger
#60 • *Ice Trap* • L.A. Graf
#61 • *Sanctuary* • John Vornholt
#62 • *Death Count* • L.A. Graf
#63 • *Shell Game* • Melissa Crandall
#64 • *The Starship Trap* • Mel Gilden
#65 • *Windows on a Lost World* • V.E. Mitchell
#66 • *From the Depths* • Victor Milan
#67 • *The Great Starship Race* • Diane Carey
#68 • *Firestorm* • L.A. Graf
#69 • *The Patrian Transgression* • Simon Hawke
#70 • *Traitor Winds* • L.A. Graf
#71 • *Crossroad* • Barbara Hambly
#72 • *The Better Man* • Howard Weinstein
#73 • *Recovery* • J.M. Dillard
#74 • *The Fearful Summons* • Denny Martin Flinn
#75 • *First Frontier* • Diane Carey & Dr. James I. Kirkland
#76 • *The Captain's Daughter* • Peter David
#77 • *Twilight's End* • Jerry Oltion
#78 • *The Rings of Tautee* • Dean Wesley Smith & Kristine Kathryn Rusch
#79 • *Invasion!* #1: *First Strike* • Diane Carey
#80 • *The Joy Machine* • James Gunn
#81 • *Mudd in Your Eye* • Jerry Oltion
#82 • *Mind Meld* • John Vornholt
#83 • *Heart of the Sun* • Pamela Sargent & George Zebrowski
#84 • *Assignment: Eternity* • Greg Cox
#85-87 • *My Brother's Keeper* • Michael Jan Friedman
    #85 • *Republic*
    #86 • *Constitution*
    #87 • *Enterprise*
#88 • *Across the Universe* • Pamela Sargent & George Zebrowski
#89-94 • *New Earth*

#89 • *Wagon Train to the Stars* • Diane Carey
#90 • *Belle Terre* • Dean Wesley Smith with Diane Carey
#91 • *Rough Trails* • L.A. Graf
#92 • *The Flaming Arrow* • Kathy and Jerry Oltion
#93 • *Thin Air* • Kristine Kathryn Rusch & Dean Wesley Smith
#94 • *Challenger* • Diane Carey
#95-96 • *Rihannsu* • Diane Duane
#95 • *Swordhunt*
#96 • *Honor Blade*
#97 • *In the Name of Honor* • Dayton Ward

Star Trek®: The Original Series

The Janus Gate • L.A. Graf
#1 • *Present Tense*
#2 • *Future Imperfect*
#3 • *Past Prologue*
Errand of Vengeance • Kevin Ryan
#1 • *The Edge of the Sword*
#2 • *Killing Blow*
#3 • *River of Blood*

Star Trek: The Next Generation®

Metamorphosis • Jean Lorrah
Vendetta • Peter David
Reunion • Michael Jan Friedman
Imzadi • Peter David
The Devil's Heart • Carmen Carter
Dark Mirror • Diane Duane
Q-Squared • Peter David
Crossover • Michael Jan Friedman
Kahless • Michael Jan Friedman
Ship of the Line • Diane Carey
The Best and the Brightest • Susan Wright
Planet X • Michael Jan Friedman
Imzadi II: Triangle • Peter David
I, Q • John de Lancie & Peter David
The Valiant • Michael Jan Friedman
The Genesis Wave, Books One, Two, and *Three* • John Vornholt
Immortal Coil • Jeffrey Lang
A Hard Rain • Dean Wesley Smith
The Battle of Betazed • Charlotte Douglas & Susan Kearney
Genesis Force • John Vornholt

Novelizations

Encounter at Farpoint • David Gerrold
Unification • Jeri Taylor
Relics • Michael Jan Friedman
Descent • Diane Carey
All Good Things... • Michael Jan Friedman
Star Trek: Klingon • Dean Wesley Smith & Kristine Kathryn Rusch
Star Trek Generations • J.M. Dillard
Star Trek: First Contact • J.M. Dillard
Star Trek: Insurrection • J.M. Dillard
Star Trek: Nemesis • J.M. Dillard

#1 • *Ghost Ship* • Diane Carey
#2 • *The Peacekeepers* • Gene DeWeese
#3 • *The Children of Hamlin* • Carmen Carter
#4 • *Survivors* • Jean Lorrah
#5 • *Strike Zone* • Peter David
#6 • *Power Hungry* • Howard Weinstein
#7 • *Masks* • John Vornholt
#8 • *The Captain's Honor* • David & Daniel Dvorkin
#9 • *A Call to Darkness* • Michael Jan Friedman
#10 • *A Rock and a Hard Place* • Peter David
#11 • *Gulliver's Fugitives* • Keith Sharee
#12 • *Doomsday World* • Carter, David, Friedman & Greenberger
#13 • *The Eyes of the Beholders* • A.C. Crispin
#14 • *Exiles* • Howard Weinstein
#15 • *Fortune's Light* • Michael Jan Friedman
#16 • *Contamination* • John Vornholt
#17 • *Boogeymen* • Mel Gilden
#18 • *Q-in-Law* • Peter David
#19 • *Perchance to Dream* • Howard Weinstein
#20 • *Spartacus* • T.L. Mancour
#21 • *Chains of Command* • W.A. McCay & E.L. Flood
#22 • *Imbalance* • V.E. Mitchell
#23 • *War Drums* • John Vornholt
#24 • *Nightshade* • Laurell K. Hamilton
#25 • *Grounded* • David Bischoff
#26 • *The Romulan Prize* • Simon Hawke
#27 • *Guises of the Mind* • Rebecca Neason
#28 • *Here There Be Dragons* • John Peel
#29 • *Sins of Commission* • Susan Wright
#30 • *Debtor's Planet* • W.R. Thompson
#31 • *Foreign Foes* • Dave Galanter & Greg Brodeur
#32 • *Requiem* • Michael Jan Friedman & Kevin Ryan
#33 • *Balance of Power* • Dafydd ab Hugh

#34 • *Blaze of Glory* • Simon Hawke
#35 • *The Romulan Stratagem* • Robert Greenberger
#36 • *Into the Nebula* • Gene DeWeese
#37 • *The Last Stand* • Brad Ferguson
#38 • *Dragon's Honor* • Kij Johnson & Greg Cox
#39 • *Rogue Saucer* • John Vornholt
#40 • *Possession* • J.M. Dillard & Kathleen O'Malley
#41 • *Invasion! #2: The Soldiers of Fear* • Dean Wesley Smith & Kristine Kathryn Rusch
#42 • *Infiltrator* • W.R. Thompson
#43 • *A Fury Scorned* • Pamela Sargent & George Zebrowski
#44 • *The Death of Princes* • John Peel
#45 • *Intellivore* • Diane Duane
#46 • *To Storm Heaven* • Esther Friesner
#47-49 • *The Q Continuum* • Greg Cox
  #47 • *Q-Space*
  #48 • *Q-Zone*
  #49 • *Q-Strike*
#50 • *Dyson Sphere* • Charles Pellegrino & George Zebrowski
#51-56 • *Double Helix*
  #51 • *Infection* • John Gregory Betancourt
  #52 • *Vectors* • Dean Wesley Smith & Kristine Kathryn Rusch
  #53 • *Red Sector* • Diane Carey
  #54 • *Quarantine* • John Vornholt
  #55 • *Double or Nothing* • Peter David
  #56 • *The First Virtue* • Michael Jan Friedman & Christie Golden
#57 • *The Forgotten War* • William R. Forstchen
#58 • *Gemworld, Book One* • John Vornholt
#59 • *Gemworld, Book Two* • John Vornholt
#60 • *Tooth and Claw* • Doranna Durgin
#61 • *Diplomatic Implausibility* • Keith R.A. DeCandido
#62-63 • *Maximum Warp* • Dave Galanter & Greg Brodeur
  #62 • *Dead Zone*
  #63 • *Forever Dark*

Star Trek: Deep Space Nine®

Warped • K.W. Jeter
Legends of the Ferengi • Ira Steven Behr & Robert Hewitt Wolfe

Novelizations

Emissary • J.M. Dillard
The Search • Diane Carey
The Way of the Warrior • Diane Carey
Star Trek: Klingon • Dean Wesley Smith & Kristine Kathryn Rusch
Trials and Tribble-ations • Diane Carey

Far Beyond the Stars • Steve Barnes
What You Leave Behind • Diane Carey

#1 • *Emissary* • J.M. Dillard
#2 • *The Siege* • Peter David
#3 • *Bloodletter* • K.W. Jeter
#4 • *The Big Game* • Sandy Schofield
#5 • *Fallen Heroes* • Dafydd ab Hugh
#6 • *Betrayal* • Lois Tilton
#7 • *Warchild* • Esther Friesner
#8 • *Antimatter* • John Vornholt
#9 • *Proud Helios* • Melissa Scott
#10 • *Valhalla* • Nathan Archer
#11 • *Devil in the Sky* • Greg Cox & John Gregory Betancourt
#12 • *The Laertian Gamble* • Robert Sheckley
#13 • *Station Rage* • Diane Carey
#14 • *The Long Night* • Dean Wesley Smith & Kristine Kathryn Rusch
#15 • *Objective: Bajor* • John Peel
#16 • *Invasion!* #3: *Time's Enemy* • L.A. Graf
#17 • *The Heart of the Warrior* • John Gregory Betancourt
#18 • *Saratoga* • Michael Jan Friedman
#19 • *The Tempest* • Susan Wright
#20 • *Wrath of the Prophets* • David, Friedman & Greenberger
#21 • *Trial by Error* • Mark Garland
#22 • *Vengeance* • Dafydd ab Hugh
#23 • *The 34th Rule* • Armin Shimerman & David R. George III
#24-26 • *Rebels* • Dafydd ab Hugh
#24 • *The Conquered*
#25 • *The Courageous*
#26 • *The Liberated*

Books set after the series
The Lives of Dax • Marco Palmieri, ed.
Millennium Omnibus • Judith and Garfield Reeves-Stevens
#1 • *The Fall of Terok Nor*
#2 • *The War of the Prophets*
#3 • *Inferno*
A Stitch in Time • Andrew J. Robinson
Avatar, Books One and *Two* • S.D. Perry
Section 31: Abyss • David Weddle & Jeffrey Lang
Gateways #4: *Demons of Air and Darkness* • Keith R.A. DeCandido
Gateways #7: *What Lay Beyond:* "Horn and Ivory" • Keith R.A. DeCandido
Mission: Gamma
#1 • *Twilight* • David R. George III
#2 • *This Gray Spirit* • Heather Jarman

#3 • *Cathedral* • Michael A. Martin & Andy Mangels
#4 • *Lesser Evil* • Robert Simpson
Rising Son • S.D. Perry
Unity • S.D. Perry
The Left Hand of Destiny, Books One and *Two* • J.G. Hertzler & Jeffrey Lang

Star Trek: Voyager®

Mosaic • Jeri Taylor
Pathways • Jeri Taylor
Captain Proton: Defender of the Earth • D.W. "Prof" Smith
The Nanotech War • Steve Piziks

Novelizations
Caretaker • L.A. Graf
Flashback • Diane Carey
Day of Honor • Michael Jan Friedman
Equinox • Diane Carey
Endgame • Diane Carey & Christie Golden

#1 • *Caretaker* • L.A. Graf
#2 • *The Escape* • Dean Wesley Smith & Kristine Kathryn Rusch
#3 • *Ragnarok* • Nathan Archer
#4 • *Violations* • Susan Wright
#5 • *Incident at Arbuk* • John Gregory Betancourt
#6 • *The Murdered Sun* • Christie Golden
#7 • *Ghost of a Chance* • Mark A. Garland & Charles G. McGraw
#8 • *Cybersong* • S.N. Lewitt
#9 • *Invasion! #4: The Final Fury* • Dafydd ab Hugh
#10 • *Bless the Beasts* • Karen Haber
#11 • *The Garden* • Melissa Scott
#12 • *Chrysalis* • David Niall Wilson
#13 • *The Black Shore* • Greg Cox
#14 • *Marooned* • Christie Golden
#15 • *Echoes* • Dean Wesley Smith, Kristine Kathryn Rusch & Nina Kiriki Hoffman
#16 • *Seven of Nine* • Christie Golden
#17 • *Death of a Neutron Star* • Eric Kotani
#18 • *Battle Lines* • Dave Galanter & Greg Brodeur
#19-21 • *Dark Matters* • Christie Golden
#19 • *Cloak and Dagger*
#20 • *Ghost Dance*
#21 • *Shadow of Heaven*

Books set after the series

Homecoming • Christie Golden

The Farther Shore • Christie Golden

Enterprise®

Novelizations

Broken Bow • Diane Carey

Shockwave • Paul Ruditis

By the Book • Dean Wesley Smith & Kristine Kathryn Rusch

What Price Honor • Dave Stern

Surak's Soul • J.M. Dillard

Star Trek®: New Frontier

New Frontier #1-4 Collector's Edition • Peter David

#1 • *House of Cards*

#2 • *Into the Void*

#3 • *The Two-Front War*

#4 • *End Game*

#5 • *Martyr* • Peter David

#6 • *Fire on High* • Peter David

The Captain's Table #5 • *Once Burned* • Peter David

Double Helix #5 • *Double or Nothing* • Peter David

#7 • *The Quiet Place* • Peter David

#8 • *Dark Allies* • Peter David

#9-11 • *Excalibur* • Peter David

#9 • *Requiem*

#10 • *Renaissance*

#11 • *Restoration*

Gateways #6: *Cold Wars* • Peter David

Gateways #7: *What Lay Beyond:* "Death After Life" • Peter David

#12 • *Being Human* • Peter David

Star Trek®: Stargazer

The Valiant • Michael Jan Friedman

Double Helix #6: *The First Virtue* • Michael Jan Friedman and Christie Golden

Gauntlet • Michael Jan Friedman

Progenitor • Michael Jan Friedman

Star Trek®: Starfleet Corps of Engineers (eBooks)

Have Tech, Will Travel (paperback) • various

#1 • *The Belly of the Beast* • Dean Wesley Smith

#2 • *Fatal Error* • Keith R.A. DeCandido

#3 • *Hard Crash* • Christie Golden

#4 • *Interphase, Book One* • Dayton Ward & Kevin Dilmore
Miracle Workers (paperback) • various
#5 • *Interphase, Book Two* • Dayton Ward & Kevin Dilmore
#6 • *Cold Fusion* • Keith R.A. DeCandido
#7 • *Invincible, Book One* • Keith R.A. DeCandido & David Mack
#8 • *Invincible, Book Two* • Keith R.A. DeCandido & David Mack
Some Assembly Required (paperback) • various
#9 • *The Riddled Post* • Aaron Rosenberg
#10 • *Gateways Epilogue: Here There Be Monsters* • Keith R.A. DeCandido
#11 • *Ambush* • Dave Galanter & Greg Brodeur
#12 • *Some Assembly Required* • Scott Ciencin & Dan Jolley
No Surrender (paperback) • various
#13 • *No Surrender* • Jeff Mariotte
#14 • *Caveat Emptor* • Ian Edginton
#15 • *Past Life* • Robert Greenberger
#16 • *Oaths* • Glenn Hauman
#17 • *Foundations, Book One* • Dayton Ward & Kevin Dilmore
#18 • *Foundations, Book Two* • Dayton Ward & Kevin Dilmore
#19 • *Foundations, Book Three* • Dayton Ward & Kevin Dilmore
#20 • *Enigma Ship* • J. Steven and Christina F. York
#21 • *War Stories, Book One* • Keith R.A. DeCandido
#22 • *War Stories, Book Two* • Keith R.A. DeCandido
#23 • *Wildfire, Book One* • David Mack
#24 • *Wildfire, Book Two* • David Mack
#25 • *Home Fires* • Dayton Ward & Kevin Dilmore
#26 • *Age of Unreason* • Scott Ciencin
#27 • *Balance of Nature* • Heather Jarman
#28 • *Breakdowns* • Keith R.A. DeCandido

Star Trek®: Invasion!

#1 • *First Strike* • Diane Carey
#2 • *The Soldiers of Fear* • Dean Wesley Smith & Kristine Kathryn Rusch
#3 • *Time's Enemy* • L.A. Graf
#4 • *The Final Fury* • Dafydd ab Hugh
Invasion! Omnibus • various

Star Trek®: Day of Honor

#1 • *Ancient Blood* • Diane Carey
#2 • *Armageddon Sky* • L.A. Graf
#3 • *Her Klingon Soul* • Michael Jan Friedman
#4 • *Treaty's Law* • Dean Wesley Smith & Kristine Kathryn Rusch
The Television Episode • Michael Jan Friedman
Day of Honor Omnibus • various

Star Trek®: The Captain's Table

#1 • *War Dragons* • L.A. Graf
#2 • *Dujonian's Hoard* • Michael Jan Friedman
#3 • *The Mist* • Dean Wesley Smith & Kristine Kathryn Rusch
#4 • *Fire Ship* • Diane Carey
#5 • *Once Burned* • Peter David
#6 • *Where Sea Meets Sky* • Jerry Oltion
The Captain's Table Omnibus • various

Star Trek®: The Dominion War

#1 • *Behind Enemy Lines* • John Vornholt
#2 • *Call to Arms...* • Diane Carey
#3 • *Tunnel Through the Stars* • John Vornholt
#4 • *...Sacrifice of Angels* • Diane Carey

Star Trek®: Section 31™

Rogue • Andy Mangels & Michael A. Martin
Shadow • Dean Wesley Smith & Kristine Kathryn Rusch
Cloak • S.D. Perry
Abyss • Dean Weddle & Jeffrey Lang

Star Trek®: Gateways

#1 • *One Small Step* • Susan Wright
#2 • *Chainmail* • Diane Carey
#3 • *Doors Into Chaos* • Robert Greenberger
#4 • *Demons of Air and Darkness* • Keith R.A. DeCandido
#5 • *No Man's Land* • Christie Golden
#6 • *Cold Wars* • Peter David
#7 • *What Lay Beyond* • various
Epilogue: Here There Be Monsters • Keith R.A. DeCandido

Star Trek® Omnibus Editions

Invasion! Omnibus • various
Day of Honor Omnibus • various
The Captain's Table Omnibus • various
Double Helix Omnibus • various
Star Trek: Odyssey • William Shatner with Judith and Garfield Reeves-Stevens
Millennium Omnibus • Judith and Garfield Reeves-Stevens
Starfleet: Year One • Michael Jan Friedman

Star Trek® Short Story Anthologies

Strange New Worlds, vol. I, II, III, IV, V, and VI • Dean Wesley Smith, ed.
The Lives of Dax • Marco Palmieri, ed.

Enterprise Logs • Carol Greenburg, ed.
The Amazing Stories • various

Other Star Trek® Fiction

Legends of the Ferengi • Ira Steven Behr & Robert Hewitt Wolfe
Adventures in Time and Space • Mary P. Taylor, ed.
Captain Proton: Defender of the Earth • D.W. "Prof" Smith
New Worlds, New Civilizations • Michael Jan Friedman
The Badlands, Books One and *Two* • Susan Wright
The Klingon Hamlet • Wil'yam Shex'pir
Dark Passions, Books One and *Two* • Susan Wright
The Brave and the Bold, Books One and *Two* • Keith R.A. DeCandido